Safe KEEPING

OTHER TITLES BY KRISTEN PROBY

Triple Creek Ranch

Safe Haven

The Blackwells of Montana

When We Burn

When We Break

Where We Bloom

When You Blush

Where You Belong

The Wilds of Montana

Wild for You

Chasing Wild

Wildest Dreams

On the Wild Side

She's a Wild One

With Me in Seattle

Come Away With Me

Under The Mistletoe With Me

Fight With Me

Play With Me

Rock With Me

Safe With Me

Tied With Me

Breathe With Me

Forever With Me

Stay With Me

Indulge With Me

Love With Me

Dance With Me

Dream With Me

You Belong With Me

Imagine With Me

Escape With Me

Flirt With Me

Take a Chance With Me

Single in Seattle

The Secret

The Surprise

The Scandal

The Score

The Setup

The Stand-In

Martinelli Mafia

Underboss

Headhunter

Off the Record

Love Under the Big Sky

Loving Cara

Seducing Lauren

Falling for Jillian

Saving Grace

Big Sky

Charming Hannah

Kissing Jenna

Waiting for Willa

Soaring with Fallon

Big Sky Royals

Enchanting Sebastian

Enticing Liam

Taunting Callum

Heroes of Big Sky

Honor

Courage

Shelter

Curse of the Blood Moon

Hallows End

Cauldrons Call

Salems Song

Bayou Magic

Shadows

Spells

Serendipity

Romancing Manhattan

All the Way

All It Takes

After All

Boudreaux

Easy Love

Easy Charm

Easy Melody

Easy Kisses

Easy Magic

Easy Fortune

Easy Nights

Fusion

Listen to Me

Close to You

Blush for Me

The Beauty of Us

Savor You

Safe Keeping

KRISTEN PROBY

Montlake

Published by Montlake, Seattle

www.apub.com

EU product safety contact:
Amazon Media EU S. à r.l.
38, avenue John F. Kennedy, L-1855 Luxembourg
amazonpublishing-gpsr@amazon.com

ISBN-13: 9781662532979 (paperback)
ISBN-13: 9781662532986 (digital)

Cover design by Hang Le
Cover image: © Regina Wamba of MaeIDesign.com; © Kris Pace / Shutterstock

Printed in the United States of America

This is for anyone who feels like they don't belong.

Prologue

Gideon

Fifteen Years Old

"Gideon, I need to see you in my office." Reggie's standing just outside the bedroom I share with three other guys. He doesn't look mad, but I'm always in trouble, so he's probably just used to it by now, and it isn't showing in his expression.

At least Reggie doesn't knock us around.

"What did you do now?" Seth, a kid that's on my last nerve, says with a smirk that I'd like to wipe off his face.

What a moron.

I ignore him and follow Reggie down the hall, past the dining and living rooms to his office, and when he closes the door behind us, unease settles in my gut.

I freaking hate it here at this boys' home. We all call it hell house. Basically, no one wants a foster kid like me. No one wants to adopt me. So I'm here. I mean, it could be a lot worse, but it's not great. The food sucks. I'm always cold. My eye aches thanks to the punch from that jerk, Ryker.

I hate that guy. We're always coming to blows. If he would just keep his big mouth shut, I could ignore him, but he must be allergic to shutting the hell up.

"I probably did whatever you're accusing me of," I say, starting the conversation and doing my best to look bored. "So go ahead and just give me extra chores."

Reggie's quiet long enough to make me nervous, and I shift in my seat.

"We have a few things to discuss," he finally says and drags his hand down his face. "First of all, your dad—"

"No."

Reggie sighs. "I get it."

"No, you don't."

No one will ever *get it*, and that's the way it should be. I fucking hate that this is my life.

I hate my life.

"You're right." Reggie looks down at the paper on his desk. "I don't. But I'm trying to empathize with you, Gideon. He's written you letters every week."

"Throw them away."

His face is grim. "I do. But there are about to be some changes, and I need to know, before that happens, if you'd like me to take you to see him."

The thought of coming face-to-face with my murderous bastard of a sperm donor makes my stomach twist.

"Fuck. No."

Reggie nods. "Okay."

My eyes narrow, and my hands fist on my lap. "You really won't make me go?"

"I'm not in the habit of forcing teenage boys to visit their fathers in prison."

"But the state—"

"They can't make you go either. I'm asking because while you don't want to read what your father has to say, I have to read it to make sure he's not saying anything incriminating or abusive to you. I know you don't like me very much, but I'm on your side, kiddo."

I don't reply to that. My hands ball into fists, and I wait for him to keep talking.

"He's asked to see you."

"No."

He nods. "You've already said that. You don't have to go. Now, you *do* need to pack your stuff up because you're being moved to a house."

My gaze whips up, and nerves immediately settle in my chest, making my throat close.

This could be worse than hell house.

"I'll be driving you this afternoon."

"Where?"

"It's a ranch about three hours from here. The owners, Debbie and Ray, are really good people, and you're going to spend the summer with them."

I get to spend the summer on a ranch? It feels like I just won the lottery.

"Ryker is going with you."

Nope. Didn't win the fucking lottery.

"I'm not going."

"Unfortunately, this isn't something you have a choice in. You have thirty minutes to pack your bag."

He stands, like that's the end of the conversation.

"What if I refuse?"

Reggie sighs and shakes his head. "You don't get to refuse, Gideon. You're fifteen, and you go where the state says you go. But I can tell you that it's better than here. If you give it a chance, you just might like it."

It's a big freaking house.

That's the first thing that comes to mind when Reggie comes to a stop in front of the house on the ranch and cuts the engine. Ryker and I are both quiet as we take it in.

It looks like something out of a movie. A gigantic house with mountains in the background that don't look real. There's a wraparound porch, and an older couple standing on the steps, who meet us when we all get out of the car.

Reggie sets our bags at our feet.

"Ryker, Gideon, I want to introduce you to Ray and Debbie," Reggie says.

Ryker steps forward to shake Ray's hand, and then Ray turns to me and shakes mine too.

"Hello," I mumble, looking him in the eye. He doesn't look mean. His hand is firm, but not too rough.

"I'm Deb," the little wisp of a woman says, folding me down in her arms. She's *so short.* So little, I'm afraid I might break her if I hug her too hard, and she's clinging to me like I'm her own kid.

I look at Ryker over her shoulder, and he just shrugs.

"You'll be staying in the bunkhouse with the hands," Ray tells us, and starts to explain what's expected of us out here. "I have one hard rule."

He narrows his eyes now, making sure we're listening to him as he gestures to Debbie.

"This is my *wife*. The love of my life. The only reason I do anything. No one sasses her on this ranch. You treat her with the kindness and respect that she'll show you. You'll get no second chances. If I find out that you even look at her sideways, you're out of here. Everything else we'll figure out as we go."

Watching them together makes my stomach hurt.

I wish my dad had loved my mom like that.

"Yes, sir," I mutter along with Ryker, and then there's a girl riding up to us on a horse, her blond hair blowing around her. She looks about our age.

"This is my niece, Willow," Debbie says as the girl joins us.

"Same rule applies to Willow," Ray says, and Willow smiles at him.

"You'll love it here," she says. She's so . . . *happy*. Like a little ray of sunshine.

As the day goes on, we're shown to the bunkhouse, where I take the top bunk, and then the barn. We meet the other hands that work on the ranch, and then it's time for dinner.

"Debbie makes the best fried chicken," Willow says as we walk to the house.

She's been hanging out with us all day. Ryker and I haven't said much to each other, which is new for us. The asshole is always running his mouth.

I freaking hate him. He's a jerk.

But Willow says we're all going to be friends. Ryker's looking at her like she hung the moon, which I'd usually make fun of him for, but I don't want to hurt *her* feelings.

I suspect we'll give her whatever she wants. She's sweet.

Whatever.

"Come on in, kids," Debbie says with a bright smile that makes my chest hurt again. "Dinner's on the table. Go wash your hands first."

Willow was right.

Debbie makes some good fried chicken.

"I'll help you clean up," I find myself saying after we're all done eating.

"Oh, you don't have to do that tonight," Debbie says, patting my back. "But I'm going to keep feeding you lots of food because you're too skinny."

There is never enough food at hell house.

She stops and looks up at me, narrows her eyes, and it feels like she's staring into my soul.

No one should look at me this deep.

"You're safe here, Gideon," she says softly as the others file outside to the porch. "You're safe with Ray and me. If you need anything, you just ask me. If you have questions, same goes."

I nod because I have a lump in my throat.

When was the last time someone was so . . . *nice* to me? I don't remember.

"I'm happy you're here," she continues.

"Thanks."

"Go on." She pats my back again. "Go rest up. You're going to be putting in long hours this summer."

"I'm okay with the work."

That makes her smile again, and I'd do just about anything for more of her smiles. I think I might have fallen in love with this tiny woman today.

"I know you are. You're going to do great. Now, you go out with the others and get some rest. Tomorrow, I want to know what all your favorite foods are so I can get them from the grocery when I go."

Nodding, I head to the door.

"And Gideon?"

"Yes, ma'am?" I turn, and my breath catches when she smiles at me again.

"Welcome home, sweetheart."

Chapter One

LENA

"Holy lobster, Batman, look at this."

My best friend, Chelsea, snickers into her glass of champagne and points to the enormous painting in front of her.

It's a lobster.

Dancing with a squid.

This painting is the size of the windows that span behind my mother's desk in the Oval Office. I should know. I was just in there this morning.

Sipping my one and only glass of champagne, I tilt my head to the side, still staring at the painting. There's a *lot* going on. "Is that a—"

"Starfish fucking a clam? Yeah, I think so."

I blink over at Chelsea, and she grins at me.

"What did you bring me to?"

Chelsea laughs and pats my shoulder. "An art exhibit opening in New York City. Come on, it's fun. We're dressed up, drinking bomb champagne, surrounded by your hot security guys."

I glance over to my Secret Service men. There they are, like always. Dressed in suits, with things in their ears, just like in the movies. Only difference is, we're not outside, so they're not wearing sunglasses. Richie has been with me since I was a teenager. But the other one is new. I don't remember his name. The rest are scattered throughout the gallery and outside.

I frown at my best friend of twenty years, since our first day of kindergarten.

"They're not *hot*." Only one has ever been hot, and he hasn't worked for me for years. "They're annoying."

"If you have to have annoying security, they might as well be hot. They can be both." She winks at me, and we move along to another piece that features a sink full of dirty dishes and a golden retriever humping a poodle.

"My eyes may never recover from this," I mutter, making her cackle with delight. Chelsea's laugh always makes me smile.

We couldn't be more different. She's the wild one. The risk-taker, the loud person with no filter.

She's also stunning, with long blond hair, bright-cerulean eyes, and an hourglass figure that fills out her blue dress perfectly.

She's a showstopper.

I can never tell her no about anything, including this last-minute trip into New York City for this exhibit. Chels loves the city, and I would rather be anywhere else.

Somewhere quiet, where I can think, where there aren't many people. Or any people at all.

"You should have an exhibit of your own, Lena," Chelsea says, sobering. "You're way better than this."

"You can't compare my art to this. It's not the same."

Chelsea rolls her eyes as she loops her arm through mine, and we click on our stilettos to another room, another gallery. And of course security follows.

"You know what I mean," she says. "Your art is fucking beautiful, and it should be displayed for others to enjoy. To buy. You could make a *killing*."

Shaking my head, I give her arm a squeeze. "Thanks for the vote of confidence, but I'm okay."

I've told her before, I don't want to draw more attention to myself. My mother is the president of the United States. I get plenty of attention already, and I hate it with a passion.

"Maybe once your mom's term is over, and things settle down a bit," she says and tips her head against my shoulder.

Probably not.

But in my usual fashion, because I can't tell her no, I simply say, "Maybe."

"Oh! I could totally be your manager. You could just do the art side, and I could run the business side."

Not in this lifetime.

I love her, but Chelsea can't manage her own allowance from her parents. She's twenty-four and has already spent her entire trust fund, and her parents *still* give her ten grand a month for living expenses.

And yet by the middle of the month, she's broke and asking me for a *loan.*

Which I always give her.

And I hate myself for it. I know I'm enabling the shit out of her, but damn it, she's like a sister to me. I don't have siblings. Just Chelsea. She battled a cocaine addiction for years, and she's finally clean. She has so much potential—she just doesn't have any self-esteem.

Because her parents, while filthy fucking rich, are assholes.

"Oh, look!" She points to the side of the room. "A dessert buffet. Let's be naughty and eat some calories rather than just drink them."

I blink over at her. "Chels."

With a huff of her breath, she shakes her head. "Come on, *Mom,* I want some of that cake."

I nod at people that I know as we walk through. This is definitely a who's who of New York's elite, and I know the only reason I was invited is who my mom is.

"Well, you look delicious."

I know that voice.

Pasting on a plastic smile, I take a steadying breath and turn to find Howard Tobias Matthews III ogling my tits as he lifts his glass to his lips.

Not champagne.

Bourbon.

His diamond-studded Rolex flashes beneath the cuff of his white dress shirt. He's in a custom black suit, which molds over his body perfectly.

On paper, Howey is the perfect man.

A Harvard Law grad, attorney with a prestigious New York City firm, tall, dark, and handsome, with a muscled body and an impressive financial portfolio, and he comes from the kind of family that would have hosted grand balls during the Gilded Age.

He's also a selfish, narcissistic asshole, and I only learned that after I dated him for a year.

"Hello, Howey."

"Goodbye, Howey," Chelsea says and flips the man the bird, and I have to press my lips together so I don't laugh.

Chels always hated this guy.

"Still have your yappy friend by your side, I see." Howey's voice is like honey.

If he wasn't such a monumental asshole, he really would be a catch.

Seeing him makes me feel *nothing*. I never thought I was in love with him, but I enjoyed dating him. Especially in the beginning, when he was attentive and kind. Sexy. He really was good in bed. He didn't cause trouble with my detail, and he was respectful to my mother.

And then, it all went to shit so fast, my head spun. So no, I don't feel anything at all when I look at him. No remorse. No longing or sadness.

"Are you enjoying the exhibit?" I ask him, ignoring the dig at Chelsea.

"It's interesting." He glances around the room, and then his brown eyes fall on me once more, flicking down to my cleavage. "It just got better."

"Yeah, well, I think we were getting ready to head out. I need to get back to DC tonight."

That's a bald-faced lie. We're staying in the city for the weekend to shop and eat at our favorite restaurants.

But Howey isn't invited to tag along.

"Come out on the veranda with me," Howey says, and I shake my head.

"I need the restroom." I turn to Chelsea, who's suddenly chatting with a woman I don't recognize. "I'll be back."

"Okay, I'll grab you some cake," she says with a smile, and I turn to walk away.

"Lena," Howey says, stopping me. His eyes have softened, and he reaches out to tuck my hair behind my ear. "I'd really just like to talk to you."

I sigh and back out of his reach, which makes his eyes narrow.

"You lost that right the day you smacked me across the face. Goodbye, Howey."

I walk across the room, toward the hallway where I noticed the sign for the public restroom. My detail is right behind me, and I glance back at them, directing my comment to Richie.

"I don't want him near me again."

"Yes, ma'am."

My detail makes me wait to enter the restroom until it's empty, and then they stand outside the door, making sure no one can get in with me.

It's over the top and ridiculous. It's always driven me *nuts.* I wonder if they can hear me pee out there. When I was a teenager, I rebelled against the security. Chelsea would talk me into ditching them all the time, which we'd do, and then go get ice cream, or go shopping. We never did anything too crazy—we just loved the adrenaline rush of losing the security guys.

And then I always got into a heap of trouble afterward.

When the *incident* happened five years ago, I put my foot down and told Chelsea we'd never do it again. Because people got hurt that day, all because of me.

And it still haunts my dreams.

Once I've washed my hands, I open the door and step out of the restroom, but then frown when I don't see Richie. The new guy glances my way, and I look down the hallway.

"Where's Richie?"

"He had to handle something."

No, that's wrong.

My guys *never* leave my side. Not for anything.

The hair on the nape of my neck stands on end as I hold this guy's stare.

"What did he have to handle?"

"Don't worry about it. He'll be right back. Your friend's waiting for you in the car out back."

He points with his thumb toward the opposite end of the hallway, where there's an exit sign.

I can hear Gideon's voice in my head. He was with me from the minute my mom took office until the night of the incident.

"Trust your gut. If something feels off, it likely is."

My heart beats faster, but I manage to keep my face calm.

"Chelsea wasn't ready to go yet."

"She is now. She's out back with Richie."

I tilt my head to the side. "You said he was taking care of something."

"He's taking care of Chelsea." His jaw tightens, that muscle twitching with his frustration. "Come on, we need to go."

Slowly shaking my head, I start to move to the other end of the hallway where the party is still happening, but his hand catches my upper arm, and he starts to drag me away.

I have an emergency button on my watch, which I immediately press, and within seconds, more Secret Service rush in.

Cold metal is pressed against my neck.

"I'm taking her," this asshole says. His voice shakes a bit, and my eyes find Richie's. *Where was he?*

Without hesitation, Richie raises his gun and fires, and my would-be kidnapper falls to the ground, dead.

Oh, God.

I stare down in horror at the blood as it spreads over the floor, and then I'm flanked by three men and taken out to the SUV. They're talking into phones and communicators, but the blood is rushing so loudly in my head, I can't hear a word they're saying.

He was going to take me.

"How?" Is that *my* voice? So small and breathy.

Richie turns to me, but I don't understand the words coming out of his lips. His face is set in concerned lines.

Was he in on it?

He wasn't there.

He was supposed to be there.

"Blackbird is secure. ETA two hours," I hear someone say as we zoom through Manhattan, just as I start to shake, and I'm hurled back in time five years.

"Get her out of here!" Gideon pushes me toward Richie, but I don't want to leave him. No one makes me feel as safe as Gideon. No one can protect me like him.

I shake my head, clinging to him.

"No. I'll go with you."

"Go with Richie. That's an order."

I shake my head again, but then shots ring out, and Gideon grunts, then collapses to the ground.

"Oh my God!"

"Go," Gideon says. His face is white, his voice strained. "Get the fuck out of here, Lena."

Strong arms pull me back, but I'm yelling for Gideon. I won't leave him.

"Lena." Richie shakes my shoulder, pulling me out of the past. "Shit, she's going into shock."

"Of course she is. She just saw a man die."

"I've told you exactly what happened five times," I tell my mother, who's sitting with me and my detail in the living room of the White House, in sweats. Her eyes are cold and hard. She's in scary executive-president mode right now.

Which is better than the terrified-mama mode she was in about an hour ago. I don't know what to do with that. My mother is not emotional. And she's *never* gone into mama-bear mode with me.

My dad's pacing behind the couch, pushing his hand through his salt-and-pepper hair over and over again.

"He passed *everything*," Richie says for the fifth time. "There were no red flags to make us think that he was a threat."

"Well, he clearly was," Mom says. Her voice is like ice, and it makes Richie shift on his feet. "The mess has been dealt with?"

"Yes, Madam President," Bishop, the head of the Secret Service, says. "It's been dealt with, and it won't make the press. The other people in the gallery have been debriefed. There won't be any mention of it anywhere."

The press only knows what those in charge want them to know. Politics is like the Mafia on steroids.

"You'll stay here for the immediate future," Dad says to me.

"I have a life—"

"And you'll be here, where we can protect you better," Mom adds, her voice leaving no room for disagreement.

I love my apartment. I don't want to live in the White House.

I hate this haunted house.

Resigned, I let out a sigh. "Do you need me for anything else, or can I go to bed?"

“Go on up,” Mom replies, and catches my hand as I walk by. “Try to get some sleep.”

“I’m sure that won’t happen.” I kiss her cheek, then give Dad a side hug before climbing the stairs to my old bedroom. But suddenly, a thought occurs to me, and I turn back. “Wait. What about Chelsea?”

“She’s fine,” Richie says. “She’s at the hotel, and she’ll be back in DC on Monday.”

“She’s staying in New York after everything that happened tonight?” I frown and reach for my phone, but there aren’t any missed calls or texts from her.

“She doesn’t know what happened,” Bishop replies, with no emotion on his face. “She thinks you were pulled back here on official business.”

“And you won’t tell her otherwise,” Mom adds. “Good night, Lena.”

Fuck my life.

Chapter Two

Gideon

"You have good aim." Nodding with approval, I cross my arms over my chest and stand back as the guys I'm training continue to shoot. Today is their last day here on my property in Montana, and after this, they'll be out in the field, protecting celebrities, politicians, and billionaires.

My phone rings in my pocket. When I see "Bishop" on the screen, I send it to voicemail—for the fifth time today—and turn my attention back to the guys.

We go through my obstacle course, and I evaluate every one of them to make sure they're ready to guard someone with their lives.

We started with ten trainees a month ago.

Six survived to today.

By the time we're finished, Bishop has tried to call three more times, but I've ignored all of them. My old boss from Washington, DC, hasn't called me in four years. He can wait another hour until my guys have left the property.

"Thank you," Roberts says, shaking my hand. "You're fucking brilliant."

"I know." I smirk and pat him on the back. "You've got this. You have my number if you have questions."

They pack up into the van that'll take them to their hotel in town, and when they're gone, I walk into my house and take a breath.

I like training new guys. They're motivated and dedicated, and they're here to learn. If they're not, they're kicked out. I don't tolerate bullshit.

But it's always a relief when they leave, and I have a few weeks between sessions.

I'm ready to work the ranch with my brother, Ryker, for a couple of weeks. I have some work to do on the firing range, since I want to add another lane and extend it farther, for sharpshooting. I need to clean the armory.

There's always shit to do.

My phone rings again, but this time it isn't Bishop.

It's *Eagle*.

"Madam President," I say in greeting. "What can I do for you?"

"Why are you avoiding Bishop's calls?" she asks.

"Because I've been working, ma'am."

"I have a situation, Gid," she says, and I can hear fatigue in her voice. "I won't tell you what it is over the phone. I need your help with Blackbird."

What the fuck has she done now?

Lena is the bane of my existence. She made every day on the job difficult. Every. Fucking. Day.

"I'm no longer—"

"I don't give a rat's ass," she says, cutting me off. "I need you here in twenty-four hours. And Gideon?"

"Yes, ma'am?"

"You're taking her back with you."

Stunned, I hold the phone against my ear, sure I've heard her wrong. "I'm sorry, could you please say that again, ma'am?"

"You heard me. Twenty-four hours."

She hangs up, and I pull my hand down my face.

What the fuck is going on? What has she gotten herself into now?

"No." Willow shakes her head adamantly as she wipes down her kitchen counter. "Absolutely not, Gideon. I don't want her here on this property. She's the reason you got hurt and lost your career."

It wasn't her fault.

But I can't tell my best friend that because it's all classified.

"You're getting worked up, Trouble," Ryker says as he pulls her into his arms and kisses the top of her head. He's watching me with sober eyes. Ryker is my brother in every way that counts, including in name. Ray and Debbie adopted us the year we moved here.

And then, after twenty years of life as a family, of Ry going pro in hockey and kicking ass, me going into the Rangers and then the Secret Service, we lost them both. Debbie passed seven years ago, and Ray followed her two years later. I miss them like crazy every single day.

But Ryker, Willow, and I, along with Willow's nephew, Aiden, are a family. These are my people, my best friends. We all live on the Triple Creek Ranch, and they need to know that Lena's coming here.

"I have security locked down," I continue, as if I'm giving a report to a superior. "No one gets on this land unless we want them to. I don't know why they want her to come here. I haven't had any contact with any of them since I retired four years ago."

"Then tell them no," Willow insists, and it about kills me when she has tears in her eyes. "*No*, handsome."

"The president of the United States has asked for my help, and although I don't work for the government anymore, she wouldn't have called me unless there was no other option. They would *never* involve a civilian unless it was necessary."

Fucking civilian. I hate that word. I'm not a goddamn civilian.

Except, I am.

"When?" Ryker asks, rubbing his hands up and down his wife's back.

It's been four years, and it still gives me a little jolt when I'm reminded that Ry married Willow. We're still the Three Amigos, but it's different. Not worse or better, just different. Ryker retired from professional hockey when Ray died, and moved home to take over the ranch. And then, he and Willow reconnected and fell in love.

Or admitted that they belonged together. I'd seen the writing on the wall for twenty years, but no one listens to me.

"I'm leaving in the morning. We'll likely be back by tomorrow night."

"I don't like it." She shakes her head again. "Gid, your leg—"

"Is fine. And I'm not asking you to like it," I remind Willow. "I'm telling you what's happening. I don't know how long she'll be here. I don't know what kind of shitstorm is going on. And I likely can't tell you about it once I'm filled in."

"This is your home," Ryker reminds me. "You don't have to ask our permission for this."

"I know. But you're my family, and I need to keep you in the loop."

"Do I have to be nice to her?" Willow asks.

"You're nice to everyone, sweetheart," Ryker says.

"She hurt him," she whispers and buries her face in Ry's chest. "So I don't want to be nice to her."

"She didn't hurt me," I say before I can keep the words back. "I can't tell you more than that."

I want to defend Lena. I hate that Willow has so much animosity toward the First Daughter. Sure, she caused a lot of irritation in the time that I was on her detail, and I wanted to take her over my knee more than once, but my injury wasn't her fault.

"I just love you," Willow says.

"I know." I smile at her, and her face softens the way it always does when I send a grin her way. "I love you too. This is going to be okay."

She nods and then sighs. "Fine. I'll be nice. Until I have a reason to *not* be nice."

"You're kind of scary, Trouble." Ryker lifts an eyebrow.

"I know. I learned it from Gid."

"Say that again." My voice is cold steel, my arms are crossed, and I'm staring at Bishop as he rubs his hand over his forehead.

Bishop has been the director of the Secret Service for almost twenty years. I worked well with him in my time here. I trust him.

And he looks fucking exhausted.

"There was a kidnapping attempt by one of our own." *One of our own.* "He was taken down during the incident, but there are rumblings that he wasn't working alone. We need to get Blackbird out of here and hidden away somewhere safe. That's why we called you. No one would guess that she's in the middle of nowhere, Montana."

I shake my head. "You're telling me there's an inside job happening? What about the president?"

"What about her?"

"Is she going into hiding?"

"No." The woman herself strides into the room and holds her hand out for me to shake. "I'm not hiding out. The intel we have says that I'm not the target."

"Only Blackbird."

Her chin goes up. "That's right. There are theories as to why, but no concrete information. I want her out of DC, where no one will look for her."

"For how long?" I ask.

"Until it's over," Bishop replies. "And we have no idea how long that might be. A week. Six months. Your guess is as good as mine."

I don't want her on my ranch for a million reasons, starting with, she's a pain in the ass. She's spoiled and does what she wants. She'll be in my way, underfoot, likely spouting off with her smart mouth. I like quiet and orderly.

Did I mention she's a pain in the ass?

"I'm not asking," Madam President adds, raising an eyebrow. "You'll be well compensated, Gideon. I'm going to be candid and say that you're the only person on this planet that I trust with my daughter's life right now. I don't trust anyone else."

Well, fuck.

"Looks like your daughter's going on a trip."

She doesn't smile. Her eyes, so much like Lena's, are sharp, but I also see fear there. "Thank you. She's in her old bedroom now. She knows she's going somewhere, but I haven't told her where. I wanted to get you here and debrief you first. You'll leave in the next thirty minutes, so go on up. She's packed."

Why is she speaking about Lena as if she's a child? She's not. She's a twenty-four-year-old woman.

But I'll never question the president of the United States. That's way above my pay grade.

With a nod, I walk out of Bishop's office, into the private residence, and up the stairs that lead to the bedrooms.

Lena's is the last room on the right.

I rap my knuckles on the door twice, and she calls out, "Come in."

I haven't seen her in four years. I remember a twenty-year-old woman who was rebellious and feisty, despite being relatively quiet, unless she was with her troublemaker of a best friend, Chelsea. She dressed mostly in jeans and T-shirts, her raven-black hair barely hit her shoulders, and she never wore makeup.

But when I open the door, that girl is gone, replaced by a fucking gorgeous woman. She's in black slacks and a purple silk blouse unbuttoned far enough to show off just a hint of cleavage. Her hair is long, almost to her ass, and she's wearing just enough makeup to accentuate her lavender eyes and high cheekbones.

She's . . . *stunning.*

I can picture that hair wrapped around my fist.

Those eyes shining up at me as I fuck her senseless.

This is bad. This is so motherfucking bad.

Chapter Three

Lena

It's him.

My tongue is stuck to the roof of my mouth, and I can't move, because standing at the threshold of my old bedroom is Gideon James.

And holy Christ in a rowboat, this man is beautiful.

I always had a crush on him. I never admitted it to anyone, especially not Chelsea because she would have tormented me ruthlessly, but Gideon is sexy. He's stupidly tall, well past six feet. Maybe six foot five? With thick dark hair and steel gray eyes that can cut you to the bone with just one look. Some might say that Gideon has blue eyes, but that's too simple for them. His eyes change with his moods, and more often than not, they're stormy, like gray thunderclouds.

He also used to make me so mad because he was strict and hard.

But when he smiles, which isn't often, those gray eyes lighten up, and it's like the sun has come out from behind a cloud, making everything bright and warm.

He's not smiling right now. In fact, he looks . . . *mad.*

And that's fine because so am I. My life is being ripped out from under me.

Gideon's jaw tightens, and then he finally speaks. "We're leaving."

I blink in response. "Who's *we*?"

My voice sounds scratchy to my own ears.

"You and me. I'll carry your bag. Leave your phone and computer and any other electronics here."

With a frown, I open my tote bag and start to unload the electronics, but I can't help but ask, "Why?"

"Because they can be traced."

I nod and reach inside.

"You're not going to fight me on this?"

I shake my head as I finish laying my iPad on the bed, next to my laptop and phone. I feel bad that I haven't spoken to Chelsea. She'll worry when she can't reach me.

"Maybe I should text—"

"Don't text anyone," he interrupts.

"Chelsea will worry when she doesn't hear from me."

He's quiet for so long that I glance his way and see that he's grinding his teeth together.

"No texts."

Rubbing my lips together, I start to think up something to say. I know he didn't like my best friend. He called her a bad influence.

If he only knew.

But then I remember that man holding a gun to my neck, and then the jerk of his body when he was shot and the blood flowing out of him when he fell.

I'll never forget that.

It's one more nightmare I'll have for the rest of my life, and I already had more than my share.

So without tapping out a quick message to Chelsea, I set the phone on the bed and turn to Gideon.

"Okay, I'm ready."

His eyes narrow, as if he doesn't trust me. "You're really not arguing with me."

I shake my head once and take a step toward him. "No, I'm not. Get me out of this fucking house."

Without a word, he lifts my bag, and I step into the hallway with him and then scowl when no one else is waiting for us.

"Where are the others?"

"The other what?" His voice is just like I remember it. Hard. Gruff. And it makes goose bumps erupt on my skin.

"Members of my detail."

"It's just me."

I stop and turn to him. "But you're not—"

"I'll tell you more once we're on the fucking airplane. Let's move. We're going out the side exit, through the tunnel, to a waiting car. You know it well. You escaped through there many times."

Pressing my lips together, I resume walking. I can't even be mad at him for his snarky comment.

He's not wrong. I know that tunnel well.

Surprisingly, we don't run into anyone on our way through the house. My parents said their goodbyes about an hour ago, and I haven't seen my other detail guys.

I still don't know what was going on with Richie at the gallery exhibit the other night. All of it felt so damn shady.

It's all a jumbled mess in my head, and when I think about it too hard, I want to cry.

Gideon is right next to me, not touching me, but so close that I can feel the warmth of him, and for the first time in four years, I feel like I can exhale. Like I finally feel *safe*.

He leads me down the tunnel and outside to the waiting car. When he joins me in the back seat, I realize that it's *Bishop* driving.

I never see the director anymore. Why is *he* our escort?

"What the hell is going on?" I ask him, and he flicks his eyes over to me in the rearview mirror but doesn't answer me. "Come on. Some guy who is supposed to be protecting me tries to take me, is shot and bleeds all over me—"

Gideon stiffens next to me. His hands tighten into fists.

"—and Richie disappeared on me, leaving me alone with the bad guy."

"What the fuck," Gideon says. "You didn't tell me that part."

"He didn't disappear," Bishop says.

"He wasn't *with* me," I reply. "And my guys *never* walk away from me."

"He was distracted. Pulled away. It was part of the setup."

I shake my head and lean back in the seat, resigned to the fact that *no one* will tell me what's really going on. It's always the same. This is what it is to be the daughter of the most powerful woman in the world.

I do what I'm told, and I'm not told much. It's infuriating.

"Where are we going?" I ask again.

No one answers me.

"And you all wonder why I'm a pain in the ass," I mutter, shaking my head as I look out the window as Washington, DC, whizzes by.

We end up at the airport, and I'm escorted onto a private jet. When the door closes, it's just me and Gideon on the plane.

My eyes fly to his. His face is stony, his eyes flat and calm, showing no emotion. Which is pretty on brand for this man. He never had much to say, and it looks like that hasn't changed.

Before long, we're airborne. I hate flying, and that sucks for me because I've had to fly all over the freaking world. I haven't said a word since setting foot on this aircraft, and we're not even looking at each other.

My hands aren't altogether steady, and I hate that no one will tell me where I'm going. I don't know *anything*.

The only reason I'm not throwing an all-out fit is that Gideon is with me. He wouldn't let anything bad happen to me.

"Montana."

My eyes return to his, and I tilt my head to the side. "Pardon?"

"We're going to my ranch in Montana."

The pieces start to fit together.

"You're not coming back to work for the Secret Service."

He shakes his head and stays silent.

"You're taking me to your *home*."

That makes my stomach jitter. I get to see where he lives?

Gideon nods.

"Because my mother wants to hide me away. Because someone wants to hurt her through hurting me."

"That's the theory."

"How long?"

He shrugs those broad shoulders. He's in a black suit, just like he always was every day that I saw him while he worked for us. His hands are perfectly steady as he reaches for his phone.

"You don't know how long I'll be staying with you?"

He shakes his head again, and frustration bubbles up in my chest.

"It's going to be awesome to live with you. Since you're so freaking chatty."

He takes a deep breath and then leans forward, resting his forearms on his knees.

"I'm not here to chat with you, Lena. This isn't a spa retreat," he says. This might be the most words he's ever said to me in a row. "You're not coming to hang out on vacation. You're going to be there because you're—"

"In danger. Yeah, I get it." I nod once and move to a seat a little farther away from him. I can smell the woodsy cologne or shower gel he uses, and it does things to me that are completely inappropriate. "Thank you for your help."

He blinks in surprise. "You're really not fighting this."

"Look, I'm not a kid anymore, Gideon. I'm not stupid. The incident at the gallery scared the shit out of me. I'm not used to being covered in blood and brain matter or having a pistol pushed against my throat." His jaw tightens. "I don't know what's going on. One minute, Chelsea and I were checking out an art exhibit, and I was trying to ditch my asshole of an ex-boyfriend while she sampled the dessert buffet. The next, I come out of the restroom to find that Richie's gone, and the *new guy* is threatening me."

"Fuck," he growls and pushes his hand through his hair.

"Yeah. *Fuck* might be an understatement. So no, I'm not fighting you or giving you shit about this. I haven't pulled anything since . . ." I swallow hard and shake my head, and now he does fist his hands because he knows exactly what I'm thinking. I glance at his leg. I can't say the words. "I grew up. I don't have to sneak around because I'm an adult who does her own thing, except I have security with me. I wish I'd been able to go back to my apartment to get *actual* clothes that fit me and that I like, rather than the castoffs I left at Mom's place when I moved out four years ago. I also wish I had my art supplies with me, because if I'm hanging out in the woods with no one to talk to, I'll be able to get a lot of work done."

"We'll get you supplies," he mutters. "And clothes."

"You'll take me shopping?"

His face says *keep dreaming.*

"You can order whatever you want from my computer at home. We may be in the boonies, but we do get deliveries."

At least there's that.

"Okay."

"For the record, I don't like this. I don't want you in my house or on my property. I don't want to bring whatever shitstorm you're tangled up in to my home and to my family."

Oh shit. I blink as I sit back in my seat, staring at him. It didn't occur to me that Gideon would be married and have kids. But it makes sense. Of course he does. He's handsome and smart, and he's living his life in Montana.

I clear my throat and can't look him in the eye, so I stare over his shoulder as I answer him.

"I'm sure your wife will be lovely, and I'll do my best to stay out of everyone's way. I'm good at fading into the background, I've had plenty of practice. Just please don't ask me to babysit your kids. I'm not good with little ones."

His eyes jerk up in surprise, and then he scowls.

"What the fuck, Lena?"

"Your family, Gideon. Of course you don't want me to intrude on your family."

He swears under his breath and rubs his hand over his mouth, and I wad up an old jacket that I wore in high school and prop it against the window.

"I'm going to nap. I haven't slept well"—*in years*—"and I think everything is just catching up to me."

I close my eyes, and he doesn't reply. I hear him sigh, but he doesn't say anything more.

I wonder what his wife's like. What kind of woman did he marry? I bet she's gorgeous. Tall and thin and looks perfect by his side. Maybe she's a redhead. Maybe they have little ginger kids.

Am I jealous?

Of course I am. But I'm not here to crush over my former bodyguard. I'm here because someone is out to hurt me, and Gideon is the only one who can keep me safe. And it does hurt my feelings that he doesn't want me around, but I'll be damned if I let him know that.

Because that's pretty much par for the course in my life. I'm typically in the way.

The whirl of the engines and movement of the plane make me extra sleepy, and finally, I feel myself drift off.

Chapter Four

Gideon

She slept the entire flight.

She even drooled, which I found to be kind of adorable, not that I'd ever admit that to anyone. Now that I've had the opportunity to really take her in, I can see the fatigue, the purple bruises under her stunning eyes, and the way her shoulders are almost up around her ears, even with sleep.

She's scared, which she absolutely *should* be. It pisses me the fuck off that Richie walked away from her, even for a second, leaving her vulnerable. My body hums with rage at the thought of anyone holding a weapon on her, threatening her.

That any piece of shit would even *think* about hurting her.

There are more questions than answers regarding what happened that night, and I don't like it.

I can't stop looking at her. She's fucking beautiful. She was always a pretty girl, but now she's stunning, and that is not something that I should be noticing. I shouldn't see the curves of her breasts under the blouse, or the way her thighs look, one crossed over the other, and imagine them wrapped around my waist. She's slender but has curves in all the right damn places. I don't know if she still likes to run for exercise.

I used to run with her every morning at seven sharp.

I don't know if she still prefers nachos over tacos, or if she likes that little restaurant near the White House that had sub sandwiches.

The truth is, a lot can happen in four years, and I don't really know her at all.

Lena murmurs in her sleep, and scowls as she shifts as if agitated. A tear rolls down one cheek, alerting me that something isn't right. She starts to shake her head back and forth, and then she cries out and sits up straight, breathing hard, her eyes glassy, and I shift over to her, take one hand in mine, and wrap the other around her shoulders, trying to soothe her. I brush the tear away with my thumb, not oblivious to her soft-as-fuck skin.

"Shh. You're okay. Hey, you're okay, Lena."

She sucks in a breath and pulls away from me, shifting so she's not pressed against me, and I take the hint and move back to my own seat, feeling the distance between us.

You're not supposed to touch her, you idiot.

"Sorry," she whispers.

"You didn't do anything wrong."

She bites her lower lip and closes her eyes. Her hands aren't steady. I want to ask her what the nightmare was about, but the pilot comes over the intercom to tell us we're about to land in Missoula.

"You live in Missoula?" she asks me, visibly trying to steady herself.

"No, it's just the closest airport. We have an hour's drive ahead of us."

She blows out a breath. "Can we pick up something to eat on the way? I'm starving."

"Sure."

Two hours later, after hitting a drive-through for burgers and fries and then making the long drive out to the ranch, I drive past the farmhouse that Ryker and Willow live in, and over to my own house by the lake. It's dark, so Lena can't see the mountains, but she'll see them in the morning.

I can feel Lena's lavender gaze staring at me.

"What?"

"Who else lives out here?"

"My brother and his wife are in the house that we just passed. There are ranch hands out at the bunkhouse, about a quarter mile away."

"Lots of people," she murmurs as I pull into my garage. Summer's over and we're well into fall, but all the hands are staying on full-time through the winter this year because Ryker has expanded operations, and it's not just a summer job anymore.

Lena and I get out of my SUV, and I carry her bag inside with her following behind me. I don't stop in the kitchen. I lead her through and up the stairs to the bedrooms, then open the door of her suite and set her bag on the bed.

"This is you," I tell her. "Bathroom is attached, and all yours. I need to make a couple of calls, so I'll be downstairs."

I turn to leave, but she stops me.

"Where is everyone?"

I lift an eyebrow. "Who's *everyone*?"

"Your family, Gideon. Your wife and kids."

"I'm not married. No kids." I shake my head. "My brother and Willow are my family. Their kiddo, Aiden, is my family."

Her brows pull together in a frown.

"You can get settled. If you need anything, just let me know. We're getting up early tomorrow."

"Why?"

"Because we're going to start training. Like I said before, this isn't vacation. You'll be working while you're here."

"What does that *mean*, Gideon?"

"You'll find out in the morning."

"And if I'm not tired?"

I reach up and lean on the doorjamb. I took my suit jacket off once we landed, along with my tie, and rolled my sleeves to get more comfortable. She's hardly taken her eyes off the tattoos on my left arm, and it occurred to me that she'd never seen me without the full suit.

She saw me in T-shirts when we ran together, but I've added to the tattoos over the past four years, filling in the sleeve.

Does she have ink?

Lena's eyes trail over my chest and stomach. She can't see skin, but she's checking me out, and then, as if catching herself, she clears her throat.

"You can wander around the house if you want. I wouldn't go outside at night because there are critters around. Bear, mountain lion, you name it. Go down and watch TV if you want."

She nods once. "Thank you. What time should I set my alarm for?"

"Five."

That has her balking. *"Five?"*

"That's seven in DC."

"Oh. Right. Okay, five it is."

I turn to leave, but she stops me yet again.

"Gideon?"

"Yeah."

"Thank you."

Shaking my head, I walk away. Christ, I could be with her for *months*. Which god did I piss off so bad that I'd get stuck with Blackbird in my house, under my nose, for God knows how long?

She's different from how she was before.

She's not argumentative. She's not brash or defiant.

I didn't think I'd ever see her again, and now she's sleeping upstairs, under my roof.

A lot can happen in two days.

Walking into my office, I close the door behind me and call Ryker.

"I saw you drive by," he says in greeting. "I take it everything went well?"

"We're here," I confirm and rub my hand over my face.

Fuck, I'm tired.

"How is she?" he asks.

Fucking beautiful.

"Scared. Different. She's grown up."

"She'll be safe here."

I nod and walk to the wall of windows. I can see the lake from here, and in the daytime, the mountains beyond.

"I've decided to start training her tomorrow. She was put in a position that she could have gotten out of if she'd been trained. So if you hear gunfire, that's us."

"Good to know. You okay, Gid?"

No. I'm not okay. I have a woman living in my house, and I don't want her here. I don't want any reminders of what I lost.

"Fine. I'm tired. It was a long fucking day."

"Get some rest."

"See you tomorrow."

After hanging up, I turn and sit at my desk. Debbie and Ray smile at me from the framed photo next to my computer.

I wish you were here.

I miss my mom. I miss them both, but Debbie and I had a special bond. She was the tiniest thing, probably didn't even weigh a hundred pounds, but man, her heart was so big. She loved Ryker and me like we were her own.

Because we were.

She and Ray had wanted a big family, and when Ray built the farmhouse for her after they first married, he included eight bedrooms.

Eight.

For all the kids they wanted to have and raise on this ranch.

But it turned out that Debbie couldn't have kids. So they took Ryker and me in. And Willow, too, in the summers. Debbie was Willow's aunt.

And that woman was *made* to be a mom. The fact that she couldn't have her own was an injustice that still pisses me off, because no one was better than my mom.

If she were here, she'd tell me to welcome Lena into my home, to take care of her and make her feel like she belongs. Hell, Mom would have spoiled the shit out of Lena.

It was just her way.

She'd have made fried chicken for dinner tomorrow, and Lena would have fallen in love with her.

Because everyone who knew my mom loved her.

"I think I brought a mess home," I say to my parents. "I hope I don't live to regret it. I don't like bringing anything here that could hurt Wills or Ryker."

So I need to make sure that doesn't happen.

Clicking the keys on the computer, I bring up my cameras. They have night vision, and I arrow through, examining each one to make sure everything is as it should be. There's a raccoon in front of camera three. Everything else is quiet.

I double-check all the alarms around the property, pleased when I see that everything is armed.

Movement in the doorway has me looking up, and the breath is stolen from my lungs.

Fucking hell, this is a bad idea.

Lena's standing there in a pair of black yoga shorts and a loose T-shirt. Her hair is up in a knot on top of her head, and she's washed her face.

It's not a provocative look. The look on her face tells me that she's not here to seduce me. She's simply ready for bed.

So why is my cock suddenly awake?

"What's up?" I ask her, glad that I'm sitting behind my desk.

"Can we order the supplies I need tonight? I'd like to get them as soon as possible."

I open a browser window on the computer and take a deep breath before I stand, willing my cock to calm the fuck down, and gesture for her to have a seat.

"I can't use my credit card," she says, biting her lip as she approaches. She smells like oranges as she shuffles by me to sit down. "It can be traced."

Smart girl.

"I'll use mine."

She shakes her head, but I stand firm.

"I'll bill your mom, Lena. Don't worry about it."

"My supplies aren't cheap."

"Don't worry about it," I tell her again, and walk away. I don't need to hover over her while she shops online, and I have to get away from her heat, her scent. "Do you want some tea? I'm going to make some."

"Sure. That would be great. Thank you."

I take my time in the kitchen. I've said that I don't want her here because of the potential dangers associated with her, and I can't have any of that touch the people I love.

I *won't.*

But it's more than that.

I'm fucking drawn to that woman. It's like she's a goddamn magnet. Starting literally *anything* with her is out of the fucking question.

And I need to remember that.

With the tea made, I pad back up to my office and walk in carrying both mugs. Lena glances up and smiles for the first time since I saw her in the White House.

And my stomach clenches.

Did she always smile like that?

"I'm about done here," she says as she accepts the hot mug from me. "The supplies are already in the cart on this page. Clothes and odds and ends I just grabbed from Amazon. Those don't have to be fancy."

My eyebrow lifts in surprise. "No fancy clothes?"

"I mean, we're on a ranch in Montana, so I don't think I have to get dressed up. Right?"

"Right." I want to kiss that smirk off her face.

Fuck.

"I snagged jeans and sweaters and T-shirts. The usual underwear. I also grabbed some skin care and other toiletries. I'm not sure what to get for shoes."

"Your feet need to be protected. Also, add workout gear."

"Oh, right. Good call."

She clicks the mouse several times and then nods.

"Done."

"That didn't take long."

"I know what I like." She shrugs and sips her tea. "Okay, show me what shoes to buy. We might as well knock this all out now."

For the next thirty minutes, I hover over her shoulder and point at the screen, trying to ignore her orange scent and how soft her hair looks. She chooses colors and sizes, and several thousand dollars later, she has everything she needs on the way.

"Jesus. Make sure my mom pays you back right away."

The money doesn't matter. I'm a wealthy man. But it's cute that she's worried about it.

Lena yawns and stands out of the chair, and she's suddenly pressed against me, her side to my front, and we both still.

"Sorry," she whispers. "Should have warned you."

I take a step back, letting her slip by.

"See you in the morning, Blackbird."

Her cheeks darken at the use of her call sign.

"Good night."

Chapter Five

Lena

I slept like the dead. And for someone who doesn't typically sleep well, it felt like heaven. This bed is cozy, the sheets crisp and not too hot, and it's so *quiet* here. There's no traffic noise, no lights from the city.

It's dark and still, and it settles my nervous system. The best part? No nightmares.

I roll over and check the time on the old-fashioned alarm clock and see that it's just past four, but that's six on the East Coast, and that's when I usually wake up. I only got about five hours of sleep, but it was *good* sleep. Add that to the few hours on the plane yesterday, and I feel refreshed.

I like to go for a jog in the morning to start my day, so rolling right into working out, which is what I *think* Gideon meant when he said training, is just fine with me.

I hope my Amazon order arrives quickly, because I don't have much to wear for workout gear. I had to pack what I had on hand at my parents' place, and that wasn't much. Thankfully, I do have a pair of yoga pants and a couple of T-shirts to tide me over, but they don't fit the best, and they're old.

Sitting up, I rub my hands over my face and glance out the window. It's still dark, still the middle of the night here. But I climb out of bed and do my business in the bathroom, then pull my hair back into a braid and get dressed.

I snagged some old running shoes from my closet, thank goodness, and I slide them on and wrinkle my nose. Ugh, they're not great. I must have run four hundred miles in these.

Please let deliveries happen soon.

I silently open the door of the bedroom and poke my head out. The house is still, but there are little night-lights along the wall that come on when you walk past, illuminating my way down the stairs. Finding the kitchen is easy enough, since it's open to the huge living area and dining space. The house is obviously newer, or recently remodeled. I expected a lot of dark wood and heavy leather furniture, but that's not how Gideon decorated his space.

It's airy, with light wood floors and big windows. The furniture looks comfortable, with camel-colored leather. There's even a wall of bookshelves.

I'm dying to see what the view is beyond those windows. I bet it's beautiful.

We *are* in Montana.

I've been to this state before, when my mom was on the campaign trail, but never really got to enjoy it. We would fly into a city, I'd listen to her give a speech and we would smile for the cameras as a family, and then we were back on another plane.

So I'm excited to actually *enjoy* being here. I already like the peace and quiet.

After walking to the coffee maker, I find the coffee pods and slip one in, then locate a mug and brew my first cup of mountain coffee.

I may not like the reasons for being here, and Gideon made it perfectly clear that he'd like me to be literally anywhere else, but it already feels good.

Aside from these horrible shoes.

Once my mug is full, I lift it to my lips and take a sip and then sigh in happiness.

"You drink it black?"

"Holy fuck." I gasp and jerk, spilling a little over the side, scorching my hand, and before I can move, Gideon's beside me, his hand gripping my wrist, yanking me to the kitchen sink, where he turns on the tap and holds my hand under it. "I'm fine."

"Didn't mean to startle you," he says, his voice gruff.

"It's okay."

Every time he's close to me like this, my body hums and my nipples pucker, which he'll be able to see through this T-shirt from five years ago that hugs my girls just a little too tight, and I *really* wish he'd stop touching me. I don't want to make a fool out of myself.

"Really, it's okay."

I tug free of his hold and reach for the towel to dry my hand.

"You're up early," he says and walks over to brew his own mug.

"It's almost six thirty where I came from." I sip my coffee before I steel myself to turn around and look at him, and then my eyes go wide, and I'm pretty sure my stomach is full of angry hornets because *holy Christ on a cracker.*

I've never seen him like *this.*

I know I'm staring, but I can't stop.

He's in black cargo pants, black boots, and a black T-shirt that molds to his torso and arms. Fucking hell, he's built. He's all muscle. There isn't an ounce of fat on him.

No dad bod here.

And he looks like he's ready to go to war and kick some serious ass.

Down, hormones.

I knew he had tattoos because he used to run with me back when he was my lead detail guy. But shit, it's been a long time since I've seen him, and it's like a punch in the gut because he's way hotter than I remembered.

And the *abs.*

His shirt hugs his stomach, and every molecule in my hands itches to touch him.

So I press them behind me against the countertop and lift my eyes to his face, only to find him smirking at me.

"You done?" he asks.

"I've never seen you out of a suit." I'm impressed that my mouth remembers how to speak because my brain is misfiring.

"Not true. We used to jog every morning, Rebel."

Rebel?

I didn't think he'd remember our morning jogs, but of course he's calling me out on my little lie.

"I'm going to make us breakfast before we head out," he says.

"Oh, coffee's fine for me."

"No, it isn't." He shakes his head and opens the fridge, starts pulling out eggs and veggies and even some cheese.

I miss cheese.

"I can't do dairy," I tell him softly, and he raises an eyebrow. "It kills my stomach."

He nods and keeps working, so I sit on a stool on the other side of the island to watch as he scrambles eggs and chops the onions, mushrooms, and peppers. His hand looks so big on the handle of the knife, it makes me swallow hard.

You are not *supposed to be lusting after the bodyguard who's keeping you safe, Lena. Absolutely not. It's highly unprofessional, and he isn't interested anyway. Don't make an ass out of yourself.*

"Did you just call me an ass?"

I blink rapidly. Shit, did I say that last part out loud?

"No, my brain was just waking up. Ignore me until after my second cup of coffee. Nothing that comes out of my mouth makes sense."

His lips quirk up on the side, and I wish with all my heart he'd smile at me. But then the moment is gone, and he turns to the stove to cook our food. Less than ten minutes later, we're both eating.

"I'll never eat all this," I tell him after I swallow a bite. "I mean, it's really good, but it's too much."

"You need the calories," he says. "You're going to work them off."

"So what are we doing this morning?" I pop a mushroom in my mouth. "Also, where did you learn to cook? Because this is delicious."

"Spent a lot of time in the kitchen with my mom." His brows pull together, and before I can ask more about his parents, he keeps talking. "You'll see what we're up to when we get out there."

"Am I at least dressed appropriately?"

He doesn't even look my way as he nods. In fact, he's hardly looked at me at all after the coffee spilled on my hand.

Great. I'm over here lusting after his hot body, and he's *barely* tolerating me. It's so flattering. Such a boost to my ego.

Mentally sighing, I shake it off. Who cares what he thinks? I'll only be here for a short time, I'll go on his little jogs in the morning, and when my art supplies get here, I'll shut myself away and work. Maybe I'll find places to hike. I'll figure it out.

When we're both finished eating, we clean up our dishes and set them in the dishwasher, and then we step out onto the porch off the kitchen, and my jaw drops.

The sun is just coming up over the mountains, and the sky looks like it's on fire, with reds and oranges shooting through wispy clouds. I had no idea that there's a lake out here, along with those jagged mountains, already topped with snow, in the background. The trees have started to change color, so along with the burning sky, the trees are yellow and orange, with a touch of red, and I'm pretty sure I just found what heaven looks like.

If heaven exists at all.

I swallow hard and sit on the top step when my knees give out, just taking it all in.

A tear spills out of the corner of my eye, but I don't care. My breaths are coming faster, and I can feel the pulse in my neck, but I'm not on the verge of a panic attack. That's not what this is.

I'm . . . *awestruck.*

There's no other word for it, and I don't think that word has ever been in my vocabulary before.

Because I've never seen *this* before.

Suddenly, Gideon lowers himself next to me, leaving at least a foot of space between us, and rests his elbows on his knees, silently waiting for me as he watches the sky change over those rugged peaks.

"I don't even know what to say." It's a whisper, because I feel like if I speak any louder, I'll shatter this moment.

"I know." He whispers it back to me. I wish he'd touch me. Maybe just hold my hand. Because this feels like a big moment, and I don't even know why. I'm a visitor here. This view isn't mine to keep.

After a few minutes, my tears dry up, and I stand, then shiver.

"Are you cold?" Gideon's frowning at me.

"It's cold here," I reply with a nod. The air is crisp, making goose bumps rise on my skin. "But I'll warm up. I could sit right here all day, so we'd better go."

He watches me for one long moment, and then he leads me down the stairs and starts to jog.

It's easy to keep up with him. It's as if he remembers my pace from all those years ago, and that's the pace he's setting for me.

There's a worn path that meanders around the lake and then into the woods, where the temperature dips even more. My teeth chatter, but I don't say anything because I'll be damned if I complain, and I have a sweatshirt on the way from last night's shopping spree. I'll be sure to wear it after it arrives.

As my muscles warm up, I settle into the run and enjoy the smell of the trees. We jog into a clearing, or a pasture, and there are men out here on horseback.

Gideon waves, and they wave back, and I offer them a smile. These must be the ranch hands that he talked about last night. I feel their eyes on me, but I ignore it, and soon we're circling back the way we came, which I only know because the mountains are in front of us again.

But we don't make our way back to the house. Instead, there are other structures in the distance. I want to ask him about them, but he's been quiet, hardly breathing hard as we've been on our run.

And I am struggling. Maybe because of the elevation change? I don't know, but I don't like it. My lungs are on fire, and I'm getting blisters on my heels from these stupid shoes.

Because of course I am.

As we get closer to the structures, I see that there are two buildings, and to the left, what looks like an obstacle course with big tires, climbing walls, ropes. It looks like something from a reality TV show.

He's going to make me do that. Shit, I don't want to do that.

But rather than lead me over there, he has us stop near one of the buildings, and I lean forward, my hands on my knees, trying to catch my breath.

"Whoa, you okay?"

I nod, then stand and press my hands into my low back, pacing. I'm a little dizzy, and there are dark spots around my vision. I haven't been this wrecked after a run in *years.*

"Altitude," I manage to get out. "Killing me."

His jaw firms, and he waits for me to cool down a bit.

"What's all this?" I ask.

Gideon points behind us. "Obstacle course. We're not starting there today. I don't like how you're breathing."

"I can—"

"Not today," he interrupts, scowling. "This is the armory. Only my brother, Ryker, and I have the combination to this building."

"You have a whole *armory*?" I blink at him in surprise. "Wow."

"The shooting range is over there."

He points off into the distance, but I can't see it from here.

"This building is the gym. Weights and machines. There's also a boxing ring in there."

"Gideon. What do you do out here? This can't just be for your entertainment."

"Sometimes it is, depending on how bad my recruits are." He smirks and crosses his arms. "I run a training center for new security officers who will be in high-profile jobs. Celebrities, the wealthy, that sort of thing."

"So they come out here and you decide whether they're badass enough to do the job?"

"Pretty much."

"That's cool." I nod, looking around, and then I shiver again, because now that I'm not running anymore, the cold air is lowering my body temperature fast.

"Come on," he says, gesturing for me to follow him into the gym. When he turns the lights on, I feel my eyebrows climb in surprise.

"This isn't a gym. This is . . . I don't even know. Gideon, this is something you'd find in New York City."

It looks like a massive warehouse, with two staircases on either side of the room that lead to a loft where cardio machines are. Down here are the free weights and the boxing ring. There are also punching bags, kettlebells, medicine balls.

You name it, this gym has it.

"We're in the ring today," he says as he reaches for what looks like tape and takes my hand in his. He brushes his thumb over the spot where the coffee splashed earlier. "Is this okay?"

"It's fine. You're going to tape my hands?"

He nods and starts to wrap it around my skin.

"Am I going to punch something?"

His steel gray eyes climb to mine. "You're going to try."

"I don't want to punch you, Gideon."

"Yeah, well, like I said, you're going to *try*. If you manage to connect, I don't want you to tear up your knuckles."

Every inch that he touches tingles. He's so close, I can smell that woodsy scent. He's hardly sweating from our run, and I can only imagine how I smell.

"You didn't have to slow down for me today," I inform him.

"I didn't."

Scowling up at him, I shake my head. "Yes, you did. You didn't get any workout in at all."

"It's not about me. I'm training *you*. I'll do my own thing later."

I don't like that.

But before I can argue, he finishes with my hands and then leads me to the ring.

"You're not going to wrap your hands?" I ask.

"I'm not punching anything."

I blink at him.

"Lena, I'm not the one on the defensive in this scenario. You are. Now, get your butt in here."

I climb in after him and try not to be distracted by all the muscles before me.

"I want to see where you're starting from in self-defense."

"I had classes in college," I reply with a shrug. "But it was mostly for exercise."

His jaw firms. He doesn't like that answer.

"I wanted to teach you self-defense when you were seventeen. I was outvoted."

"Why do I need it? I always have a crowd of testosterone-fueled men surrounding me. Hell, Howey managed to smack me *once*, and—"

"Fucking say that again," he growls, stepping into me. "Who the fuck is *Howey*?"

I roll my eyes. "The idiot ex. He was nice until he wasn't."

"He slapped you with witnesses around? What the fuck did he do when you were alone, Lena?"

Now he's breathing hard, and every muscle is tight with anger. It's a good thing Howey isn't here right now because he'd likely be getting his ass handed to him.

"He didn't do anything bad when we were alone. I mouthed off at a party"—he starts to speak, but I cut him off—"which I know is *not* a reason to ever raise your hand in anger. He slapped me across the face, my guys jumped in right away, and I never went out with him again because I may be a pushover, but I don't put up with that nonsense. No second chances."

He swallows hard. "When?"

I frown, thinking it over. "About a year ago, I guess. I saw him at the gallery the other night, and I basically told him to go fuck himself."

"Good."

"I also told my detail that I don't ever want him near me again."

"Also good." He steps away and walks to the middle of the ring. "Come here. I'm going to be the pretend bad guy."

"And I'm the damsel in distress."

He shakes his head. "No, you're not. You're going to kick my ass." He raises his hand and gestures for me to come closer. "I'm about to act like I'm going to slap you, and I want you to deflect."

"If we're in the heat of the moment, and you suddenly hit me, I can't see that coming and push your hand away."

"Yes. You can."

Chapter Six

Gideon

She's exhausted. We've been in this ring for an hour, going over self-defense and hand-to-hand moves, and she's barely standing.

But she won't complain.

I'm not trying to push her to collapse—I'm trying to get her to tell me that she's done. But this woman never would complain. For all the times I was frustrated with her, or even scared for her, she never complained.

It seems that hasn't changed.

"You're going easy on me," she says with a scowl and pushes the hair that's escaped her braid from her face with shaking hands.

For fuck's sake, Rebel, call it already.

"If I didn't go easy on you, every bone in your body would be broken by now."

She rolls her eyes, and it makes my cock twitch.

"Okay, big guy, come on. Come at me, but don't go easy."

"We're done, Lena. You've had enough."

She scowls and props her hands on her hips, but not before I see the relief move through her eyes. "I don't know why you bothered to put this tape on my knuckles, because I didn't get to hit you even once."

"You managed to elbow me in the gut, and that didn't feel good."

I barely even noticed it, but I don't want her to feel totally defeated.

Which is fucking new for me, because when I'm training, I don't give a rat's ass about feelings.

But Lena smiles with satisfaction at my words, and I'll tell her that she ruptured my spleen if it keeps that grin there.

"Good." She sighs and moves to walk out of the ring. "What are we doing next?"

The door of the gym opens, and Aiden saunters in. His eyes scan the room, looking for me. This kid grew into a monster of almost six foot five, and he's all muscle. After two years of college, he decided to enter the NHL draft and was picked up by Seattle.

My brother's old team.

He leaves next week to start the season, and I'm going to miss having him on the ranch.

"Hey," Aiden says as he saunters our way. "Wills sent me out here to find you. You're not answering your phone."

"I'm working," I reply. "Is everyone okay?"

"Yeah, she just wants you and the princess to come to breakfast." Aiden grins and winks at Lena, and for the first time in his life, I feel like punching the kid. "No offense or anything. But you're kind of a princess."

"Nope, I wasn't born into politics—my mother was elected into them. There's a difference. I don't have a tiara or anything." She's not offended at all as she walks over and holds her hand out to Aiden.

I want to pull it back. I don't want him touching her.

Get a grip, asshole.

"Lena," she says as he takes her hand and shakes it. Then the little brat kisses her knuckles.

Don't make me kill you today, buddy.

"Aiden," he says with a grin. "I'm the favorite around here. Wills raised me, and the rest of the family history requires a spreadsheet and a presentation. Anyway, she's making something delicious and wants everyone there."

"And does she always get what she wants?" Lena asks as she pulls the black tape off her knuckles.

"Duh," Aiden says with a laugh. "Of course she does. Otherwise, Ryker kicks ass. I'll see you guys over there. She said to be there in an hour."

"Oh, good, that gives me time to go wash the filth off me," Lena mutters as Aiden walks out of my gym.

I don't know why it bothers me that he's flirting with Lena. He's closer in age to her than I am. He's a good kid. He's one of my favorite people in the world, and I only have three of those.

Nope, still don't like it.

"Come on, we'll head back to the house."

Lena's chin firms, and she takes a breath before she walks ahead of me. Something isn't right. My eyes move over her, watching her stilted gait, and then I see the blood on the backs of her heels.

"Stop."

Immediately doing as she's told, she glances over her shoulder and raises an eyebrow. "Problem?"

"Fuck yes, there's a goddamn problem."

"You never used to swear this much."

"I've always sworn like this, just not at work. What the fuck, Lena? Why didn't you tell me that you'd torn apart your heels?"

She glances down and then winces. "It's okay."

"It's not okay."

"Look, if we weren't about to traipse all over the wilderness, I'd go barefoot. It doesn't bother me, but I don't want to step on woodland creatures or slimy things, or whatever. So I'll deal. I've had worse."

"I want you to listen to every word I'm about to say. If you tear your skin up like this, you can't train. You can't be reckless here. I know you're tired. You should be. You've been through hell this week, and now you're in a strange place. It makes sense that you'd be adjusting to the altitude and everything else. But you have to *talk to me*, Rebel. You can't just keep injuries and fatigue to yourself, because I can't read your mind, and I'm responsible for you."

"I'll tell you when I want you to know something, Gideon."

That's the wrong fucking answer.

She stumbles away from me, but I take two strides and I'm in front of her, my back to her, and I squat down.

"Hop on."

"You're kidding."

"Get on my back."

There's no movement, and I finally look back at her. She's biting her lip and staring at my ass.

Christ.

"Lena, jump on my back, or I'll throw you over my shoulder. You're not walking a mile like that. Fuck, I don't want you walking ten feet with your heels torn up like that."

"The house is a mile away?" That caught her attention.

"Just over."

"You can't carry me for more than a mile."

I turn to her. "Yeah, I can. You're tiny. I'll carry you around all day if you want." My leg aches like a bitch, but I won't have a problem toting this little thing around. "Now get on my fucking back so I can take you home. Wills doesn't like it when we're late."

"So Willow runs a tight ship around here."

"She's the only woman on this ranch, and we all adore her. What do you think?"

I turn back around, squat, and wait, and finally, Lena's hands grip my shoulders, and she bounces onto my back and wraps her arms around me, and I hold on to her thighs.

This was a bad fucking idea.

I should have jogged home and gotten the car.

Because now, the most beautiful woman I've ever seen is wrapped around me. Her breasts are pressed to my shoulders, her pussy to my low back, and she's *warm*. Not to mention, I can smell her oranges, and now I'll be walking with a goddamn semi all the way back to the house.

Hockey.

Fishing.

Terrorist attacks.

Running into a grizzly.

Getting shot in the knee.

I'm trying to think of anything that'll take my mind off the sexy woman clinging to me like a sloth on a tree.

"Can I ask you something?" Her lips are inches from my neck, and all my distraction tactics evaporate into thin air.

"Ask."

"You don't limp."

I pause in the middle of the field and look back at her. Her eyes are wide, and then she looks away and rests her forehead on my shoulder, so I keep walking.

"That wasn't a question."

"How?" It's whispered.

I don't want to talk about this. Not today or any other day. It was the worst night of both of our lives. What we went through together is something I wouldn't wish on my worst enemy, or my biological father, and that's saying something.

"A lot of fucking work" is all I say.

And yeah, the leg aches like a bitch today, but I'll push through it the way I always do.

She tightens her arms around me, and I pick up the pace because I need to get her off me. I can't touch her like this. I can't be this close to her and not want more.

And wanting more is absolutely *not* an option.

She's my job. She's the president's daughter. She's completely out of my league and off limits.

Finally, the house comes into view, and once we're inside, I carry her up to her room and set her on her feet.

My knee fucking aches.

No, I don't limp, because I make sure I don't limp. It's a weakness I'm not willing to show.

"Thanks," she murmurs. She still won't look me in the eye as she turns away and toes off the sneakers.

"Throw those away."

"I will when the new ones get here."

"Throw them away today. We won't train again until your new stuff arrives. That'll give you a few days to heal."

"I can—"

"For fuck's sake." I push my hands through my hair and pace the room. "Just do what you're told for once in your life."

Her gaze snaps up to mine, her eyes flashing with indignation. "I'm not your prisoner, your child, *or* your wife, Gideon."

Wife. Fuck.

"I don't have to do every single thing you say. I'm also not stupid. I'll be tossing these when the new ones get here. Trust me, I don't want to keep them, because they're trying to kill me and now my DNA is smeared all over the heels. But I don't have any other casual shoes here. Now stop being a bossy ass and get out of here so I can take a shower. Or don't and get a show—I don't really care."

She rips her T-shirt over her head, tosses it aside, and stalks to the bathroom, where she doesn't close the door. She keeps her back to me and pushes her thumbs into the waistband of her yoga pants, and as she starts to wiggle them down her hips, I turn my back to her and stomp out of the bedroom.

I'm going to spank her tight little ass.

I storm into my own bedroom, close the door, and strip down, then get into a cold shower. I'm going to be taking a lot of cold showers while that little rebel is in my house. Because I wanted to wrap that braid around my fist, rip the leggings in two, and fuck her into submission.

And that's the last thing that I can do.

I *never* saw Lena like this. Of course, she was a child for the majority of the time I was on her detail.

But she's not a kid now. Not by a long shot.

I've never had issues with keeping my hands to myself. I'm damn picky when it comes to women and who I fuck. I used to spend a lot of time with Ryker at hockey games, at after-parties where puck bunnies were plentiful and thought fucking the army Ranger turned Secret Service guy was pretty damn great.

And once in a while, I indulged.

But I'm not handsy with women. I'm not flirty. That's all Ryker. He can charm the pants off a pineapple.

I tend to scare people away.

Maybe I just need to get laid and work off some steam.

Shaking my head, I lean my palm on the tile and fist my aching cock as visions of Lena stripping out of her shirt fill my mind. She had a simple white bra on that cupped her tits perfectly. She's all soft, smooth skin and lean muscle and *fuck*.

I pump my fist quickly and grunt when the orgasm moves through me, then pull the nozzle off the wall and wash the cum down the drain.

Thirty minutes later, dressed in clean cargo pants and a T-shirt, I walk downstairs and find Lena outside sitting on the steps, staring at the mountains. Her reaction to the view this morning didn't surprise me. It still knocks me on my ass every day.

"I'm going to sketch it," she says, not looking my way, as I step out with her. "Probably over and over again. Do you mind tracking my order for me?"

"I don't mind." I pull out my phone and check my email. "Looks like two more days and it'll be here."

She nods. "Do you have regular paper and pencils here?"

Frowning, I sit next to her, just like this morning, sure to keep my distance from her.

"Yeah, I have those. You can have them."

"Thanks."

Feeling her gaze on me, I glance her way, and before I realize what I'm doing, I tuck her hair behind her ear.

Keep your hands to yourself, James.

"Sorry I snapped at you," she says softly.

"No, you're not."

Those lips tip up into a soft smile. "Not really, but I don't want to make you mad."

"Why not?"

A line appears between her brows. "What do you mean?"

"Why don't you want to piss me off? It never bothered you before. You pushed my buttons every chance you got."

She takes a deep breath and turns her gaze back to the mountains. "That's not true. It's always bothered me, but I'm not good at saying no."

As Lena falls silent, a bald eagle flies overhead, dips down to the surface of the lake, and then pulls up with a fish caught in its talons.

"Wow." Lena gasps, her eyes pinned to the bird as it flies away, probably to its nest in the woods. "Holy shit, that was cool."

"We should get over to the farmhouse for breakfast."

I stand and hold out my hand, which she takes, and I pull her to her feet. She doesn't flinch, but she's careful when she walks down the steps.

"We're taking the ATV." I point to the four-wheeler sitting next to the garage. "Hop on."

"Would you take this if I wasn't here?"

"No, I'd walk."

"Then let's walk."

"Get on, Rebel."

"Why have you started calling me that?"

I always called her that in my head, but I could never say it out loud.

"Because you're stubborn as fuck and you don't do what you're told. Let's go."

I get on, and she slides on behind me, and I immediately regret my life choices. Because for the second time in one day, Lena has her front pressed to me, and she rests her cheek in the center of my back.

It's intimate.

It's too fucking much.

So I hop off and grip her by the hips, scooting her forward.

"This is the gas," I tell her. "This is the brake. It's easy to steer, and you don't have to shift gears. I'll meet you there."

"I can—"

"Go." I take off at a jog, not glancing back to see if she's going to drive the stupid thing. If she gets off and goes inside, I don't care. I'll tell Willow that Lena was tired or not feeling well.

But the engine revs, and a few seconds later, she comes inching up next to me.

She doesn't pull away from me, keeping pace as I run faster than she ever could, stretching my muscles and lungs, finally getting a good workout in for the day, even if it is a short half a mile.

When we reach the farmhouse, I cut the engine on the four-wheeler, and Lena hops off, frowning at me.

"Were you trying to make me feel like shit?"

"About what?"

"About how fast I can't run. Jesus, who are you, Captain America?"

I can't help but laugh at that, and Lena's face softens as she laughs with me, breaking the tension between us.

"I can't do that with you," she says, shaking her head sadly. "Not even once I get used to the altitude."

"I have longer legs than you."

"Yeah, and you must take your Flintstones vitamins too."

Lips twitching, I gesture for her to climb the stairs to the front door. "I take two a day."

"I knew it."

I open the door and find Willow already walking our way.

She's *not* smiling.

Fuck, this could be bad.

"Hello, I'm—" Lena begins, but Willow cuts her off.

"Lena," Willow finishes for her. She actually takes Lena's offered hand, which surprises me. But she must squeeze it hard, because Lena gives her hand a little shake after Willow lets go, and looks up at me with wide eyes.

Fuck.

Ryker walks up behind Willow, his face grim, and he shakes his head. Aiden's watching with a blank face from the living room.

"You have a lovely home," Lena says. I can tell that she's nervous, and I wish Wills would smile and put Lena at ease, the way I know she normally would.

But she doesn't.

No smile. No warm welcome.

Fuck.

"Would you like something to drink?" Willow asks and turns to lead us all to the kitchen.

"Oh, I'd love some water, thanks."

"Gid?" she asks and finally smiles at me.

"I'm okay."

With a nod, Willow pulls a bottle of water from the fridge and offers it to Lena, who takes it but doesn't open it right away. She sets it on the island and shifts on her feet.

"You can have a seat," I tell her, gesturing to the stool, but she shakes her head and stays standing. Her whole body is tense. She doesn't want to be here.

And based on the lack of welcome from the woman I consider my sister, I can't blame her.

"What do you think of the ranch so far, Lena?" Ryker asks, cutting through the tension in the room.

"It's *so* beautiful," Lena says with a smile. "The mountains take my breath away. That and the altitude. I'm adjusting to that. I had no idea that Gideon had a place in Montana, let alone a gorgeous ranch like this—"

"Why would you know that?" Willow asks, and I see anger in her cheeks.

Shit.

"Trouble—"

"Why would you think that you'd know *anything* about him? All you ever were was a pain in his ass, making him work harder than he needed to, pulling him away from his family."

"Wills—"

"You're the little girl who hurt my guy," Willow continues, and Lena's entire body stiffens, her face goes white, and I step in front of her, blocking her from Willow's wrath. Lena's hands bunch into the back of my T-shirt, and then she pulls back.

"No." My voice is granite. "You won't speak to her like that, baby girl."

"She's in *my* house, and I'll—"

I hear footsteps, the front door opens and then closes behind me, the engine of the four-wheeler starts, and I look out the window to see Lena headed back to my place, the wind whipping through her dark hair.

"You're out of fucking line," I say to Willow. "Don't ever do that again."

I turn to follow Lena, but Willow grabs my arm.

"Gid—"

"You know, I love you," I tell her, pulling away from her. I'm *so* frustrated with her. What the fuck does she think she just proved? "And you've been with me through a lot of shit. I don't know where you ever got it in that head of yours that what happened to my leg was Lena's fault. I never said or implied that."

"You were protecting her, and—"

"Yeah. I was *protecting her.* She didn't fire that gun. She didn't do anything except have the misfortune of being in the wrong place at the wrong time. But the thing that disappoints me the most is, I've never heard you speak like that to *anyone*. Never. You invited us over here so you could put her in her place and bully the fuck out of her, but all you did was piss me off."

"Gid—"

Shaking my head, I ignore Ryker and run back to the house. The ATV is sitting by the back door, and I expect to find Lena upset in her bedroom.

Instead, I find her vacuuming the living room.

And she's singing at the top of her lungs.

Badly.

Chapter Seven

Lena

As I sing a Shakira song, I wiggle my own hips and push the vacuum out and then back to me, belting out the lyrics with all my might. When I'm frustrated, I either sketch or play the piano or clean.

And I'm a whole lot of frustrated right now. But all I can do is clean.

Did Gideon know that I'd be walking into that mess? *No.* He immediately tensed up, the way he does when he senses a threat, and stood in front of me. He told her to stop.

He didn't know.

What a lovely welcome to the ranch.

I guess I'll be staying close to home and keeping to myself while I'm here. Aiden seemed nice enough, but if everyone here hates me, I'll hide away.

It doesn't bother me.

I've done it before.

"I won't deny . . ." I turn and then come up short and let out a little squeal when I see Gideon standing at the edge of the living room, his arms crossed, showing off bulging biceps that I'm quite sure are illegal in all fifty states.

And if they're not, I'm sure my mom could sign an executive order if I asked her.

Gideon says something, but I can't hear him over the vacuum, so I shut it off and lift an eyebrow.

"Sorry, what did you say?"

"I asked if you're okay."

Shrugging a shoulder, I grab the feather duster I found in the closet with the vacuum and start wiggling it over surfaces.

"I'm fine, Gideon. A whole lot of people don't like me. If I cried every time they threw it in my face, I'd have some sort of eye disorder. But if it's all the same to you, I'll remove myself from that situation and make myself something different for breakfast."

Willow doesn't just dislike me. She hates me. She was breathing fire at me, and if looks could kill, I'd be six feet under.

"But did you tell them that it was my fault?" I can't help the question that falls out of my mouth, and then I instantly regret it. "Never mind. It doesn't matter."

"I didn't tell them anything," he replies. "Because it's all classified. So no, Blackbird, I didn't tell them that it was your fault. Besides, it *wasn't* your fault."

Except, it was.

It absolutely was my fault, and it's my biggest regret. My worst nightmare, one that I relive over and over again.

"It really doesn't matter. It's over. You're fine. It was a long time ago." I swallow hard because *now* the tears want to come.

"Gideon!"

"Go with Richie! Get the fuck out of here, Lena!"

Christ, I'll never forget the helplessness, the despair. The panic. The fear. And how the rain fell so hard, in sheets, soaking us all to the bone and making Gideon's blood run faster.

I whimper and then slap my hand over my mouth and play it off as a cough.

"Something in my throat."

"Lena . . ."

"You should have stayed for the food. It smelled good." *Do not cry. Do not cry.* "I'm just going to clean a bit, if that's okay? Maybe later I'll take a nap."

That's a lie. I won't nap because I'll dream, and that can't happen today.

"You don't have to clean my house."

"I know." My voice sounds so cheerfully fake that Gideon's eyes narrow. "It's all good—I like it. I can't sketch, and I can't play the piano, and I can't listen to music because I don't have access to any electronics—"

"Fuck."

"—so I'll clean. I can't cook, though. Never got the hang of it, and the chef at the White House always chased me off. I'd order in, but I don't think DoorDash is a thing in the boonies, and we swing back to the no-electronics thing. Otherwise, I'd put a pot roast in the oven or something, but it would burn and then your house would stink, and no one wants that."

I can't stop babbling. Someone make it stop!

"Lena."

"I'll see you later." I shoot him the fakest smile I've ever given anyone, even when my mother was running for president, and then turn away so he can't see my face.

Why do I feel like I'm breaking?

This is stupid.

This is *so stupid.*

I've had so many horrible things said to me in the seven years that my mother has held office that I let it roll off like water on a duck. It *never* affects me. Death threats, men describing in detail what they want to do to my body—you name it, I've heard it. Hell, *Gideon* has heard it because he was there with me.

So why now? Is it because I felt safe with Gideon, and I wasn't expecting it? I should never assume that just because I can relax a little I can let my guard down with anyone.

I learned that a decade ago.

Dragging the feathers up the handrail, I decide to clean my bedroom, where I can close the door and just *be* for a while.

Because I'll lose it if I have to be in a room with Gideon for even one more minute. And I'll want him to hug me, and I know that he won't do that.

I don't remember the last time anyone did. I never see my parents. Chelsea isn't a hugger. And I don't *trust* people.

Once in my room, I close the door and take a shaky breath, and then let the tears come.

You're the little girl who hurt my guy.

Fuck.

Why did he bring me here? Why couldn't he have taken me literally *anywhere else* to hide? I know there are safe houses, and places that are off the grid that don't involve his family. I don't want to be here.

I'll demand to speak with my mom or Bishop and ask to be reassigned. I just have to get through the next year of Mom's last term, and then I can disappear. I'll have no obligations, and I can do whatever I want.

No security detail.

No reporters.

No more threats, since I won't be connected to anyone with any power anymore.

God, that sounds so nice.

I let the duster fall to the floor and walk to the bed, but I don't sit on the side of it. I sit on the carpet with my back against the mattress, facing the wall, hidden from the doorway.

And I bury my face in my hands and cry.

I must have fallen asleep. Someone is knocking on the door, and when I blink my eyes open, it's dark. *Did I sleep all damn day?*

"Lena, are you in there?"

Gideon.

I didn't dream, which shocks the hell out of me because all I've done since this morning is think about that night. It would usually be a living entity in my body, terrorizing me relentlessly.

But I slept hard, and dreamlessly.

"Lena?"

"Sorry," I call out, and the door opens.

"Where are you?"

The light from the hallway shines in, and Gideon walks around the room, then sees me on the far side of the bed.

His face hardens.

"Why are you hiding?"

Because it's instinct.

"I'm not. I fell asleep down here."

"On the floor."

"I guess so, yeah."

"Why?"

I take a deep breath and let it out slowly. "Because I had a minor meltdown and sat closest to the wall for a few minutes and accidentally fell asleep. Okay? Is that what you want to hear, Gideon?"

"Lena—"

"It's not a big deal. But I'm super hungry, and I have no idea what time it is."

"It's after nine." His face is grim. "I just got back."

"From where?"

"First, I stopped to have another heart-to-heart with Willow."

I sigh, shaking my head. "You don't have to do that."

"Then, I went to town so I could get some groceries and some takeout. I also got you this."

He passes me an iPad. I blink at it and then up at him.

"It's connected to my secure Wi-Fi, but any messaging capabilities have been disabled. No texts and no email. I mean it, Lena, I'm trusting you. However, you can listen to music, or watch movies, or surf the internet all you want."

I can listen to music.

"Thank you."

"You're welcome. I grabbed tacos and chips and guac—"

"Say no more. I'm totally down for this adventure. Tacos are my love language." I stand and grin at him, but he's not smiling back, and I feel my face fall. "Something's wrong."

But he shakes his head, denying it.

"Nothing's wrong. Let's go eat."

"Gideon, are you and Willow okay?"

He blows out a breath, clenches his jaw, and then meets my gaze with his. "No. We're not okay. But we will be. Come on, I'm hungry too."

"I don't want—"

"Let's go, Rebel. I'm fucking hungry."

He didn't just get tacos and chips.

The man bought out the restaurant.

"There's enough here to feed eight people."

He shrugs and pops the staples on the top of a brown paper bag, revealing the freshly fried corn chips, then opens a tub of guac, another tub of queso, and yet another of salsa.

"I have tacos, burritos, and quesadillas. I didn't know what you would order."

He got everything.

Because he didn't know what I would want.

But I need to play this cool. It's not a romantic gesture. We have to eat, and it's not like he can text me to ask me what I want.

"Thanks." I dip a chip in the queso and sigh when I chew. "We'll have leftovers."

Gideon passes me a plate, and we dig in, and less than five minutes later, I'm sitting crisscross in a plush leather chair while he's sitting on the couch, and the beginning credits of *The Goonies* come on.

"A classic," I say, nodding in satisfaction.

"Never seen it."

I stop chewing and stare at him. "How? I thought this was a staple in everyone's childhood."

"I didn't have a normal childhood" is all he says, and the hard look of his face tells me that he won't say more.

"Well, then you can watch it now."

This burrito is *bomb*, and when all my food is gone, the chips are just a memory, reduced to crumbs on the coffee table, and my belly is as full as it's been in a long time, we lounge back and watch the movie.

"This town is full of idiots. All of them should have CPS called for losing their kids."

"It's a *movie*, Gideon. It doesn't have to be realistic."

He smirks but crosses his arms over his chest and stays quiet for a while.

The kids have just found the pirate ship when Gideon lets out a huff. "No way."

"It's a *freaking movie*. Are you like this during Marvel movies? Or *Star Wars*?"

"No, those are science fiction."

"You're entertained. I can see it. Your teeth aren't clenched so hard that it looks like they're going to break."

He scowls over at me. "I don't do that."

"On the daily, big guy."

"Why do you call me that?"

I blink over at him. "You have nicknames for me. I can have one for you. Besides, have you seen you? You're a *big guy*. And if you make a joke about your dick right now, I will choke you out with that burrito wrapper."

"I'd love to see you try, Rebel."

He holds my gaze, those steel gray eyes full of humor, and the room is suddenly consumed with humming electricity. My breathing increases. My pulse is hammering. And Gideon's eyes spark with interest as he licks his lower lip.

"Walk the plank!"

Gideon's the first to break the stare, and I feel like I should fan my face.

It's hot in here.

"Those restraints are not tied very tight. The kids are lazy. They could get out of those. Amateurs."

I can't keep the giggle in. "Okay, *expert*."

"I *am* an expert."

"They're kids. They're scared."

"Doesn't matter."

"I think you just don't want to like this movie because *I* like it."

"Not true." He shakes his head and then smirks when the two oldest teenagers share a kiss after falling off the plank. "He's thinking about scoring *now*?"

"Duh. He's sixteen." I take a sip of my water. "Don't ruin the ending."

He manages to stay quiet until the credits roll.

"That's two hours of my life that I'll never get back."

I glare at him. "Did you really hate it that much?"

"No." His lips twitch, and I throw a pillow at his face. "You're so fucking violent, Blackbird."

"Not usually. You must bring it out in me." I stretch my arms over my head and yawn. I don't really want to go to sleep. I don't want to dream.

But my eyes are heavy, and we have an early morning tomorrow.

"Back at it at five?" I ask him.

"No. Not until your new gear arrives."

"There has to be something we can do that doesn't involve shoes."

And just like that, the air is heavy again, and Gideon's eyes drop to my lips.

I want to climb into this man's lap so bad, it almost hurts.

"We can shoot," he finally says, interrupting my thoughts. "But we don't have to get up that early. Let's meet in the kitchen at eight."

I nod and stand, then start to pick up our mess from dinner.

"Leave it. I'll get it."

"I don't mind—"

"Good night, Lena."

With a sigh, I take my own plate to the kitchen, then offer him a wave as I walk through to the stairs and up to my room.

Chapter Eight

Lena

The nightmare tears me out of sleep, my heart racing, sweat pouring down my back, tears streaming down my face, and memories that I wish with all my heart I could forget so vivid, I feel sick to my stomach.

So much blood.

Gideon hurt.

My screams.

Sitting up, I bend my knees, rest my elbows on them, and then bury my face in my hands and give in to the tears.

You're the little girl who hurt my guy.

"You have to get a grip, Lena." I sniffle and wipe the tears away, then check the time.

Five.

I guess I'm not sleeping in this morning after all.

After washing my face and pulling my hair up into a high ponytail, I pull on some jeans and a T-shirt.

These jeans are too tight. My ass has grown since high school.

Please let my clothes get here today.

Not wanting to wake Gideon, I pad quietly out of my room and down the stairs to the kitchen, where there's a light on above the stove.

While the coffee brews, I take a deep breath and glance outside. The sky is lightening, and I can see the outline of the mountains.

I want to sit outside with my coffee, but it's chilly in the morning, so I check the coat closet by the front door and find a green army hoodie and slip it over my head.

God, it smells like him.

And it's huge on me.

But it's warm, and it almost feels like he's hugging me, and damn it, even if I won't admit it to anyone else, it's the comfort I need this morning after that fucked-up nightmare and the altercation with his family yesterday.

I'm only in socks this morning, but my heels are still sore as I walk out the back door and sit on the steps, ready for Mother Nature's show to begin.

I love that I have this front-row seat for this view. And I can picture this lake frozen in the winter, with snow falling and sticking to the trees, and I bet that's just as beautiful.

Sipping the coffee, I take a deep breath and then let it out, watching the steam from my breath fill the air. It's so peaceful here. So *quiet.*

Except for that rustling coming from the path that leads—

"Ah!" I jump up and narrowly avoid spilling my coffee when a figure rounds the house, and she squeals too. "Holy shit."

"Sorry." She puts a hand up to her chest and shakes her head. "I'm so sorry. I didn't mean to startle you."

Willow.

"It's pretty early to be lurking around." I swallow hard and sit back down, and butterflies erupt in my belly. I'm not mentally stable enough to have it out with her right now. I don't want another lecture, or to have her yell at me. I haven't even had half this coffee yet, and the nightmare is fresh in my mind. I needed this time alone out here to settle, and now it looks like I won't get it.

"Gid's usually up by now, and I wanted to come over and talk. I brought muffins." She holds up the covered plate and then sighs when I don't reply. "Is he around?"

"Haven't seen him yet today." I shrug a shoulder, and I see her eyes narrow when she recognizes the sweatshirt that I'm wearing.

Fuck.

One more thing for her to judge me over.

"I was cold, and I don't have any clothes here, but I'll put it back in the closet if it bothers you."

"Listen, we got off on the wrong foot."

"You think?" I stand and move to go inside. "If I see Gideon, I'll tell him you're looking for him. Or you can call him—"

"He never answers the phone. Please don't go."

I pause and look over at her.

"Can I sit with you?" she asks.

"This isn't my home. It's yours. You can sit wherever you want."

Willow huffs out a breath, sets the plate on the rail of the deck, and sits, gesturing for me to return to my spot and join her.

I could be a bitch and go inside.

But I'm not a bitch.

And I'm not good at telling people no.

So I sit and take a sip of coffee.

"Gideon and Ryker both think I owe you an apology," she begins softly. "And they're probably right. But before I do that, I need to explain where my anger is coming from."

"You don't have—"

"Yeah, I do." She rubs her palms up and down her denim-covered thigh. "I met Gideon and Ryker when I was fourteen. They're a year older than me. They came to the ranch under . . . difficult circumstances. I lived here every summer because I stayed with my aunt and uncle, who owned the ranch, and I loved it here. Then Ry and Gid came, and we became the Three Amigos."

I'm so jealous of that. That friendship, that connection to each other. I don't think I've ever had that with anyone. Even with Chelsea, it feels like her love for me is conditional, and there are things I know I can't tell her. Can't confide in her.

"Ray and Debbie adopted Ry and Gid the following year, and for almost twenty-five years, we've been a family."

"Where are Ray and Debbie now?" I ask softly.

"In a tiny graveyard about a mile from here."

My head jerks up, and my gaze latches on to hers.

"We lost them a while ago. It was the hardest thing we've ever gone through. When we lost Ray two years after Debbie, Ryker retired from hockey, and Gid came home for almost a month so we could settle the estate and figure out what the next steps were."

I remember that.

I remember Gideon being gone for longer than he ever had been before. He never took vacations, but there was a time, not long before that horrible night, when he took leave. I never knew why.

I didn't ask.

"I was struggling with Aiden at the time. He was going through a rough patch. I'd just lost Ray. And it was awesome to have my guys home. To heal together and help each other. Romantic feelings started to develop between Ry and me. I never saw Gid that way. He's my brother. Always has been. He had to cut his vacation short and go back to work—"

"Because of me." I nod, remembering.

Chelsea talked me into going to the tattoo parlor that night. We snuck out, and some tattoo artist she knew opened his shop late for us. I didn't want ink, but I agreed to piercings.

My nipples still hurt when I think about it.

"Yeah. Then, a few weeks later, Ry officially retired from hockey, and we were in Seattle for the press conference and celebration. Gid came for it, but he was too late to be at the announcement. He barely made it to the party, but he was there. Then, the next morning at breakfast, he got a call back to DC."

I swallow hard as I watch the sky turn peach and blue. I don't remember what I did that time to pull him back. It could have been anything, but it was likely Chelsea and me evading my detail so we could party.

So *she* could party and have me with her.

"Then, the next thing we knew, he was calling to tell us he'd been shot, he wouldn't let Ry come help him, and then his career was over. A career that he loved."

I blink rapidly, but I can't keep the tears back because *God,* how I missed him after that night. I was terrified, and no one would tell me if he was okay. I didn't know for more than a week how bad his injuries were, or where he was. I knew that I was just a job for him, but Gideon was the one person that I felt the safest with, and he was suddenly ripped away, and I didn't even know if he was okay.

Finally, I begged my mom to fill me in, and she reluctantly did.

But I was never allowed to see him. To thank him.

"I can't tell you what happened," I whisper and wipe the tears away. "I would if I could. I'd tell you everything, but—"

"You can't." Those two words hold so much hostility, I wish she'd just slap me. "Yeah, Gideon says that all the damn time. It's really annoying. The point is, we're his family. We're the ones who have his back, no matter what. Even when he's doing his job at the order of a president, and that job blows up in his face, we're the ones who pick up the pieces."

She shakes her head and brushes her own tears away.

"I'm sure you're not a bad person, Lena. But whatever decisions you made when you were a young, silly teenager shaped who that man is today. And it almost destroyed him there for a while. Maybe I was out of line yesterday. Maybe I *do* owe you that apology, but I love him so much, and love isn't always something that the three of us had until we found each other, and Ray and Debbie."

"Don't apologize. I don't need it." I shake my head and stand, brush off the seat of my jeans. "I'll stay out of your way, Willow. I'm not a kid now, and the shit that's going on is scary. Otherwise, I wouldn't be here. I'll ask to call my mother—I'm not allowed to have electronics—to have me reassigned and get me off your property as soon as possible."

"Bullshit."

Neither of us noticed Gideon approach. He didn't come from inside. He'd been running, or working out, based on his black running shorts and long-sleeved T-shirt and the sweat coating his skin. He's clenching his jaw in that way he does when he's pissed off.

Which, if I'm being honest, is a lot.

"It's for the best," I reply, lifting my chin, but he won't look at me. He's staring daggers at Willow.

"Go inside, Lena."

"Gideon, I'm not going to stay on private property when the owner of said property is angry and uncomfortable with me being here."

That gets his attention, and his eyes narrow at me.

"What the hell does that mean?"

Shaking my head, I sigh. "Just make the call. Have me reassigned. Drop me off on an island somewhere. Or take me home. I'd rather deal with potentially being kidnapped and killed."

Willow gasps, and I turn to walk inside, but then turn around.

"You have a lovely family. I like that you defend it. That you'd burn the world down for it. That's not something everyone has. Good for you, Willow."

I turn and walk inside and straight up to my room, where I start to shove my things into a bag.

Chapter Nine

Gideon

I want to run in after Lena, hug her to me, and tell her she's not going any-fucking-where. Goddamn it, I *like* having her around. It's been less than two days, but I'm already used to her presence. Her sass. Her smile. And fuck me if I don't want to touch her.

I can't.

But I want to.

"Gideon," Willow begins, and I shake my head, rounding on her.

"What the fuck, Wills?"

"I came over to talk to you, and I found her here on the deck—"

"So you decided to attack her again before the sun is even up? Christ, did you let her take a sip of coffee first?"

"No." Her shoulders slump, and she closes her eyes. "I mean, yes, she had coffee. No, I didn't attack her. I was trying to explain why I feel the way I do, and of course she told me that she can't explain what happened before."

"You really have to let that shit go." I push my hand through my sweat-soaked hair. "It's been five fucking years, Wills. I have a great life here at the ranch. I like my career. I'm good at it, and I make a shit ton of money. So seriously, *stop*."

"I had no intention of it escalating. Honest, I was talking to her, she was a little defensive—"

"I wonder why."

"And then she was telling me that she'll leave."

"She's not leaving."

Willow's lips thin as she watches me, and then her eyes narrow. "Wait. She's not leaving now, or when whatever this is is over, or she's not leaving *ever*, Gideon?"

The question is a kick to the solar plexus.

Of course she'll eventually move on from the ranch. She's not mine to keep.

But that thought leaves a bad fucking taste in my mouth.

"For now, it's my job to keep her safe, apparently even from my best friend. So let me make myself *crystal* clear. We'll stay out of your way, and while she's here, you're not welcome at my place. She deserves to feel safe and comfortable, and apparently I can't trust you for that."

Willow shakes her head, but I keep talking.

"Go home, Wills."

"Gid, I love you."

"Yeah, I know. I love you too. Go home."

Turning away, I push through my back door, head straight to the stairs and up to Lena's room. The door stands open, and she's stuffing things into the one duffel bag she brought with her.

She's still wearing my army hoodie, which makes me want to bend her over that bed and fuck her. Hard. Then come all over her back, marking her.

Jesus.

"Lena, you're not going anywhere." *No fucking way.*

"They didn't approve it?" Her pretty lavender eyes round, and something similar to despair takes up residence behind them, and it makes me want to punch a goddamn hole through the wall.

"I'm not asking," I reply and step closer. "This is where you're the safest."

She shakes her head and starts to pace.

"No, I don't want to be in the way. I don't want to make your family uneasy, and—"

"I told Willow that she's not welcome to come here while you're living here."

That makes her stop cold, and she shakes her head. "No, Gideon. I'm not going to be the reason there's a rift in your family. I won't be a burden, or an imposition. I don't want to be anywhere that I'm not welcome. Damn it."

Her lower lip quivers, and it's almost my undoing. Who is this woman? The Blackbird I knew never cried in front of me, not until that horrible night. She was almost obstinate, and strong willed.

This little rebel before me is about to have a panic attack.

"Why can't I ever tell Chelsea no?" she mutters, wringing her hands together. "Why do I let her get me into trouble like this?"

"You're not in trouble."

"I ruined your vacation, and then Ryker's retirement—"

I'm going to kill Willow.

"I ruin everything."

"Nothing is ruined, Lena."

The tears are falling now, and I'm not sure if she even hears what I'm saying, so I do the only thing I can think of.

I move right into her and wrap my arms around her, hugging her to me.

She stiffens and tries to hold herself away, but after two short seconds, she gives in and leans into me, her cheek pressed against my chest, and her arms loop around my waist.

"Listen very carefully to me. Do you hear me?"

My lips rest next to her ear, and I'm rubbing my hands up and down her slender back, rocking her back and forth, doing my best to soothe her.

Lena sniffles and nods. "Yeah."

"I want you here. You're staying because that's what *I* want." I swallow hard because she smells so good, and I want to kiss her head, but I have to keep it together. "I'm not going to ask for you to be reassigned because I'm what's best for you right now. I've got you here with me for safe keeping. This *is* your safe space. Nothing and no one will hurt you."

"I might hurt them." It's the tiniest whisper, and it breaks my heart.

"No, you won't."

"I already am. Willow—"

"Is fine. Apparently she has some misdirected anger, but she's going to be just fine. You're important, too, you know."

That has her pulling back and frowning up at me as she blinks through her tears.

"So you're going to unpack that bag, and take a deep breath, and then we're going to have some breakfast."

She licks her lips and wipes the tears off her face. She's not crying anymore, which is a huge relief.

I can't handle it when any woman cries, but Lena? Hell no.

"Do you like it here so far?" I ask her as I tuck her hair behind her ear. I can't stop touching her.

"It might be the best place I've ever been." She swallows hard. "Your mountains are just so amazing."

My mountains. She's adorable.

"Yes, I like it here, but I honestly don't want to be a burden. This is not the panic attack talking. I never want to make anyone uncomfortable."

"You're in *my* house, and you're not a burden to me. If Willow has a problem, she can stay at her house."

Lena shakes her head, but I catch her chin in my fingers.

"Keep shaking your head like that, and you'll give yourself whiplash. Tell me you'll stay, Lena."

Only a second passes before she whispers, "I'll stay."

"Good. I'm making steak and eggs for breakfast." Her stomach growls, making me grin. "I'm hungry too."

She nods, but she's not smiling. "I'll just freshen up and meet you downstairs."

"Take your time."

I have to make myself turn to walk away, because every cell in my body wants me to stay here with her. To hold her and comfort her.

Before I reach the door, Lena says, "Gideon?"

"Yeah." I turn back to find her pulling my hoodie over her head, showing me her bare midriff and the bottom of her white bra. *Jesus fuck.* Her skin looks smooth and inviting, and I want to know what it tastes like.

"Here, you can have this back." Her head pops out, her hair in disarray, and she offers it to me.

"Nah, you keep it. You look better in it than I do. See you in a few."

"You grilled these steaks at six in the morning," she says as she takes the last bite and closes her eyes. "Like, on the barbecue."

"How else am I supposed to make them?"

She lifts one shoulder and then finally smiles at me. "It was really good. I can probably hit a target today. We're shooting, right?"

"That was the plan." I eye her as I push my empty plate away and pick up my mug of coffee. "But I have questions first."

"Okay."

"Have you ever shot a gun?"

"No."

"Have you ever held one?"

"Not that I remember." I narrow my eyes, and she smirks. "No."

"We'll start here with some instruction, then. Never point the barrel of a weapon at a person, unless you plan to shoot them. So if you're holding it, keep it pointed at the floor."

"Okay. Point it at the floor or kill someone. Got it."

"Some of the weapons I'll be training you on will have some kick."

"But you'll tell me before I shoot it, right?"

"Of course."

"Okay, let's go."

I chuckle and stand to put my dishes in the dishwasher, and Lena follows me. "You're excited for this."

"Look, I have some aggression to get out, okay? Sure, I could go punch one of those bags in the gym, and I might do that later, but shooting the hell out of something sounds cathartic."

It definitely can be, yeah.

But before we can head out of the house, my phone rings, and our ranch manager's name is on the screen.

"Hey, Dusty."

"Hey, boss," the old man says. "A big delivery was just made over at Ryker's, and we thought it was for the barn, since there's so much of it. But it's not for us. It all has your name on it. Want me to bring it over?"

An idea starts to form in my head.

"No, keep it all there. I'll come get it. It'll be a couple of hours before I get there."

"You got it."

He hangs up, and I turn to Lena. "Change of plans today. You're getting a tour of the ranch."

Her eyebrows climb in surprise. "So no target practice?"

"We'll save it for tomorrow."

"Cool. How big is it, anyway?"

"About fifty thousand acres."

Lena coughs. "Holy shit, Gideon. That's *huge*."

I grin at her, and that sassy roll of the eyes has my cock paying close attention.

"The ranch, big guy. Not, *you know*."

"No, I don't know what you could possibly mean." I cross my arms over my chest, my lips twitching as she scowls, her lips tipped down in the corners. *I want to kiss her.* "Enlighten me."

"You have a dirty mind."

"*I* have a dirty mind? I'm not the one who went there."

"Yes, you did. You totally did."

Yeah, baby, my dick would wreck you, and then you'd beg for more.

That's definitely a line I can't cross with this woman, no matter how much I want her.

"Come on." Without a second thought, I reach for her hand, and she pauses, as if surprised by my touch. "You okay?"

"No, I'm fine." She slides her palm over mine, and I link our fingers. "I'm just . . . You know that hug earlier?"

"Yeah."

"It was nice. I don't remember the last time someone hugged me. I guess I needed it."

Stepping in front of her, I tip her chin up so her lavender gaze meets my own. "What do you mean?"

"What do you mean, what do I mean?"

"You haven't been hugged?"

She bites that plump lower lip and glances down at my chest.

"I mean, *of course* I've been hugged. Just not in a long time. Sometimes a person just needs to be touched."

"Why?"

"Because hugs feel good."

"Not that. Why haven't you *been* hugged?"

She starts to pull away, but I hold on firmly, keeping her hand in mine.

"My parents aren't warm and fuzzy. Chelsea definitely isn't a toucher." She shrugs those shoulders again. She's back in my hoodie, and I was right. She looks fucking adorable in it. "It's okay."

It's not fucking okay.

But instead of saying that, I grab the keys to the side-by-side that's sitting by the four-wheeler and lead her outside.

"You have all kinds of fun toys," she says as she gets in the passenger seat.

"We're on a ranch. We either get around on one of these, or on a horse."

"You have horses?"

She doesn't know anything about this place.

"Yeah, about a dozen of them. Ryker and Willow have a bunch of chickens. We have cattle that we sell for the beef."

"Did we eat one of your cows this morning?"

"Of course." I wink at her as I pull away from the house. "The eggs are from here too. Those are the Bitterroot Mountains."

"They already have snow," she says, admiring them. "When will it snow down here?"

"Could be anytime, but it won't stick until December. Then, we won't see grass again until April at the earliest."

"I *love* snow," she says with a happy sigh. "I like being cold. I hate summer."

"You *hate* summer?"

"Okay, that's a strong word, but I'm not one of those girls who loves to lay out and get skin cancer and get hot or stung by bees. I don't like to sweat."

"You jog every day."

"That's different. When I jog, I'm sweating because I was productive. In the summer, it's just sweat. I don't like it."

"You always used to go to Mexico with Chelsea in the summer," I remind her. "We went at least three times."

"*Chelsea* likes hot weather. Not me."

"Then why did you go?"

When she doesn't answer for a minute, I glance in her direction. "Because I never tell her no."

"Never?"

"Even when I definitely should. Anyway, I prefer the cold, because then you can get cozy inside. Are you still able to train people in the winter?"

"I train people all year round," I confirm. "Whether it's forty below or a hundred and ten, we're training."

"Put me down for a balmy seventy degrees. Otherwise, I'll tap out."

I smirk, enjoying the fuck out of her. I had no idea she was this funny.

"What's that old wall over there?" she asks, pointing off to the right.

"Ruins. We don't know for sure what it used to be. Ryker, Willow, and I used to play around there all the time when we were kids."

"I'll come check it out sometime."

"We can go look now."

I turn the wheel and steer us over to the old rock building that crumbled a long, long time ago.

Lena hops out and walks over, runs her hand over the wall.

"It makes me wonder who built this. Was it a home for a family? Was it a storage place for food? An outhouse?"

"Little big for an outhouse," I reply.

"It's pretty cool." Shoving her hair off her face, Lena turns back to look at the mountains again.

She's enamored with them.

"I want to draw them from here. Maybe from everywhere."

"You can do that."

We get back in the little vehicle, and I set off for the barn. Aiden's walking out of it as we approach and waves when he sees us get closer.

"Hey," he says with a smile. "I saw the pile of loot in there. I didn't know you liked to shop so much, Gid."

"It's cathartic," I reply and then grin when Aiden laughs. "It's all for Lena. Where is everyone?"

"Most everyone's inside," he says. "Storm's coming later, so we're getting ready for it."

I nod and see Ryker step out to join us.

"Do you need my help?" I ask him.

"Nah, we have it covered." He turns to Lena and offers her a smile. "I'm Ryker. We didn't get to meet yesterday."

"Lena." She holds her hand out to shake, but I see the way she tenses, as if she's waiting for Ryker to go on the offensive the way Willow did. "It's nice to meet you."

"Same," Ry says.

"Ignore Aunt Wills," Aiden adds. "She's just in mama-bear mode, and that can be intense."

"Oh, it's fine—" Lena begins, but Ryker shakes his head.

"Welcome to the Triple Creek," he says, and I can't help but smile.

This is exactly how she should have been welcomed yesterday.

"All the horses are put away," Malachi, one of our young ranch hands, says as he comes outside, but when he spots Lena, he blinks, and a slow smile spreads over his handsome face as his eyes travel up and down her body, pausing at the sight of her tight jeans. "Well, hi there."

"Hello," Lena says. "I'm—"

"My dream come true," Malachi says, and before he can reach out and touch her, I step in front of her and pin the man in a hard stare. "Um. Sorry. Didn't realize—"

"Don't you have something to do?"

"Sure." He looks around me and waves at Lena. "Nice to meetcha. Have a good day."

He walks back inside, and Ryker and Aiden are both laughing. Lena's hiding a smile behind her hand.

"What?"

"You could have just peed on her," Aiden says, making me growl. Lena lets her laugh loose, and it sends electricity through me, and all I want in the world is to be alone with her right now.

Forty-eight hours and this woman is under my skin.

I'm fucked.

"Funny. Where are the packages?"

"Inside," Aiden says, pointing with his thumb over his shoulder. "Big pile of them, but they should fit in the back of your rig."

"I want to see the horses," Lena says with a sweet grin. And then she ruins it with her next comment. "Maybe Malachi will give me a tour of the barn."

I narrow my eyes at her, then step closer and lower my lips beside her ear. "Keep it up, Rebel."

"And what?"

"You'll find out."

"Well then, come on. Show me the horses, big guy."

She's sweet with them. Her voice is soft and soothing, and my horse, Rascal, nuzzles her neck.

Yeah, I get it, buddy. She's fucking magical.

"Doesn't anyone have a dog on this ranch?" Lena asks.

"We have a golden retriever," Ryker says. "He's only two, and a pain in the ass. He's also attached to Willow, so he doesn't come out to the barn much."

"What about barn cats?" she counters.

"I didn't know you liked animals."

She shrugs. "They're usually better than people."

"You're not wrong," Aiden agrees. "There's a few mousers around."

Lena's eyes find mine. "You need a couple of cats. Inside ones, so predators can't get to them."

Why am I suddenly considering adopting pets just for her?

Shaking my head, I lift some of the boxes. "I'm out training too much to have animals. Aiden, help me load these up."

It only takes Aiden and me a few minutes to get all Lena's things loaded into the back of the side-by-side, and then Lena and I are headed out so I can show her the rest of the ranch on the way back to my house.

"Are those your cows?" she asks, gesturing to the Black Angus cattle in the pasture.

"About half of them," I confirm and turn to the left to loop back around.

There's a fenced area nearby with a locking gate to keep animals out. Two headstones sit in the middle of it, and there's plenty of room around them for the rest of us, when our times come.

"Your mom and dad?" Lena asks with a soft voice.

My gaze whips over to her, and she shrugs.

"Willow told me."

"She told you too much."

"She was just trying to make me understand, Gideon. I'm sorry that you lost them. And I'm sorry that I made that time more difficult for you."

I brake next to the cemetery and turn to face Lena.

"You have to stop apologizing. You *have* to, Lena. None of it was your fault. My parents dying wasn't on you. The shooting wasn't your fault. *None of it.* I told Willow that she needs to let it go earlier, but you do too. You don't need to carry around any guilt. Not for me."

She nibbles that bitable lip and then offers me a smile. "Okay. I won't apologize anymore. It's annoying. This is a great place for a cemetery."

"We thought so too."

Putting the side-by-side back in gear, I point us toward the house. "Let's go look at your loot."

Chapter Ten

Lena

"I need a sharp knife."

Gideon's eyebrow shoots up, and I can't help but grin at him. *He's so freaking handsome.*

"To open the boxes, not for nefarious acts."

"Box cutter coming up," he says and opens a drawer in the kitchen that's obviously a junk drawer. Every home in America has one of these.

Except the White House. But that's not a normal home.

"Be careful," he warns me as he passes it to me, and I push the blade out with a triumphant grin. "Seriously."

"Seriously, I'm twenty-four," I remind him. "I've used a blade before. But maybe stay over there. Just in case. I wouldn't want to accidentally draw blood."

He chuckles, and the sound moves through me like music. I can probably count on two hands the number of times I've heard this man laugh in all the years that I've known him.

If he'd cracked a smile more often, or let out a chuckle like that, I would have been so gone over him, I would have humiliated myself on the daily.

But it was the hug earlier that made the butterflies erupt and my skin prickle, and my freaking vagina do the two-step. Being held by

Gideon James is an experience that everyone should have at least once in their lives, and yet, if one single woman were to touch him right now, I'd scratch her eyes out.

After I cut her hands off with this box cutter.

"You have a devious grin on that gorgeous face of yours."

Wait. He thinks my face is gorgeous?

Since when?

"What were you thinking about?" he asks.

"Psh. Nothing." I slice through the tape of the first box and rejoice when I find three pairs of jeans. "Thank God, denim in my actual size. The ones I'm wearing are about to sever me in half. My ass has grown. I think my kidneys are shutting down. Turn around."

He lifts a brow. "What?"

"Turn. Around. I have to put these on. Everything else is getting washed before I wear it, but I'm trashing these torturous jeans that I'm wearing immediately. Maybe we'll burn them. Incinerate them. They deserve it."

He just stares at me.

"I'm going to strip, big guy. If you would please turn around, I'd appreciate it." Shrugging, I pop the button on the fly, and he turns his back to me.

And what a backside it is.

Broad shoulders are encased in his black T-shirt, with muscles that ripple with every movement. That back tapers to a slim waist and the best damn ass I've ever seen. You could totally bounce a quarter off his ass. His thighs are like tree trunks. No wonder he could carry me on his back for more than a mile.

My nipples tingle at that reminder.

Down, nipples.

I work the jeans over my hips and am shimmying back and forth, peeling them down my thighs, but suddenly they're caught around my ankles, and I hop twice before I face-plant on the hardwood, narrowly missing breaking my nose.

"Ouch."

"Shit, are you okay?"

"Don't turn around."

"Too late."

I wince before opening my eyes and looking up at Gideon, who's now standing over me, his eyes raking over my body.

My ass is in the air. Covered only in a pair of red satin panties circa seven years ago because the hoodie has ridden up my back.

And his eyes are pinned to my backside.

"Gideon?"

"Stay where you are."

Narrowing my eyes, I push up onto my hands and knees, and he lets out a string of curses that would make a sailor blush.

Or an army Ranger.

"Just get my feet untangled, and do not check out my ass."

"Also too late."

I whimper, but he's suddenly at my feet, tugging on the legs of the denim until he wiggles them over my feet, freeing me.

"Thanks. Now, turn back around."

"Not a chance in hell," he replies. His voice is deeper now, almost growly, and I push up onto my feet and reach for the new jeans, begging my core to calm the hell down. "How did you get that scar?"

I pause before pushing my feet into the legs and twist so I'm looking back at my upper thigh and the white scar that spans from left to right.

"I was shaving in the shower and slipped. Cut myself on the way down."

His jaw works and eyes heat with that explanation.

"So you're saying you're a fall risk. Do I need to have handrails installed everywhere in my house?"

"Har har. You're funny. That cut hurt, too, but not nearly as bad as the nipples."

I push my feet into the jeans and grin when I zip them up and they feel *amazing.*

"That's so much better."

"If you say so."

"Are you flirting with me, big guy?"

I tilt my head to the side, set my hands on my hips, watching him.

"What happened to your nipples?"

"Huh?"

"You said it didn't hurt as bad as the nipples. What happened?"

He's slowly walking closer to me, and my breaths speed up with every step. His muscles are coiled tight, as if he's going to strike.

I really want him to strike.

"Doesn't matter."

"Tell me."

Pressing my lips together, I wince. "They're pierced."

He stops moving. His gray eyes go wide, and his jaw drops in surprise.

"Didn't expect that, did you?"

"Your fucking nipples are *pierced*?" His gaze drops to my boobs, which are hidden beneath his hoodie.

"Yeah." I shrug, reach for the knife, and resume opening boxes. After pulling out the contents, I toss the empty cardboard aside, getting excited with every new garment I uncover. "This is going to be so cute with leggings."

"Why did you pierce yourself, Rebel?"

"I didn't. Some guy did it. He was kind of cute, and very respectful."

The air is thick with Gideon's frustration at my answer.

"Why?"

I open another box and pull out two packages of underwear—*thank God*—and then set them aside to go in the wash before reaching for another box.

Why do they send everything separately? This is a lot of packaging.

"Lena."

"Remember when you were gone for almost a month?"

The room goes silent.

"Go on."

I clear my throat and slice open a box, internally rejoicing at the sight of fresh charcoal and pencils. The sketch paper and pads must be around here somewhere.

"So no one knows this. *No one*, Gideon."

"I don't know if you're aware, but I have the highest security clearance there is."

"Yeah, well, I'm just saying. I mean, Chelsea and the piercing guy know, but that's it. Oh, and Howey, but he didn't like them. He was afraid of chipping a tooth."

"Look at me."

"Nope." I shake my head and pull clothes out of their protective plastic bags. "I can't look at you while I tell this story because you're going to be *so mad* at me."

"No, I'm not."

I huff out a laugh and shake my head. "Yeah, okay. Chelsea wanted to meet up with this guy who owns a tattoo-and-piercing shop, but she wanted to go after hours because she had a crush on him, and she didn't want my detail to follow us. Which, in hindsight, was probably a good call because I did *not* need my guys seeing my nipples being pierced."

"Christ."

"Anyway, she decided that we both should get tattoos. Not necessarily matching ones, but still have them done on the same night."

I'm running out of boxes to open, and then I'm going to have to look at him, and I really don't want to do that.

"I didn't want a tattoo. It's not that I would never get one, or have issues with them in any way. I love yours."

I glance over and take in the sleeve that runs down his left arm.

Yeah, those are hot as shit.

"But I was only nineteen, and there wasn't really anything I could think of to put on my skin for the rest of my life. A unicorn? No. A heart? Stupid. They had some premade designs that they tried to push on me, but nothing spoke to me."

"It's your fucking choice, Lena."

"Exactly, so I said no thanks. No ink for me on that night. And I felt guilty for giving the guys the slip, like always, and Chelsea was annoying the hell out of me. The girl doesn't know how to take no for an answer. She just keeps badgering and poking and won't let up. Then, the guy mentions that I could get something pierced, since that's not permanent if I don't want to keep it. I could always take it out."

I bite my lip, remembering how pressured I felt that night. I hated being there.

"And you chose your nipples."

"I didn't want it on my face, and there was no way in hell he was getting anywhere near my pussy."

He swears some more.

"So yeah. I had the nipples done. And you know what? I like them."

I turn and see his gaze whip over to mine in surprise.

"I thought I'd end up taking them out, but once they healed, which took a long-ass time, I liked them. I don't love the way I got them, but I'm definitely keeping them." I peek over at him.

"Why would this make me mad?"

"Because it was the night you got called back to DC after being gone for a few weeks. *My nipples* ruined your life that week, and I feel really bad."

He's quiet for a minute, and then he takes a deep breath and shakes his head.

"Never a dull moment with you, Rebel."

He doesn't look mad.

If anything, he looks a little . . . turned on.

"I'll help clean this mess up." I stare at the pile of boxes and wrappings as if it's Christmas. "I just sort of tossed stuff around."

"Go put your new clothes in the wash. I've got this."

But I shake my head and dig in, helping him, and within five minutes we have the boxes broken down and everything else in a big trash bag, and we're carrying it all out to his truck so he can haul it away later. We work silently, but it's not an uncomfortable silence.

I just wish I knew what he was thinking.

"Do you mind showing me where the laundry room is?"

"Sure. Come on."

I gather all my new clothes in my arms and follow Gideon up the stairs and down the hall past my bedroom to a gorgeous laundry room.

"This is nice."

He nods. "There's soap here, softener here. Everything you'll need. Do you know how to operate the machines?"

I frown at him. "I do laundry every Sunday at home, Gideon. I have an apartment."

"Right." He backs out of the room, and I sort the clothes, then put a load into the washer, measure in soap and softener, and start it.

When I get to my room, I see that Gideon has already brought the rest of my things upstairs. The shoeboxes sit by the end of the bed. My art supplies are on the desk by the window, and there's a small box of the few toiletries I ordered as well.

After getting all that stowed away, I grab my new charcoal set and a pad and walk downstairs and out to the deck, plant my ass on the top step, in what I've now claimed as *my spot*, and start to sketch, and it feels like I can finally, fully breathe.

God, I've needed this.

I usually only work with black charcoal, but I also ordered colors. Today I'll work with gray scale, but I can't wait to try to capture the sunrise on another day.

Time is irrelevant when I'm drawing. I'm so absorbed in it that I don't even realize that Gideon has joined me until he sits next to me and passes me a bottle of water.

"Drink this."

Pausing, I take the bottle and sip it, then set it down next to me and keep sketching.

I'm having issues shading the water just the way I want it. Rubbing it with my thumb, I pause and look up before brushing my hair off my face, taking in the view.

Gideon's hand comes up, and he swipes his thumb over the apple of my cheek.

"You have a smudge right here."

"I always make a mess when I work," I tell him. "It's part of the fun. Luckily, all this washes out of clothes easily."

"You're damn good, Lena."

For the first time since I sat down, I hold the page up and take in everything that I've already drawn. I have the mountains done, but I can't get the water quite right.

"The shoreline over here is fighting me."

"It's perfect, just the way it is."

Pressing my lips together, I glance over at him.

"You should sell your work. Why aren't you in galleries?"

"You and Chelsea actually agree on something. Hell must be chilly today." I smirk and smudge my fingertip over that shoreline again. "Art is the one thing that wasn't ruined for me by my mother's presidency. No one really knows about it, other than a few close people. I haven't had to talk about it in interviews or show it off. Do you know that during her second campaign, *People* magazine came into the White House to look at my *bedroom*?"

"Yeah." His voice is rough. "I remember."

He wasn't around anymore by then, and I hated that he was gone. Everything was still so raw and empty.

"My life is an open book." I start to shade in clouds. "Everything from my SAT scores to my prom pictures to my shoe size. My *literal* shoe size was discussed in *Marie Claire* one year. I don't know why that's important, but whatever. I didn't want to share this piece of me with anyone. Not to mention, I don't love the attention that I get because of who my mom is. It feels weird."

"Why?"

He's a really good listener.

"Because I'm not doing anything. I'm not signing executive orders or putting laws into effect or changing the world. I have no say, and it's not me in the job. Just like if my mom was a pilot. I'm not the one flying the plane. Why would anyone want to talk to me about her job?"

I shake my head and go back to that shoreline.

Why won't it work?

"I would have been happy if she lost." Those words are whispered, and I feel so guilty for voicing them out loud. "And that's a shitty attitude. I'm not complaining."

"No, you *never* complain."

I frown over at him. "I don't like to complain. I'm as privileged as it gets, Gideon. I don't even have to list all the reasons. They're glaringly obvious."

"It's okay to have opinions," he replies.

"Sure. And I have some. But it would be intensely ungrateful of me to bitch about any part of my life." I shake my head and go back to working on the trees on the other side of the lake. "Anyway, maybe someday I'll try to sell my art. But it would have to be when Mom's out of politics, and our last name isn't so recognizable."

"You could always sell it under a pseudonym."

I blink over at him.

"You know, like some authors do. Actors. You don't have to do it under your real name."

Huh. I never thought of that.

"So it would be sort of anonymously."

"It could be. You wouldn't have to put your face next to it. Have a third party handle sales and exhibitions. Maybe the mystery would make it sell for a higher price."

I grin at that. "You could be onto something."

Sighing, I stare down at the drawing in my lap.

"I'm rusty. This is shit."

"You're crazy if you think that's anything other than fucking amazing."

The clouds overhead are getting angry, and I hear thunder off in the distance.

"Storm's coming through." Gideon stands and offers me his hand to help me up. "We should go inside."

"I can smell it." Taking a deep breath, I grin when the wind kicks up, blowing through my hair. "Wow, it happened fast."

"They usually do around here. Come on."

Following him inside, I'm surprised to smell something delicious in the air.

"How long was I out there?"

"A few hours. I have that pot roast you talked about in the oven. Make yourself at home. I'm headed out to the gym for a while."

From his posture and the way he's not looking me in the eye, I can see that I'm not invited to go with him.

And why does that hurt my feelings?

It shouldn't.

"Oh, okay. Have a good workout."

Gideon nods. "Need anything before I go?"

"Nah, I'm fine."

I want him to stay. Or take me with him. I like being close to him.

I wasn't lying this morning. If I was offered another place to hide out until whatever's going on back home is over, I would have gone.

But it would have torn my heart out.

Gideon going out to the gym for a while is a good thing. I need to remember that I'm here because of a favor to my mother, not because of anything personal going on between us.

He may be attracted to me, *I think*, but nothing's going to happen.

Because this is Gideon. He does everything by the book.

And just because he might have liked the sight of my ass in red panties doesn't mean that he wants to take said panties off and do unspeakable, sexy things to me.

Damn it.

Maybe while he's out of the house I'll go take an arctic shower to calm down my hormones.

Chapter Eleven

Gideon

I had to get the fuck out of that house.

In the span of forty-eight hours, Lena has managed to get under my skin and make me question everything I thought I knew about her. I worked next to her for *years*, and I would have said, with absolute certainty, that there wasn't much I didn't know.

If I'd bet my life on it, I'd be fucking dead right now.

Granted, people change. They grow, especially over the course of years, and it's been a while since I last saw her.

But fundamentally, at the base of who they are, most people don't change *that* much.

So what I'm learning is that my little rebel may be sassy and headstrong, but she was also manipulated more than I realized at the time. She's good at putting on a brave face, but horrible at standing up for herself and telling goddamn Chelsea to fuck off.

Her artwork just about opened up my chest and squeezed the bloody organ pumping there from my body. It's breathtaking. She captured my mountains perfectly.

The dark charcoal on her cheek was sexy as fuck.

And don't even get me started on her tight little body. When she fell, and her ass was in the air, it was all I could do to keep my dick in my pants and not fuck her right there on the floor.

She's not mine.

Lena is the job, and I need to remember that. I need to keep my fucking hands to myself. *Stop* touching her.

I've never been afraid of touch. That's not something that my shit childhood took away from me. I hug my family all the time, and affection comes easy to me. I think I have Debbie to thank for that. She loved to be hugged and did it so often, it was just second nature.

Lena isn't so lucky.

But it's not my job to hug the woman. Or to strip her bare and fuck her into the mattress. Or to sit next to her and listen to her talk about how she was manipulated into having her *motherfucking nipples pierced.*

And it's absolutely not my job to want to comfort her, hold her, laugh with her, *absorb her* the way I want to.

I could want everything with her, and that's foolish.

So I'm going to work myself into oblivion and get her out of my system, starting with free weights. I haven't had a good, hard workout in days, and I'm feeling it.

I have music playing, but I can still hear the thunder raging outside. Rain and hail pelt down on the metal roof, echoing inside the gym, and I love the noise.

I finish a set of squats and then pace, listening to the building take a pounding, letting it empty my mind.

After two hours, when it sounds like the storm has calmed, and my muscles are weak and pushed to the limit, I take a shower in the gym bathroom and change my clothes, and then set off for the house.

It's wet out here, but not currently raining.

The mountains are covered in fresh snow.

And now that I've worked out some aggression, I feel better. Lena's fine. I like having her around. But she's just the job, and she'll be gone soon enough. Then, I can get back to work.

I already postponed my next round of trainees by two months, just to be on the safe side, but I can do a lot remotely.

In fact, I need to get home and spend an hour in my office before dinner.

The house is still and silent when I walk inside, and for some reason, that puts my back up. I move to the pantry and press a hidden button on the inside panel, and when it opens, I pull out the GLOCK I have stashed there, make sure there's a round in the chamber, and silently stalk through the house.

It's *too* still.

Something's going on.

Once the lower floor is cleared, I move to the stairs. There's nothing out of place. No sign of struggle or forced entry.

It's only my gut telling me that something's off.

I take the stairs two at a time, my weapon at my side, and look in each bedroom that's not currently being used.

Nothing.

Lena's door is slightly ajar, and I push it open, but I don't find her inside. She's also not on the other side of the bed, closest to the wall. But the bathroom door is pushed most of the way closed, and the light is on.

There she is.

Silently, I back out of her room and check the laundry and my office and bedroom, and find it all clear, so I tuck the gun in the waist of my pants, at my back.

Everything's fine.

I don't know what set me on edge.

But when I walk past her bedroom again, a noise catches my attention. A *moan.*

Walk away. Get your ass out of here.

My feet move, all right, but not away from the room. My traitorous body takes me right inside it, closer to the bathroom, where the shower is running now, and I can hear throaty moans coming from inside.

Jesus fuck, this is none of your business.

But I can't leave.

Like a goddamn creeper, I peek through the slight opening in the doorway, and there she is, in the shower. The glass door is fogged up, so I can't see her in detail, and I wish I could see the metal in her nipples, but I can clearly tell that she has one foot up on the bench at the end of the walk-in shower, and she's pointing that showerhead right at her pussy. Her hips move, chasing an orgasm.

Motherfucking hell, I want to be in that shower more than I want to breathe.

So I do the only thing I can do. I lock the door from the inside and slam it shut, keeping myself out.

Keeping her safe from *me*.

And then I storm down the hall and lock myself in my office while I jack off, leaning against my desk, imagining that I have her bent over, fucking her from behind.

Fuck.

I should have taken her up on having her reassigned.

But the thought of her leaving is unacceptable. It makes me feral.

I need to stay out of her way. Keep her safe. Do the job. Send her home.

Easy.

"I can't."

She's panting, bent over, shaking her head. Covered in a sheen of sweat from head to toe, Lena rests her hands on her knees, trying to catch her breath. This girl never fails to amaze me. In the past week, we've been at the range twice, and both times, her shooting has impressed me. She's not afraid of the handguns, and she hits the target every time.

We're in the ring this morning, and I've put her through the paces, but she's having a hard time getting out of a chokehold.

Ironic, since . . . same.

Of course, my chokehold is metaphorical.

Hers is literal.

"You're too strong, Gideon."

I shake my head, pacing the ring.

Since I heard her getting off in my shower a week ago, I've kept my distance. We work out every day, we eat meals together, but aside from that, she does her thing, and I do mine.

Her face was flaming red when I walked out of my office that day, and I simply told her to lock her door from now on.

She said nothing.

If we're going to get through this without me being inside her, this is how it has to be. Having my arms around her while we're sparring is torture enough.

"You *can*. Don't say that shit again."

"Stop being so moody." She reaches for her water and takes a long sip, her throat muscles working with every swallow.

I have to look away.

"I'm not here to be your bestie. I'm here to train you."

"Actually, I'm quite sure my mother never asked you to train me. But okay, big guy."

Big guy.

That's the first time she's called me that in a week, and it pisses me off that it soothes my prickly skin.

Get a fucking grip, James.

"Again." I crook my finger at her, motioning for her to come closer. "Let's go."

"Fine."

I have her walk past me as if she's striding down the sidewalk, and I attack her, wrap my arm around her neck, holding tight.

She stomps on my foot but only catches my toes, not hurting me at all. Then she tries to dig her elbow into my stomach, but I arch back.

"Damn it," she grunts, and finally, she digs her fingernails into my forearm, and when I jerk, my hold loosening, she bites my arm.

"Fuck."

I drop her, and she swings around triumphantly. "I got out!"

"You fucking *bit me.*"

"You told me to get out of your hold. If you were a kidnapper, well, I'd probably be too scared anyway, but in this scenario, I would have gotten loose."

I stare at my arm, blood trickling where the little wildcat broke skin.

"Oh shit. I didn't mean to bite that hard."

"No, it's good. Get out any way you can. Rip the skin from their fucking bones if you have to."

"Ew." She wrinkles her nose, and it's the cutest fucking thing I've ever seen.

"Do I need a rabies shot?"

Lena smirks and reaches for her water again, her energy renewed with her victory.

"We're doing the obstacle course tomorrow, now that your feet are healed up."

"Ugh, that sucks."

Lifting a brow, I walk out of the ring and drink my own water, watching her carefully. Lena doesn't tell me when she's hurting. I have to watch for it—otherwise she'll push too hard.

"Why does that suck?"

"I'm not good at stuff like that." She shakes her head and starts to stretch, bending over, and I turn my back on her.

"What do you mean?"

"I don't have the best coordination. Or balance. I'm not clumsy, but I'm no ballerina."

"Fall risk."

She barks out a laugh, and it makes my own lips tip up in a grin.

"My hands aren't the strongest."

"I hear a lot of excuses, Rebel." I shake my head and cross my arms. "I don't give a fuck about any of them. We're doing it."

"Your army Ranger is showing. You might want to tuck that in."

Damn it, I like her.

"We're running back to the house."

"Goody. Are you going to sing march songs too?"

"Your mouth is going to get you into trouble one of these days."

"Wouldn't be the first time." She's unconcerned as she shrugs a shoulder and wiggles into my old hoodie before we lock the gym and set off on our jog.

It's fucking freezing outside. We're squarely into the middle of October, and cold-weather season is upon us. Clouds hang in a moody overcast ceiling, and there's a chilly wind hitting us in the face as we jog home.

Once inside, Lena tugs the hoodie off as she heads right for the stairs.

It's now our routine that she goes up and showers after the workout, and I go to my office to get work done for a few hours.

I won't see her again until dinner.

And for the sake of my sanity, and keeping my dick to myself, that's the way it has to be. Even if being away from her makes my skin itch.

But not two minutes after I hear her door close upstairs, I hear a bloodcurdling scream, and I immediately sprint upstairs, taking them three at a time.

Her door is locked, but one hard shove with my shoulder has the doorjamb splintering and giving way to my body weight, and I find Lena standing at the doorway of the bathroom, breathing hard, her hands covering her mouth.

"What's wrong?"

She shakes her head, still staring straight ahead.

"Damn it, Lena, why did you scream?"

She points, and in the bathroom, in the center of the floor, is one giant fucking wolf spider.

Lena pulls in a shaky breath, and then she turns into me, buries her face in my chest, and clings to me.

"Why is there a spider the size of my goddamn head in this house?"

"It's cold out, so the bugs that haven't died yet try to come in. I've never seen a wolf spider inside before, though."

"Gideon."

"Okay, I'm on it. You can go."

"What if there are more?"

"There aren't. Go, Rebel. I'll get it out of here."

She's clinging to me, so I hug her tight, keeping my eye on the asshole so it doesn't hide somewhere, and rub my hand down her spine.

Thank God she hadn't gotten naked yet.

"If you want me to take care of this before it gets away, you have to let me go."

She blinks up at me, swallows hard, and then runs away from me, out the door, and toward the stairs.

I turn back to the spider.

"Fuck. How am I supposed to get rid of you?"

I'm not squishing it. Even with these boots on, it'll crunch, and that's fucking disgusting.

I could shoot it, but then I'd have a hole in my bathroom floor.

Finally, I trap it in a towel and take it outside, about a hundred yards from the house, before I flick it away.

"Burn that towel!"

I spin and see Lena standing on the back deck, watching me.

"I can just wash it."

"No! Absolutely not. It needs to be burned. The whole house might need to be burned. It's okay, I have some money. I can help pay for a new one."

"A new *house*?"

She nods solemnly as I approach, and she skitters out of the way, afraid that the spider might still be on the terry cloth in my hand.

"I can appreciate that that was a gigantic spider, and your scream and my subsequent heart attack were warranted, but I'm not burning my house down for you, Rebel."

But I would incinerate the entire fucking world for you.

"I'm terrified to use that bathroom now. I have PTSD."

"Do you need me to do a sweep to make sure it's safe?"

"Well, it *is* part of your job description." Her lips twitch, and her shoulders relax just a little when I drape the towel over the railing of the deck, leaving it outside. "You'll also have to check my bed, between the sheets, every night. Oh my God, that was horrible."

"None of the spiders here can kill you."

"That's not comforting."

"In the summer, you'd have to watch out for rattlesnakes, and the occasional bear, but that's really all that we have that's life threatening."

"You're not helping, Gideon."

"I'm giving you knowledge. Knowledge is power." I smirk and reach out to tuck a stray strand of hair behind her ear, breaking my rule on touching.

Her hair is like silk.

"Come on. I'll make sure he wasn't the daddy of a family, and the rest of the clan isn't in the shower."

"Oh my God, Gideon."

I laugh and lead her up the stairs.

Lena stands in the hallway as I clear her room of any other terrifying creatures, and when I return, we both eyeball the doorway.

"Do you want another room?" I ask her.

"You really demolished this door."

"You screamed." I shrug, as if it's a no-brainer. "I had to get to you."

And it's a sound I never want to hear again.

"I don't need another room. I don't need to hide anything from you." She squares her shoulders and lifts her chin.

She's so much stronger than she gives herself credit for.

"I'll fix this right away, but it might be a couple of days because I'll need to go to Missoula for supplies."

"Oh, I'll go—"

"No."

She deflates. "Gideon, I love this ranch, but I could really use a change of scenery."

"No."

"I'll wear a disguise. No one knows I'm here. And I'll have you with me. I won't do anything stupid, I won't leave your side. I won't even go to the bathroom without you. *Please.*"

I should say no.

I should not give a shit that those gorgeous lavender eyes are begging me, and that I would give her literally anything she asked for.

This is a bad fucking idea.

"You'll do *exactly* what I say."

Her face splits into the biggest grin, and she nods frantically.

"I promise. I won't do anything stupid. I wouldn't do that to you."

This is a bad fucking idea, James. Say no. No fucking way.

"Fine."

"Thank you."

"For the record, I don't like this."

Some of her excitement fades. "If it's really dangerous, I won't go. I'll stay here and sketch, or whatever. I don't want to put you in harm's way. Never again."

Blowing out a breath, I shake my head.

"I'm just going to a hardware store. It'll be okay. But I'm trusting you, Lena."

"You can trust me."

Chapter Twelve

Lena

"So where did you go to school?" I shift in the front seat of Gideon's truck so I can look at him better. "Did you have to ride an hour each way every day?"

"No, we went to Paradise Valley schools." He checks his mirror and then makes a lane change. "That's a small town about fifteen minutes from the ranch. There were twenty-six kids in our graduating class."

"Holy shit, that's small." I nod and glance out the windshield. When we arrived almost two weeks ago, it was dark, so I couldn't see any of the scenery on the way out to the ranch.

And I'm sad I missed it, because this is gorgeous. Brown fields flank the highway, with lots of evergreen trees rising tall into the sky. There's a little herd of deer in one of the fields, and little puffs of clouds that hang close to the ground, making it feel eerie.

The past week or so has been so . . . *hard.*

I was mortified when I realized that Gideon knew what I'd been doing in the shower. Honestly, I kind of hoped it would encourage him to actually *really* touch me.

It had the opposite effect.

He's hardly even looked at me since, let alone talked to me. It took a horrible, giant spider to break the ice again.

And what does that say about my allure?

That it's nonexistent.

We fall back into silence, and I let out a sigh.

"Are we allowed to make any other stops while we're there?"

"No." He doesn't take his eyes off the road ahead. His hand grips the wheel, his forearm flexes, with all those muscles and veins snaking down to his hands, and I have to squeeze my thighs together because *holy shit.* His arms belong in a movie, and I'm sitting two feet away, and I want to lean over and lick him.

But also, I feel bad that he has a little wound where I bit him yesterday.

"Hear me out."

"No."

Actually, I want to bite him again.

"Gid—"

"You said I could trust you."

"You *can* trust me. I'm not trying to pull a fast one on you here. I'm trying to have a conversation."

He sighs and pulls his hand down his face, and I nibble my bottom lip for a second before filling the silence with a soft voice.

"I was only going to suggest that we maybe get some takeout from that Mexican place you got food from last time. Because the queso was a religious experience, and I'm not supposed to have cheese, but it's totally worth it for that."

"We can do that."

Success shines in my chest, but I refrain from doing a happy dance.

"And maybe the bookstore."

"Lena—"

"I want to read, and I don't want to read the war books you have at your place. Which is very on brand for you, by the way."

"Willow has tons of romance books at her place."

I lift an eyebrow. "Right, because Willow loves me and would be perfectly fine with loaning me her paperbacks. Fine, no bookstore, but

I'd like to install a reading app on the iPad so I can download books, but you'll have to put your credit card in so I can buy them, and add it to the tab for when this is over."

"Fine."

"Wow, we just compromised. I'm actually proud of us. Usually you just bark orders, and I argue, but you get your way anyway."

He huffs out a laugh and glances my way, and I bat my eyelashes at him.

"I won't leave your side," I assure him, and his face sobers.

He doesn't reply.

He goes back to staring out the windshield.

"Can I ask you questions?"

Gideon mumbles something under his breath about silence and then sighs. "You can ask. No guarantees that I'll answer."

"How did you come to be at the ranch when you were a teenager?"

His fist tightens around the wheel, his knuckles go white, and his jaw clenches.

"You don't—"

"I'd been in foster care," he says in a hard voice. "Actually, it was a home for boys in Bozeman, and it fucking sucked. I hated that place. One day, I was told to pack a bag because I'd be going to a ranch for the summer with Ryker."

"Were you glad to have a friend with you?"

"I fucking hated him."

My eyes widen in surprise, and he smiles.

Fuck, I love his smile.

"I wish I could bottle that."

The smile fades, and I immediately want it back. "Bottle what?"

"Your smile. It's freaking awesome. Sorry, go ahead. You hated Ryker? How come?"

"Because he was a pain in the ass, and he had a mouth on him, and we were forever punching the shit out of each other. I had one hell of a black eye when we arrived. Asshole."

He smirks, and it makes me grin.

"But now you're brothers."

"It didn't happen overnight. Willow was already at the ranch for the summer when we got there. She spent every summer out there. And she decided on the spot that the three of us were going to be best friends. Ryker and I both took to her right away. She's the sweetest, happiest person I've ever met."

"I haven't met *that* Willow."

"No. You haven't." He changes lanes to go around a big truck. "The person you met doesn't come out often. She's protective. We all are, especially of each other. Anyway, it only took a few days before Ry and I started to soften toward each other. By the end of that first month, we'd figured out our shit."

This might be the most he's ever said to me in one sitting. I love the deep timbre of his voice, the gravel in it. I wish he was murmuring in my ear.

Just the thought makes me shiver.

"Are you cold?"

"No, just a random chill. Where are your biological parents?"

"Gone" is all he says, and I decide to leave it alone. It's really none of my business.

"Did you always want to go into the Secret Service?"

That has his hand loosening and his shoulders lowering, and I'm glad I changed the subject. I want him to be comfortable talking with me. I'm going to be here for God knows how long, and I don't want to do it in silence.

"No, I was recruited."

Okay, now I'm extra intrigued, so I shift even more in the seat and rest the side of my head against the headrest. "Tell me more."

"I'm not much of a talker."

"You're doing great." Without thinking, I reach out and brush my knuckles down his arm, from his shoulder to his elbow. "You can do it. I know you were in the army. Did you go in right after school?"

"I enlisted, yeah."

I glance down at his hoodie, which I'm still wearing. "How old is this?"

"Old as fuck. I think I got it during one of my first years of enlistment."

I love the way it smells. I hope I never have to wash it.

"I'm not giving it back."

"You can wear it while you're here. I don't mind."

"No. You misunderstand. It's mine now."

He lifts an eyebrow, glances over at me, and then nods. "I figured. Women have a habit of stealing a man's clothes. Anyway, I enlisted right out of high school. Went through all the fucking training for Ranger school, which is pretty much designed to make or break you. It didn't break me."

"I'm not surprised at all."

"By the time I got out of the army, I was a second lieutenant."

"I don't know what that means."

"I was an officer. One day, I got a call from Bishop, and he asked me to apply. And here we are."

He glossed over quite a bit there.

"You're badass, big guy."

Gideon takes a turn, and a few minutes later, we pull up to a big home improvement store, and he shuts off the engine.

"You're with me," he says. "But wait for me to come around."

Doing as I'm told, I wait for him to walk around the vehicle and open my door, and then I slide out next to him, bumping into his chest.

His hard wall of a chest.

I seriously need to settle my hormones, because he's made it clear that he's not interested, and I'm in danger of making a complete fool of myself.

He takes my hand in his, leads me into the store, and grabs a cart from the corral, and then, to my shock, he places me behind it, then stands behind *me*, his hands bracketing mine on the handle, caging me in.

"Are you serious right now?" I tip my head back to look up at him.

"If someone wants you, they have to go through me."

You'd think it would feel awkward to walk like this, but we find a rhythm and make our way through the store. Gideon only leaves me long enough to grab things off the shelf and throw them in the basket.

The rest of the time, his front is pressed to my back. His hands are mere inches from mine. I can feel his breath on the top of my head.

All that combined makes me shiver again.

"Are you getting sick or something, Rebel?"

"No, I have a sexy man pressed against me. It's a physical response."

He stills, and then mutters, "That fucking mouth."

We're silent as we check out, and when he pulls the vehicle around to have lumber put into the back of it.

Before he starts the engine to pull away, he slides his phone out of his pocket and taps the screen.

"What do you want to eat?" he asks me.

"The burrito, the quesadilla and chips, queso, and all the good stuff."

"Basically what I got before."

"Yes, please."

"That's a lot of cheese. Will you be okay?"

I kind of love that he's asking. "Worth it."

He nods and taps his screen some more, obviously placing an online order, and when he's finished, he starts the truck and drives out of the parking lot.

"You know, I thought I'd miss my electronics." I *really* need to fill this awkward silence. I basically just admitted that I think he's the sexiest man ever and my body craves him, and all he could do was swear and ignore me.

My ego has never felt so good.

"You don't?" he asks.

"No. I mean, yeah, I'd like to check in with Chelsea. I'm sure she's freaking out."

"She was told that you're on a press tour in Europe."

I stare at the side of his face. "Seriously?"

"Yes. You don't have reliable cell coverage where you are, and you'll be in touch when you get home. That part isn't a lie."

"But what if she needs me?"

"She's an adult, Lena. She's fine."

You don't know her like I do.

"Anyway, aside from texting Chels and speaking to my parents once in a blue moon, there's not much I miss. I never did look at the news much, and I don't have social media."

"Good. It's a fucking cesspool and a good way to get hurt."

Blinking over at him, I huff out a laugh. "How do you really feel about it?"

Gideon parks in a space with a number and then taps his phone again. When the delivery kid comes out with the bags and makes his way to my side, Gideon pushes out of the vehicle and intercepts him, shaking his head.

The kid shrugs, passes Gideon the bags, and walks away.

"Wow, no human interaction for me." I roll my eyes as he sets the bags in the back and then fastens his seat belt. "I don't think that kid was a security risk, big guy."

"You don't know that." Suddenly, his hand cups my chin, making me turn to him, and my skin ignites from the fire of his touch, which seeps all the way down to my bones. "Roll your pretty eyes at me again and see what happens."

Holy Jesus in a rowboat.

That threat has my vagina doing the foxtrot, and I'm not mad about it.

"You're in a mood."

He lets go and starts the engine, and within seconds we're back on the freeway, headed toward the ranch.

The food smells good, but I've lost my appetite.

I should have stayed at the ranch.

Chapter Thirteen

Gideon

She should have stayed at the goddamn ranch.

Instead, I've had her right next to me all day, her orange scent wafting over to me every time she so much as moved. She's in my hoodie, which is so big on her, it's laughable, but she won't let go of it.

And fuck if I don't like that.

Walking through that store, with my dick pressed against her back and feeling her heat against me, was the kind of torture the army never trained me for.

And they trained me for both physical and psychological warfare.

Which I'm pretty sure I'm in the middle of right now.

My control is hanging on by a fucking *thread.*

Thank fuck she finally fell asleep. Glancing her way, I make sure she's still out, and then breathe a sigh of relief.

I need a break from her sweet-as-honey voice and her questions. I wish the smell of her went away when she slept.

That would be a bonus.

But no, I can still smell her oranges, and I want to strip her naked, spread her open, and bury my nose in *her.* Inhale her and then eat my fill.

I'm going to hell for all this. I've been entrusted with her safety, and I'm not even sure I can keep her safe from *me*.

When I turn off the freeway and onto the ranch road, Lena stirs next to me. Her whimper sounds distressed, and suddenly, she gasps and sits up straight in her seat.

I brake and shove the truck into park and turn to her.

"Look at me."

Her glassy eyes find mine. She's breathing hard.

"You're okay. It was just a dream."

Rubbing her lips together, she gives a jerky nod and then exhales. "Yeah. Shit. Sorry."

After watching her for a moment longer, I drive us the rest of the way home, listening in agony as Lena tries to steady her breathing. Something terrified her, and I want to tear it apart.

"What was it about?" I ask her, fisting my hand so I don't reach out for her.

"The same as always" is all she says, and when I come to a stop at the house, she pushes out, slams the door, marches up the steps to the back door, and waits for me to unlock it.

After I grab the food out of the back seat, I join her and punch in the code, and she pushes through.

"I just need a minute," she says, and doesn't bother to go upstairs—she heads right into the half bathroom down here.

Leaving her be, I set the food on the island and go back out to get the supplies for her bedroom door. I leave the lumber where it is until I need it, and once I get back inside, I lift an eyebrow when I see Lena march out of the bathroom, pulling the hoodie over her head.

Her shirt comes off with it, leaving her in a practically see-through black bra, and there on full display is the metal in her tits.

Jesus Christ. Those sexy-as-fuck horizontal barbells will be what brings me to my knees.

When Lena lifts her head and sees me standing before her, those gorgeous eyes widen, but she doesn't hurry to cover herself.

And I don't turn away.

I stride toward her slowly, giving her plenty of opportunity to tell me to stop. To move back. To at least scowl at me.

But she does none of that, and my control is officially nowhere to be found.

"This is against every rule I follow." My voice sounds like gravel, and she swallows hard but doesn't falter. Her pupils dilate with every step I take, her chin lifting to keep her eyes on mine.

"Fuck the rules," she whispers, and that's all I need to hear.

Framing her face in my hands, I sweep my thumbs over her cheeks and lower my mouth to hers, and we both moan, as if we're starving and this is our first meal in weeks.

She's so fucking sweet.

Her lips are softer than I imagined, moving gently under my own, and when she parts her lips, inviting my tongue to dance with hers, it feels like every nerve in my body is on fire.

She whimpers against me, and my tongue slides over hers, learning her. Feasting on her. God, I couldn't stop this kiss if there was a gun to my head.

She's everything I've ever wanted in my fucking life.

Her hands land on my sides, and there's nothing gentle about them. Fisting my shirt and tugging it out of my pants so she can slide her palm over my skin—nothing has ever felt so fucking good. She groans when her hands find my abs, making me grin against her lips.

That's all for you, baby.

My fingers push into her soft dark hair, and I wrap the strands around my fingers and make a fist, keeping her exactly where I want her as I lick that bottom lip and she presses her stomach against my already-hard cock.

"God, Rebel. What are you doing to me?"

"Not as much as I want to." She wiggles my shirt up farther, and I have to break my hold on her so I can shed it and toss it aside, and just those few seconds of taking my hands off her is too much.

Pulling her against me again, I reach behind her and unhook the bra, and she lets it fall down her arms and to the floor, and my eyes make the journey down her glorious torso.

"Fuck."

"Yeah, fuck." Her eyes are making their own trip over my chest and abs. I have a lot of ink. A lot of bulk.

We couldn't be any more different, physically.

I set my hand on her hip, still covered by leggings, and run it up her side and over to one breast, letting my knuckles skim over her nipple and the warm metal there, and she groans, her eyes drifting closed.

"Eyes on me, beautiful."

Lazily, they blink open, and caught in her stare, I lean close to kiss her nose and down to her lips once more.

"You're the sweetest thing." My lips graze hers as I whisper to her, my knuckles still roaming over her skin, along her belly and up her breastbone. "So fucking soft. So damn beautiful."

"Gideon."

My name on those wet lips is pure sin.

"I'm right here."

Her hand finds my belt and works it open, and then she grasps onto my fly and pops the button. Before she can lower the zipper, I take her hand in mine and kiss her palm before I loop both of her arms around my neck.

"Hold on."

I slide my hands down her ass to the backs of her thighs and easily lift her. She wraps her legs around me and buries her face in my neck as I carry her upstairs.

I could fuck her, hard and fast, on the kitchen counter, or against the wall, or any-fucking-where, but right now I want her in my bed.

I want to spread her out and feast on her.

Savor every glorious inch.

When I reach my bedroom, I do pin her against the wall so I can sink into her again, kissing the fuck out of her.

"Take your pants off," she says. Her eyes are amethyst, full of sparkle and lust. I can't get enough of them.

"I will." I nip at her chin. "But you're not in charge right now."

That little gasp makes my cock twitch and my blood heat.

"If I fuck you—"

"You're fucking me."

I press my hand over her lips, shutting her up, and although I didn't think it was possible, her gaze heats even more.

She's loving this.

"If I fuck this perfect pussy, everything changes, Rebel. Because I won't be able to *not* touch you whenever I want. I can't go back to ignoring this bone-deep attraction that I feel for you. So you need to speak up now if this is just a way to get me out of your system and go back to the showerhead, because once I've been inside you, you're mine for as long as you're on this ranch."

She swallows hard, her eyes steady on me as she reaches up and gently tugs my hand away from her mouth, but not before pressing a kiss against my skin.

"Gideon. I would like you to touch me, kiss me, fuck me . . . do pretty much whatever that dirty mind of yours can come up with. I'm here for it. If I don't like something, I'll say so."

I spin with her in my arms and head straight for the bed and lay her right in the middle. After yanking her leggings and panties down her hips and legs, I toss them over my shoulder.

Picking up her left foot, I press a kiss to her heel, then her calf, my eyes feasting on every inch of her. Her dark hair is spread out around her, those eyes watching me, her lips parted.

I'm going to fuck that mouth.

"I didn't think you wanted me."

The admission shouldn't surprise me, but it does. How could she not know how much I want her? How fucking much I crave everything about her?

"I've imagined stripping you out of those clothes a thousand times." I drop my lips to her knee. "I'm supposed to be strong enough to leave you be. To do the right thing and then take you back when everything is over."

Hurt flashes through her eyes, making my own chest ache.

"But damn it, I can't resist you. And I've done my best to try." I kiss the inside of her thigh. "I survived in the wilderness for twenty days, on my own, evading the enemy." A kiss to that crease where leg meets pussy. "I've been tortured, had food and water withheld, been waterboarded—"

"I can't stand that."

"—and none of that holds a candle to the fucking agony of keeping my hands off you, Rebel."

"I'm right here." She cups my cheek and guides me up to her so she can kiss me so sweetly, it takes my breath away. "Don't keep your hands off me anymore."

I kiss my way down her jaw, her neck, where I nibble and make her legs scissor in agitation. Then, I pull one nipple into my mouth and gently bite around the barbell.

"Gideon!"

"Does that hurt?" I ask, sweeping my nose back and forth over the wet nub.

"No."

"Good." I repeat the motion, tugging her nipple with my teeth. "These are sexy as fuck, Lena."

"I know." She arches her back, encouraging me to keep doing what I'm doing.

She's so fucking responsive.

Once I've thoroughly lavished attention on her tits, I leave wet kisses down her torso to her pussy, spreading her legs and taking her in.

"This is the prettiest pussy I've ever seen, Rebel."

Her breath hitches, and she throws her arm over her face, but I reach up and pull it away.

"No hiding from me."

"So I'm . . ." She swallows hard.

"Talk to me." My lips press to her hip, and I take a deep breath, enjoying the way she smells. I can smell her arousal in the air, and I'm fucking drunk on it.

"I'm not a virgin."

My head comes up, and I narrow my eyes at her. "I'm not talking about anyone else fucking you right now, Lena."

"No, it's not that." She licks her lips, and she won't look at me.

"Hey." I boost myself back up to her and brush her hair off her cheek before kissing her softly. "What's wrong?"

"No one's ever done . . . *that*."

I frown, not understanding, and then it dawns on me. "No one has ever eaten you out?"

She bites her lip and shakes her head just once, and I hate seeing the uncertainty on her gorgeous face.

"Do you think that's a turnoff?"

She blinks in surprise.

"Because it's *not*. I like knowing that my mouth is the only one that's been down there. That I'm the only one who will know what you taste like when you come all over my tongue. I'm going to devour you, beautiful, and then I'm going to fuck you so thoroughly, you'll forget any motherfucker who was here before me."

She licks her lips.

"Unless you're telling me no. In which case, I won't do that."

"I'm not saying no," she replies.

"Thank fuck." I grin and kiss her hard, then dive back down, spread her wide, and lap at her core, from her ass to her clit, and the sound she makes will haunt my dreams for the rest of my life.

"Holy shit."

"That's nothing, baby."

Chapter Fourteen

Lena

Dear, sweet mother of God, he's going to suck my soul out of my vagina.

And I'm not upset about it.

My hands dive into his hair, holding on as his mouth does the most delicious things to my pussy. I can't look away. I can't stop watching as he pulls my lips into his mouth and tugs, presses his nose to my clit, and makes me see stars.

This is the best way to die ever.

Those steel gray eyes meet mine, and he's moaning as he licks and sucks, and then his fingers get in on the action.

He pushes two fingers inside me as he licks up to my clit, and then he pauses, clenches his eyes shut, and groans.

"Fuck, Rebel, you're so damn tight."

"You have thick fingers."

He chuckles as he works them in and out, stretching me just a bit, and then he turns his hand, palm facing up, and makes a little *come here* motion, hitting a spot that no one's ever hit before, and it sends me out of my damn mind.

"Oh my God!"

"He's not here, baby. It's just me."

"Fuck." My hips buck, and he keeps rubbing, keeps stretching, and then his lips pull on my clit, and I scream as the orgasm bursts through me.

He kisses up my body but doesn't take his fingers out, and when he's at my neck, he bites me, hard enough to leave a mark.

And it's fucking *everything*.

"Gideon."

"You're so fucking pretty when you come, Rebel." He kisses my cheek, and then my lips. "And we have a big problem."

My eyes find his, and I scowl. "What?"

"I don't have condoms. I don't bring women into my home, Lena."

I blink up at him. "I don't have any either. Birth control is handled, but if you sleep around—"

"Two years."

I blink up at him. "Excuse me?"

"It's been two years. I'm good to go, but I want to make sure that *you're* sure, baby, because—"

"Gideon, I need you inside me. I'm not going to get pregnant. I've only had this implant for six months. I haven't had sex in more than a year. Please don't make me wait anymore."

I cup his face and lift up to kiss him, and then he's gone, standing next to the bed, stripping out of his pants and boxer briefs.

And that's when I see it.

His leg.

And I can't stop myself from springing up and moving to the edge of the bed so I can see his scars. Without asking, I run my fingertips over the rough, pebbled skin of the two bullet holes and the long white scar that runs down the outside of his knee.

"Gideon!"

"Go with Richie. Get the fuck out of here, Lena."

"I'm so sorry."

I'm lifted up into Gideon's strong arms, and he settles us back on the bed, lying on our sides, facing each other, and I move into him, hugging him close to me.

"No more of that," he whispers, kissing the top of my head as his hands glide up and down my bare back, making me want to purr. "I'm just fine."

Peppering his chest with kisses, I loop my leg up over his hip, and his hand immediately clutches onto my ass and pulls me right on top of him as he rolls to his back, settling my pussy over his long, thick, rock-hard cock.

"It's never gonna fit."

His lips tip up in a smirk.

"You're going to take me perfectly."

I slide back and forth, bracing myself on his solid chest, and then I lift up and position him right where I need him.

With my eyes locked on his, I start to lower myself, and *holy God*, he's big.

The two-finger trick from earlier did nothing to prepare me for this man's monster dick.

But once the initial burn subsides, it feels *so damn good.*

"Talk to me, Rebel." His hands cup my ass, fingertips digging into my flesh in such a delicious way, it makes my walls clench.

"I can't." I shake my head and come up to the tip, then work my way down again. "Words are gone. It's too good."

He pushes up, takes my nipple in his mouth, and tugs, and I squeeze around him.

"Fuck, baby."

"That's what we're doing."

Suddenly, I'm on my back, and he's hovering over me, pushing inside me, until he's fully seated. With his forehead resting on mine, he whispers, "Breathe for me."

I didn't even realize that I was holding my breath.

With my inhale, he pulls out to the tip, and then pushes in all the way again, and I pull my knees back, opening myself up to him even more.

"Incredible," he murmurs against my lips. "Fuck, you're incredible, Lena."

His lips cover mine, and his hips start to *move*. Long, slow strokes, as if he's exploring every inch of my pussy, and when he licks his thumb and covers my clit, I start to see stars again.

"Gid—oh shit. Right there."

"That's it. Christ, you're gorgeous." He nibbles on the side of my mouth, and it sends tingles down my body. "Come all over my cock like a good fucking girl. You know you can do it."

My neck arches, and his lips land on that spot, just under my ear, that pushes me right over the edge.

My whole body convulses, my legs shake, and I cry out his name as the most intense climax of my life takes over.

"Fuuuuuck, I'm going with you, baby." His hips jerk as he growls, and I can feel him come inside me, and I'm incredibly smug.

I did that. I made him do that.

Go me!

We're sweaty and panting, and we made a mess of the bed. But the most pressing matter is the fact that I'm *starving*.

My stomach growls, and Gideon grins at me, and God, if I don't want to keep that smile with me forever.

"Let's clean up and eat," he says before pressing a kiss on my breastbone, right in the middle. "Then I'll bring you back here and start this all over again."

"I like that plan. When are you going to fix my bedroom door?"

He pauses and narrows his eyes at me. "*This* is your bedroom now, Rebel. And the door is just fine."

Chapter Fifteen

Gideon

"Oh my God, it's so good."

Lena's eyes are closed as she chews, and her little noises go straight to my cock.

I was inside her hot, perfect pussy less than twenty minutes ago, and I already want her again. I should keep my hands to myself, lock her in a bedroom with a functioning door, and keep her safe until it's time to send her home.

But I won't do that, because now that I've had her, staying away from this little rebel is out of the question.

"We'll move your things into my bedroom tonight."

Her hand pauses halfway to her mouth, and she stares at me with surprised lavender eyes. "We will?"

"Fuck yes."

"So that wasn't just things you said in the heat of the moment?"

I lean on the counter and cross my arms over my chest. "I meant every word I said. You'll be sleeping in my bed, baby."

"What else will change?"

I tip my head to the side. "We're still training together every day."

"Even the obstacle course?"

I can't help the smile that spreads over my face, and her eyes narrow menacingly.

"I see that you enjoy torture."

No. Been there, done that, and I do not *enjoy torture.*

"That's not what it is. It's training. You'll get stronger, your reflexes will get faster."

"I'll fall on my ass and maybe break a leg." She pops a chip in her mouth. "Fun times. You must enjoy all this."

"I live for it." I grin at her and reach over to brush her soft hair behind her ear. "But I know that it's not for everyone. For every ten new recruits I get for each session, thirty to fifty percent drop out before it's done."

She blinks rapidly at that, taking it in. "Holy shit, Gideon. I hope that's not on your brochure. I don't think it's a strong selling point."

"I don't need brochures. I have a two-year waiting list."

Her smile grows, and I want to lean down and kiss her.

So I do. I cup the side of her neck and jawline and kiss her before letting her go and crossing to the fridge to grab us some waters.

"And your leg really doesn't bother you?"

I pause at her question. Normally, I would brush it off and change the subject, but things have shifted with her, and she deserves the truth.

She lifts an eyebrow, waiting for my response.

"I have moments," I concede, "when it acts up. Usually if I've pushed myself too hard. It gets sore and needs some ice. It's why I couldn't go back to active duty and return to your detail, and I worked like crazy for a year to get it back. I'll never be a hundred percent, and in order to protect the president and their family, you have to be better than a hundred percent."

She frowns down at her burrito.

"It pissed me off that no one would tell me if you were okay," she says softly. "I wasn't allowed to see you, or talk to you, but the worst was, no one would even tell me that you survived."

She swallows hard, and I cup her head, kiss the top of her hair, and then pull her into my chest and hug her close.

"Finally, after a horrible week, I marched into Mom's office and said I wouldn't leave unless she told me. I threatened to go to the press. I threatened a lot of stuff."

"You threatened the president of the United States, Rebel?"

"No, I demanded that my *mother* fucking talk to me." She pulls back enough to look up at me. "Because yeah, she's the president, but she's also my mom. And her motherly moments are few and far between, but I'm pretty sure seeing me hysterical gave her one of those moments."

"What did she say?" Using my pinkie, I gently nudge her hair back from her face, enjoying the way she feels against me.

"Just that you lived. That's all. I got no details, and it was made clear to me that I *wouldn't* get any more information. I was to keep my mouth shut about the whole ordeal and go back to my life."

I scowl down at her. "Wait. You didn't even get any therapy?"

She snorts and shakes her head. "I mean, sure, there are probably therapists with top security clearance, but no. I was told to suck it up and get on with it."

The anger that moves through me is confusing because I've been trained to follow orders without question. If you question, you can get hurt. You can die.

But this is *wrong*.

After everything Lena went through, the answer was to sweep it under the rug and pretend it never happened?

"What are your nightmares about, Rebel?"

Her eyes dip to my chest, and I take her chin, nudging her face up to look at me once more.

"You," she whispers. "It just plays over and over again. Sometimes you die. In the truck today—"

She shakes her head, unable to finish the thought, and I pull her in once more, holding her tight.

"I didn't die."

"I know." She wipes at a tear but doesn't pull away from me. "I always liked you. Not the way I do now, because I was too young and, well . . ."

"I get it."

"But I liked trying to get you to smile, because you're always so serious, and out of all my guys, you made me feel the safest."

My chest swells. I love knowing that I did my job right, because she should always feel safe with me.

"All the guys are fine to have around. Except the one, you know."

"The traitor."

She nods. "Richie's been with me forever. Others come and go. But you were my favorite."

"I wasn't exactly nice to you."

"You were a dick." She pulls away, laughing, and wipes the last of her tears away, and I breathe a sigh of relief because I do *not* want her to cry. "Barking orders, grumpy face. You'd never answer my personal questions."

"I'm not there to—"

"—'be your friend,'" she says, doing a horrible impression of me, and then she smiles, and I feel my own lips twitch. "Yeah, yeah. But so much changed after you left."

Sobering, I pick her up and carry her into the living room and cuddle up with her on the couch.

"I never took you for a cuddler."

"If you're here, I'm a cuddler. What changed, baby?"

"I made it clear to Chelsea that there would be no more acting out on my part. No more games. And I was in such a depression for so long that—"

"What do you mean?" My voice is hard as fuck, and the anger pushes through me again.

"It had been a lot, Gideon. Not nearly as much as what you went through, but it overwhelmed me. And you were gone. Even though you weren't there to be my friend, you were a safe presence, and you got hurt because of me."

I'm shaking my head, but she continues.

"You were there because of *me*. If I didn't exist, you wouldn't have been there."

"That's bullshit, and you know it."

"I went back to college that fall. I graduated early because I actually hated college, got my own place, dated Howey the idiot for a while. I was already going to break up with him, but then we were at a party, things got heated, and he hit me. Richie had him on the ground so fast. It was quite impressive."

"Howey's lucky he isn't dead."

And he still might end up that way.

"I guess all I'm trying to say is, I'm not that girl anymore. Actually, I don't think I was *ever* that girl. Therapy probably would have helped, and maybe I should still look into it. I've never talked about it with anyone until I came here."

I scowl. I was able to talk to a therapist, and although I haven't told Ry and Willow everything because it's classified information, I've been able to talk about my feelings with them.

Lena has had no one.

"You can always talk to me, baby."

"I'm just so relieved that you're okay. That you have this great place, and a career you love. That you didn't lose the leg."

I almost did. It was touch and go there for a little while.

"It occurs to me that I don't know what you do for a living." I frown down at her and drag my fingertip down her soft cheek. "What did you major in in college? What do you do now?"

"I was a fine art major with a minor in finance. Which was a big waste of time. I'm not allowed to work as a financial advisor."

"Why the fuck not?"

"Because I'm the daughter of the president. I could be accused of insider trading. So no one will ever hire me."

One more thing she's lost or can't do because of who her mother is.

"I want to create art."

"Then that's what you should do."

"Someday." She nods slowly. "Someone suggested I use a pseudonym. I kind of like that idea."

Stay here and make your art.

I can't suggest that.

Because this has an expiration date.

And I'm nowhere near good enough for her. She deserves so much better than me.

It's five in the morning, but it's seven on the East Coast, and I have to make some calls, so I left a sexy and sleeping Lena in my bed, and I'm sitting in the office with a cup of coffee at my elbow.

I hit the call button on the phone and press it to my ear, staring out the window into the darkness.

"Bishop."

"James," I reply.

"Report, James."

If Lena thinks *I'm* short and to the point, she's never spent any time with Bishop.

"All's quiet. Blackbird is safe. There's been no movement here."

I hear the man sigh on the other end of the line, and that has the hair standing up on the back of my neck.

"We found messages on Tucker's phone to an unknown number, which has since been disconnected, indicating that it wasn't a one-man job."

I figured.

"There's been rumors, but nothing concrete. We're still digging. As of now, she stays where she is."

Every muscle in my body relaxes in relief.

She doesn't have to go yet.

"I'll touch base next week unless there's a change."

He hangs up, and I drag my hand down my face.

Who the fuck wants to hurt my Rebel, and why? And why, with all the tools at the government's disposal, is it taking them so fucking long to find out?

They should have known seconds after it all went down in that gallery.

Something doesn't add up.

But there's not much I can do from here, without official access. Nothing I can do except what I've been tasked with, which is keeping her safe.

Which I'll do with my life.

Glancing at my phone, I realize that I missed a text from Willow late last night.

Willow: I miss you. Stop being mad at me.

I blow out a breath and think about how to respond. Then, an idea takes shape.

Me: I'm not that mad, baby girl. Do you have some paperbacks that you don't mind loaning out? Some of the romance ones?

Expecting her to still be asleep, I stand to leave, but the three dots appear on my screen, and I pause.

Willow: Wow, I had no idea you were into smut. I have plenty around here. What are you in the mood for? Small town? Sports? Alien smut?

What the fuck is alien smut? You know what? I don't want to know.

Me: It's not for me, smart ass. It's for Lena. I don't know, a little of each maybe? I don't feel comfortable taking her to a bookstore.

Willow: I'll put some together for her.

Me: Thanks. Love you.

Leaving my office, I walk down the hall to the bedroom. It already smells like her. Lena's sweet oranges hit me as soon as I step through the door, and I stride right to the bed and climb over the covers, and over her body, planting kisses all over her precious face.

"Mm." She shifts beneath me, pulls her arms out from under the blankets, and loops them around my neck, hugging me close. "Morning."

"Good morning, gorgeous." I bury my face in her neck and breathe her in. "We have to get to work."

"Let's play hooky and stay here. It's too good in this bed."

"Don't fucking tempt me." I nip at her ear, then drag my nose down her cheek and kiss her lips softly. "We have to get up. I'll get you some coffee and start breakfast."

"Okay. Give me five."

By the time I've made her coffee and have scrambled eggs and bacon in the pan, Lena comes walking downstairs in her typical work-out uniform of leggings, a form-fitting tank, and a zip-up hoodie. Her bra is thinner, and I can see the outline of her metal through the material, and I can't resist moving over to her and brushing my thumbs over her nipples as I kiss her senseless.

"No one else is allowed to see these," I grumble against her lips, making her grin.

"I don't make a habit of walking around without a top on."

"Even like this. I can see them through the shirt, and if anyone else sees you this way, they won't have their eyes in their head for long."

"Have you always had violent tendencies?"

I growl against her lips, making her chuckle.

"My thicker bra was dirty today, possessive man."

"Buy more of them" is all I say before I go to check on the food and then dish us up. Thirty minutes later, we're jogging toward the gym and obstacle course.

Over the past week, Lena's breathing has improved as she's adapted to the altitude. She's hardly out of breath when we arrive at the course, and she props her hands on her curvy hips, scowling.

"You're going to do great."

"I'm going to make a fool out of myself, and you're not going to want to fuck me ever again."

I'm in front of her so fast, it startles her, my hand gripping the back of her neck, my forehead pressed to hers.

"There is *nothing* that could make me keep my hands to myself when it comes to you. This, what we do out here, has no bearing on my attraction to you. You're *not* going to make a fool out of yourself. Give yourself some grace, Rebel. No one's a master at this on the first try."

She swallows hard and gives me a little nod, and then I back away.

"This is the starting point." I point at the twenty rubber tires lined up side by side for her to run through, and then talk about the rest of the hurdles throughout the course, which spans a quarter of a mile. It's rigorous as fuck, and it's meant to be hard.

I can't adjust it for her to go easier on her. I don't think I would even if I could. She can do this. If not today, we'll get her there.

"We're going to time you on this. Eventually, I want you to be through everything, without failing, in less than fifteen minutes."

She blinks at me. "How long does it take you to do it?"

"Eight minutes."

"Christ." She shakes her head, and she looks nervous as hell.

"Do you want me to do it first, and you watch?"

"Yes. Hello, eye candy."

Shaking my head with a laugh, I hand her the stopwatch.

"Go!"

I make it through each obstacle—swinging through hanging rings, climbing over walls, crawling under rope webs, the whole thing—with Lena running beside me, watching raptly.

When I ring the bell at the end, she stops the watch and lifts an eyebrow.

"Seven minutes, fifty-six seconds."

"Your turn." I'm out of breath, but damn, it feels good. Sometimes, I come out here and run the course over and over again for exercise.

"I don't want to."

"Don't care." I cross my arms over my chest, unmoving. "Let's go. We don't have all day, Lena."

Her brows pull together for just a heartbeat, and then she firms her chin and moves to stand in front of the tires.

I hate how nervous she looks.

"Every time you give up, you start back at the beginning."

"Okay, hard-ass."

"Just spelling it out for you."

"How long are we doing this?"

"Until you're able to get through it all and finish."

"So for several months, then. You're going to get tired, Sergeant."

"That's *lieutenant*. Stop stalling. Go!"

She runs through the tires without a problem.

"Take your time through those tires."

She flips me off, and it makes me grin.

She's so fucking adorable.

But when she gets to the rings, where she has to hang and move hand over hand to the other side, she falls.

"Back to the start."

"Fuck."

Three more times, she gets to the rings and falls in the middle, so I step over to her to give her some tips.

"Use your legs when you're swinging," I tell her, demonstrating. "You want to use the momentum to move, so you're suspended in the air and taking some weight off your hands."

She's listening, watching me, her face hard with concentration.

Finally, she nods and goes back to the beginning to try again.

This time, when she gets to the rings, she gets to the end, and she looks shocked as shit.

"Don't stop. Keep going."

She runs over to the wall, where she has to use a thick rope to climb. First, she rubs her palms down her leggings, then she grabs the rope, and to my surprise, she climbs it easily and is over in seconds.

"Good job."

She doesn't answer as she runs to crawl under the rope web, immediately dropping down and shimmying under, her front pressed to the dirt below as she maneuvers through.

"This wasn't built for women with boobs," she mutters before she manages to wiggle out the other side and runs to the balance beam.

"Easy."

Her adrenaline is too high, and she falls off the middle of the beam.

"Goddamn it."

"Back to the start."

"I hate you."

I'm crazy about her.

Chapter Sixteen

Lena

This. Fucking. Sucks.

My legs feel like they're going to give out on me, but I'll be damned if I'll say something to the asshole barking orders.

No way will I admit that he's pushed me too far.

Or that I want to punch him.

This is *not* the man who said sweet things in my ear while he fucked me and kissed me awake this morning.

No, the drill sergeant is back, and I don't like him.

"Back to the beginning," he barks when I fall from the rings again.

My lungs burn, my hips ache. My hands feel like the skin is going to split open from all the hanging and climbing ropes.

Rather than flipping him the bird or telling him off, I've gone silent. I won't even look at him now. I'll do what I'm told, and when we get back to the house, I'll take a hot shower and then sketch.

Or die.

"Lena."

I shake my head and stand by the tires.

"Lena."

"Just tell me to go."

Suddenly, his fingers grip my chin, and he makes me look up at him. His eyes are hard, his jaw firm.

"What's wrong?" he asks in that growly voice.

"Nothing. Let's do this."

"Lena." I hear the warning, but I don't really care.

"We don't have all day, remember?"

He sighs. "Talk to me, Rebel. I know you too well, and something's wrong."

My chest softens with his voice, and now I want to cry.

I will absolutely not cry.

"I'm fine."

"You're not fine."

"Stop it." I tug out of his grasp, making him scowl, but I don't really care. I pace away from him and unzip my hoodie, toss it aside. It's cold out here, but I've been running my ass off, literally, and I'm a sweaty mess. "You're confusing the shit out of me, Gideon."

"Why?"

"You're sweet and sexy in the house, and as soon as we get out here, you're back to being a bossy jerk, barking orders, with that scowl on your face."

"We're *working* out here."

"Right."

"This is how I treat all trainees."

I don't want him to treat me like everyone else.

And I don't want his hard attitude, or his stern face.

I want the sweet affection back, because I haven't had it in *so long* and it feels like heaven.

"I can't go easy on you out here," he continues, "because you learning this stuff could be the difference between life and death."

"Yes, I can see how being unable to walk a balance beam could mean my demise."

His jaw flexes, and his hands ball up into fists.

"What if you're running away from someone who's trying to take you, and you have to run over something small, like a tree trunk or a board or something? You have to have the balance and the skill to get across safely."

"Whatever, let's just do this."

He's quiet as I stand in front of the tires, ready to go again, but he doesn't give me the signal.

"We're done," he says.

"No, we're not. I didn't make it through without failing."

"You'll try again another day."

I shake my head and count down from three, and then I take off, running through the tires.

I've figured out to not go too fast straight off, because I don't want to trip. I lift my knees high as well, so I don't catch my toe on the inside of a tire, which could also make me fall and smash my face or break a wrist.

The rings are my nemesis, but I remember what Gideon said about using my legs, and I actually make it across this time.

The climbing wall is the worst on my hands, but I haven't failed on that one at all, and I don't this time either. Then I have to crawl under the rope web.

I hate this one. I don't love being this close to the dirt. Maybe that wolf spider decided to make this handy premade web a home and thinks I'm the intruder this time.

Don't think about that.

When I approach the balance beam, I take a deep breath, calming my nervous system before I put my foot up to walk across. I take it fairly quickly but try to stay focused so I don't fall off, and to my surprise, I make it all the way to the end.

Next, I have to drag a pile of tires to a line about ten yards away. I grab the rope and hold on to it, putting my back and legs into it as I tug with all my might, pulling the heavy-as-fuck tires behind me.

Finally, I've crossed the line, and I can drop the big rope.

My hands are bleeding, my lungs screaming, but I don't care right now. I have to do this hop-back-and-forth thing with platforms that are tilted, and I have to jump between them. There are no railings, and I don't have the best balance, so I have to concentrate.

But I do it.

I haven't been this far before. I have two things left.

First is a long tunnel that's only about three feet high, and I have to run crouched down. No crawling allowed, and if I stumble to my knees, I have to start over.

I will not stumble.

It's also dark, and I don't like that, but I make it out the other side.

One obstacle left, and then I can tell Gideon to go fuck himself because he won't be fucking me today.

This is a super-tall rope net—I have to climb it, get myself over the top, then climb down to the ground.

This is going to suck.

I get up about halfway and hear myself groan because my hands are so torn up.

"Lena, get your ass down here."

Ignoring him, I keep climbing. I'm slow. *Really* slow, because my arms are shaking, and it's hard to breathe, and my hips are a nightmare, and I don't know why. I'm trying to avoid using the pad of my hand where the skin is split to hold on to the rope. Finally, I reach the top and lie across the board, resting my cheek against it, and psych myself up for climbing down the backside of this torture device.

"You've got this," I hear him say, but I think I might be stuck.

My limbs don't want to listen to my brain, and tears fill my eyes.

"Lena, you've got this, baby."

Oh, now *he wants to be sweet.*

"I'm stuck."

"You are so fucking badass, Lena. You can do this. Swing that sexy back leg down."

I turn and look down at him. He's smiling at me.

He's fucking smiling at me.

Damn it, I want to stay mad at him, but he's smiling at me, and I love his smiles.

"Have I mentioned I hate heights?" I say after clearing my throat, and his eyebrows climb into his hairline.

"I'll talk you through it."

"Have you jumped out of airplanes?" I ask, distracting myself. *I need all the distractions if I'm going to get out of this without an injury. Like, a brain injury from falling on my head.*

"Yes. Too many to count."

"Was it part of your training?" I lower my back leg and find the rope with my foot.

"Yes. Good job, Rebel. Your foot is secure."

"What else did you have to do for training?"

"All kinds of shit."

"Did you have to do one of these obstacle courses?"

"Yes, this is designed after the one I trained on."

"Really? Does this mean I could be an army Ranger?"

"You have to get down from there first."

I glare down at him, but he's still grinning at me, and he looks . . . proud.

And damn it, that makes me want to complete this so that pride stays there.

"I'm mad at you. Don't smile at me like that."

But the grin doesn't leave his handsome-as-hell face.

"This is nothing compared to what you just put yourself through to get here. Come on, you can do this."

With a deep breath to gather some courage, I scoot around and let the other leg drop. Slowly, I work my way down, and when I get a few feet from the ground, Gideon's hands are gripping my hips.

"No!" I shake my head. "You can't take me down. I have to do it myself, or else I've failed, and I have to start over."

He immediately moves away.

"You're right. Go ahead."

I drop to the ground, and then jog over and ring the bell, and then I'm in Gideon's arms and he's spinning me around, kissing me like crazy.

"You're the sexiest fucking woman I've ever seen in my life," he growls against my lips.

"I'm *so mad* at you."

"Good. That means you used that anger to get through the course."

He squeezes me to him and kisses my cheek, and damn it, I love being surrounded by him.

"I wish we'd timed it," I mutter.

"I did."

I blink up at him, waiting.

"Eighteen minutes, six seconds. If you hadn't paused at the top of that last one, you would have done it in under fifteen minutes."

"Well, fuck."

He laughs and takes my hand, but I wince and tug out of his grasp, and his face immediately darkens.

"What's wrong?"

I shake my head and turn away, but he catches my wrist and pulls me back to him, scowling when he sees my hands.

"I'll be fine."

"Jesus, you need to tell me—"

"I'm just a trainee, remember? Do you hug and kiss and coddle everyone who finishes the course, Lieutenant?"

His face hardens, and if I'm not mistaken, hurt moves through his eyes.

"I didn't think so. I'll clean up when I get back to the house." I pick up my sweatshirt and tug it on, wincing when the cotton scrapes against my hands. "Why do my hips hurt so bad?"

"Because of the rings. The swinging back and forth." He crowds into me and wraps my ponytail around his fist, then tugs my head back so I'm staring up at him. "You're not *just* anything. Do you understand me?"

I will not cry.

"What are we doing next?"

"I'm taking you home, and I'm going to tend to your hands and get you comfortable."

"Would you—"

"Be very careful, Lena. You're pissing me off."

"I'm just treating you like I would any trainer, Gideon." His lips firm. "Doesn't feel good, does it? You can be tough on me, that's fine. I can take it. But you don't get to fuck me one minute and then speak to me like I'm a stranger the next."

I start to walk away from him, and swear at myself when I limp, my right side already so sore.

Suddenly, I'm in Gideon's arms, and he's carrying me bridal-style back toward the house.

"D—"

"Shut that beautiful mouth," he growls. "No, I wouldn't carry anyone else. Damn it, cut me some slack. The rules shifted less than twelve hours ago, and I'm figuring it out."

Okay, now I might feel a little bad.

Wrapping my arms around his neck, I sink my fingers into his hair and my face against his neck and hug him close.

"I'm sorry," I say softly. "You hurt my feelings, and I got mad."

"That's not ever my intention."

"I know. I just need to remember that grumpy is your standard factory setting. I was scared of the obstacle course."

"Obviously, you didn't need to be. You kicked ass today. You did far better than men who have been through the military and come here to train do. Most don't make it through on their first day."

I freeze, staring at him in shock.

"You're kidding."

"I'm not kidding. I'm grumpy, remember? I don't have a sense of humor."

He carries me into the house and up the stairs to the primary bathroom, where he sets me on the vanity and gets to work starting the bath.

"I want you to soak in some Epsom salts for your joints. Let me see your hands."

Without arguing, I show him my palms, and he lifts one to his lips and gently kisses it, then raises his gaze to me.

"I'll get you gloves. You'll wear them from now on."

"I'll get calluses. It'll be okay."

"No, you'll use the gloves." He leans on the counter on either side of my hips and presses his lips to my forehead. "I'm so fucking proud of you."

"You are?"

"Hell yes. Watching you do the course, all pissed off and stubborn, determined to make it through, was the sexiest thing I've seen. And then you broke my heart when you got to the top of the rope net and froze."

"It scared me."

"You should have told me that you don't like heights."

"Why? I still would have had to do it."

His lips flatten, and he doesn't look happy, but he can't argue because he knows I'm right.

"Get in the bath," he says before kissing my lips. "I'm going to make you lunch."

The bath actually sounds really nice, so I don't argue.

Once Gideon has left the bathroom, I gingerly hop off the vanity and wince. Now that the adrenaline is all gone, I'm *really* sore. Probably because I did the first half of that course at least a dozen times before I could move on to the next thing.

I slip into the water, and it stings my hands, but then I relax against the edge of the soaking tub and take a deep breath.

This is actually really nice.

If I'm not careful, I could fall asleep in here. The warm water makes my eyes so heavy. Next thing I know, I feel lips pressed to my forehead.

"I'm not sleeping."

Gideon smiles against my skin. I love it when he does that.

"No, not at all. You snore while you're completely awake all the time."

"I wasn't snoring."

He pulls back, and I open my eyes to find him still smiling at me. "I made lunch."

"What is it?"

"Leftovers from last night."

"That sounds really good." Gideon helps me up and out of the water, and then he wraps me in a gigantic blue towel and hugs me to him, his hands rubbing up and down my back. "I need some ibuprofen or something."

"I have that ready for you too." He kisses my forehead. "Come on, my little badass rebel. I have a surprise for you."

That grabs my attention.

"What kind of surprise?"

"You'll see when you get your sexy ass downstairs."

"Is it a living thing? Did you get me a cat?" I smile hopefully, but he just smirks.

"No. It's not a living thing."

"Well, damn."

Chapter Seventeen

Lena

The end.

I finished that whole small-town romance series in a week, and that brings me to the end of the books that Willow lent me a couple of weeks ago. I was shocked when I went downstairs with Gideon after I kicked the obstacle course's ass that day and there were about ten books sitting on the kitchen counter, all on loan from Willow's personal library.

I've even seen her in passing a couple of times, and she asked me if I was enjoying them.

Recognizing the kindness for the olive branch it is, I'm going to grip onto it with both hands, because we still don't know how long I'm going to be here. It could be for months more, and although I love spending time with Gideon, I'm starting to get lonely for female companionship.

Gideon and Ryker had to drive into Missoula for supplies today, and my man warned me that they'll be gone all day, so this is good timing to return these books and extend my own peace offering.

I hope with all my heart that she likes this.

After loading the books into a couple of bags, I pull on a coat and, with the gift tucked under my arm, make my way down the long driveway toward the farmhouse that Willow and Ryker live in.

I've been here for about a month, and I've grown to love this ranch. It feels like home more than my apartment in DC ever did. The mountains speak to my soul, and I can't stop sketching them. I've probably captured them twenty times or more, with different mediums, from different views, and I could do it hundreds of times without getting tired of it.

But it's when I'm with Gideon that I *truly* feel like I'm home.

Our relationship has shifted. Or maybe *grown* is a better word for it. He's still a hard-ass when it comes to training. Every single day, he pushes me to the limit. Just this morning, we were in the shooting range, and my hands are still sore.

"You can hit that target, Rebel. You've done it a hundred times before."

I glare over at him through my clear eye-protection goggles. "Yeah, with a smaller gun and ten yards closer."

He smirks and crosses his arms over his chest. "Hit that target, and you'll get a reward."

"What's the reward?"

He steps close, his hand gliding over the small of my back, down my ass, and between my legs.

"I'll eat this sexy pussy until you're screaming and soaking my sheets. But you have to hit that target first. Otherwise, I won't let you come."

"You're a jerk."

"Never claimed differently. Come on, you've got this." He slaps my ass and steps away, and I raise the gun, my arms singing with exhaustion, and pull the trigger.

The orgasms when we got home were worth it. I'm still tingling in all the right places.

The house comes into view, and I'm immediately nervous. Sure, Willow lent me these books at Gideon's request, but that doesn't mean that she wants to be my friend or even be *friendly* with me. I should have just stayed home and let Gideon return the books when he gets back.

Don't be a coward. If she gets bitchy, you can leave. You're not stuck here.

Unlike when I had to do press conferences for my mother and had to listen to all kinds of bullshit with no way to escape.

With a deep breath, I climb the steps to the front door and knock.

"Come in!"

Shit, did she really mean that?

"Really, come in! My hands are dirty."

Okay then.

I push the door open, and to my surprise, Willow is smiling at me in welcome. There's still hesitancy in her eyes, but she's not openly scowling or hostile.

Improvements.

"Hey," I say, feeling awkward. "I wanted to return these to you."

"Oh, come on back. I'm making sourdough in the kitchen." She wiggles her fingers, which are currently caked in what looks like white dough. "It's a huge mess, I'm not good at it, and whoever claimed that it's easy is a big, fat liar."

I smirk as I follow her into the state-of-the-art kitchen and set the bags of books on stools by the island and start to unload them.

"What did you think of that Mafia series?" she asks, gesturing to the three books in my hand.

"I loved it. Book two was my favorite, but the whole series was great. I want to check out more by this author."

"The second book was my favorite too. I enjoyed recording that one."

I blink at her, and Willow grins.

"I'm an audiobook narrator. That's what I do for a living. I'll show you my booth upstairs sometime."

"Holy shit, that's *very* cool."

"I'm not saving the world or anything."

I snort out a laugh and shake my head. "Neither am I. But you're telling stories, and that's important."

Willow's cheeks flush pink, and she sighs, pausing in kneading the dough.

"The boys were right, you know. I *do* owe you an apology. I never should have come on as strong as I did when you got here, and I regret it so much, Lena. Especially because I don't know anything about you, and my opinions were all based on assumptions."

"You love him. I understand that."

"He's my brother. Maybe closer than that, because I remember what my life was like without those two men in it, so I appreciate them even more because of it. I was always worried about him when he was working with you. Every day. So when he got hurt, it sent me over the edge."

Nodding, I lean on the counter and watch as Willow gets her dough into bread pans and then slips them into the oven before washing her hands.

"I'm glad that Gideon has a family that loves him so much. Not all of us do."

She lifts a brow, but before she can ask questions, I pass her the wrapped package.

"As a thank-you for loaning me the books. And, maybe, a peace offering."

Her lips twitch as she accepts the gift, and once she's unwrapped it, Willow gasps and covers her mouth, tears instantly filling her eyes.

I don't always sketch people, but I thought this would mean more to her than a piece of the mountains.

"My guys," she whispers as her eyes roam over the framed page. "All three of them. How—"

"Gideon has a lot of photos in his office. I studied them. And of course I've met Ryker and Aiden a couple of times."

Willow nods, and then she's rounding the island and pulling me in for a big hug. "You're so freaking talented, Lena."

"Thanks." Hugging her back, I feel tears of my own want to come.

It took me more than a week to finish the charcoal drawing of all three men. They're walking down a dirt road, with the barn and mountains in the background, laughing with each other.

Honestly, I'm damn proud of that piece.

"I bet Gideon loved it."

"He hasn't seen it." Her eyes jump to mine in surprise. "It's for you. Now, it's up to you to share it."

"Thank you so much." Willow sets it against the wall on the counter so she can stare at it. "I know exactly where I'll hang it."

"I'm glad you like it."

She turns back to me and bites her lip. "Can we maybe just start over?"

"Hi, I'm Lena. It's nice to meet you."

Willow laughs, and her shoulders relax, and I think everything is going to be okay.

"How is it going with Gideon?" she asks me as she grabs a rag and some cleaner and starts to scrub the countertop.

He's everything I've ever wanted in my life, and I don't have any idea how I'm going to leave him.

"It's going well."

"He mentioned that he's training you?"

"Yeah, I pretty much want to slash all his tires at least once a day, because holy shit, it's a lot of work."

She barks out a laugh, making me grin.

"I've heard he's tough."

"He's a freaking gorgeous monster. But I've lost a few pounds, and I could probably hold my own against a really bad mugger."

Willow smirks, and I nibble my lip.

"Okay," I confess, "it feels good to know that if something bad went down, I'd be able to put up more of a fight. Because let me tell you, feeling helpless sucks ass."

"I'm glad he's training you. And the rest of it? I see the look he gets on his face when he talks about you. You're not just roommates over there."

I sigh, trying to decide how much I can tell her. Sure, she's being super nice to me right now, but I'm not good at trusting.

"I get that it's none of my business." She holds her hands up and then pulls new ingredients out of the fridge. "You don't have to tell me anything at all. I'm going to build a couple of lasagnas. Do you want to stay for dinner?"

"Um—"

"Gid will swing by here when he and Ry get back, so we can just inform him that he's staying. He loves lasagna."

"I mean, that's a few hours away. I can go and come back—"

"Stay." Willow sighs and reaches out to take my hand. "Please stay. I'd like to chat and get to know you better, and I promise not to be a bitch."

"I, too, will do my best to keep my bitch on a leash."

She snorts and walks back to the fridge. "We should drink wine while we do this."

"Wine sounds great."

Before long, we each have a glass of red, and I'm helping to assemble a lasagna.

"You've really never done this before?" she asks me.

"No. I wasn't allowed in the kitchen at the White House. The chef would shoo me away."

"Holy shit, you grew up in the White House," she says, shaking her head. "I mean, sure, I knew that, but it seems like such an unreal thing."

"Oh, it's real." I nod and sip my wine. "I wasn't allowed to do much myself. No cooking. Someone cleaned my room."

"Wow. Do you know *how* to clean?"

Laughing, I pull a noodle out of the pot. "Yes. I live alone now, and I don't have help. I do it all myself. Except the cooking. Well, if it comes in a box, I can manage it. And I'm really good at using the microwave and calling for takeout. I know, that makes me sound spoiled as hell."

"No, it doesn't. A lot of people don't cook."

"Gideon's excellent in the kitchen."

Willow grins at me. "I know. Debbie was the *best* cook, and she made sure all three of us knew the basics. But Gideon *loved* being in here with her. He'd spend hours and hours with her, learning everything he could. I don't think it was the food per se—I think it was that he wanted to be with his mom. We were all close to Debbie and Ray, but Gideon and Debbie had something special. Maybe because of the tragic way his biological mom died."

What the hell happened to her?

I want to know everything, but my gut tells me that digging into that information is probably best done with Gideon.

Instead, I keep focusing on Debbie.

"How did Debbie die?" I ask softly.

"Cancer." Her nose wrinkles as she sprinkles cheese over the sauce in her pan. "Fucking cancer. Ryker had just won the Stanley Cup the year prior, and he was going for year two in a row."

"Wow."

"He was in the middle of the season, and we found out about the cancer. It was aggressive, and already systemic. She passed when Ry was in the middle of playoffs, and he didn't get to come home for the funeral."

"Oh my God, that's horrible."

"Gideon came home when I called him and told him that time was running short. Ray wouldn't leave her side, of course. Ray and Deb had the kind of love that you read about in those novels. That you dream about. He was obsessed with her, completely devoted to her. Gideon and I took turns bringing him food, sitting with her while he freshened up, but he slept with her, held her, wouldn't budge. Not that that surprised either of us, because Ray was the OG of feral men for his woman."

She takes a breath and a sip of her wine. We've almost made it through this bottle already, and I'm feeling . . . *floaty.*

I'm also riveted. Gideon rarely talks about his adoptive parents, and hearing this tragic story only makes my heart soften toward him even more.

"Gid and I were both in the room with Ray and Debbie that morning. Just quietly sitting, listening to her breathe. And then, suddenly, she just . . . *wasn't*. Wasn't breathing. It was the calmest, most peaceful transition."

"Wow." I wipe a tear off my face.

"Debbie loved so big, so hard, and she deserved to die with complete love and peace, and she did. But man, it broke us all for a while. Ray never recovered, and he passed two years later."

No wonder the three of them are so close to one another. They've been through so much together. How can I be mad at her for wanting to jump in and defend Gideon when I first arrived? She thought I was the cause of him almost being killed.

Because I was.

But I don't want to focus on that now.

"Do you have a photo of them that I could borrow? I'd like to sketch a gift for Gideon."

"Honey, I have *hundreds*. Give me your number, and I'll text them to you so it's on the down-low. I know that Gid has a couple in his office, but I have some great ones that are better."

"I can't give you my number. I'm not allowed to have a phone." I finish my wine and then lift a brow when I see that Willow's opening a fresh bottle.

"Why can't you have a phone?"

She pours me more wine, and I try to decide how to answer her.

"Because cell phones can be traced, Willow."

She watches me for a moment and then nods slowly.

"And you're hiding here."

"Yeah, I'm hiding here. Gideon's keeping me safe, just like he's always done for me. And no one else can know where I am. But I'll happily borrow some pictures, if you don't mind."

"You got it."

We sip quietly for a moment, and then she grins at me.

"Okay, give me a hint. Are you guys having sex? Or do I have to liquor you up a bit more before you spill the beans?"

I can't help but laugh at that. "Fine, I'll talk. Yes, we are. And *holy shit.*"

Her smile is wide as she clinks her glass to mine. "Attagirl."

"I would have thought for sure that you'd be pissed that I'm sleeping with your brother."

"A month ago? Yeah, I probably would have been. But frankly, I've seen a change in him with you here. He smiles more, and that's big for him."

"He hardly ever smiled the whole time he was on my detail. And he has the *best* smile."

"He really does." She nods and puts the pan of lasagna in the oven. "He's always been ridiculously handsome, even as a gangly, awkward teenager."

"I mean, Ryker is fucking *hot*, my new friend." We cheers again, and Willow preens. She's so *pretty*. "You hit the freaking jackpot with him."

"I know, right? All those muscles just do it for me."

"THE MUSCLES!" I do a little happy dance, and Willow giggles. "You really have to thank whatever god you believe in for giving men those V's on their hips that lead to the promised land."

She flips her blond hair over her shoulder and sips her wine. "Also, the tattoos. Who knew ink was so damn hot?"

"Me. I knew." I snort and sip my wine. "But it's so much hotter on Gideon than any other man I've seen. Does Ryker have a lot of tattoos?"

"So many," she confirms with a nod. "And one of them is for me. A willow tree."

I stop and blink at her, feeling all of me melt at the admission. Is it from the sweetness of the tattoo or all this wine? Maybe both.

"That is the *sweetest*."

"I know. And the best part? He got it *years* before we fell in love. My man is the best."

"I love that."

"Do you want to see my recording studio while this bakes?"

"Hell yes, lead the way."

We grab our glasses, and Willow snags the bottle and leads me up the stairs to the second floor.

"This house is enormous," I comment as we pass a gym and many guest rooms.

"I know. Ray and Debbie wanted *tons* of kids, and Ray built this house for her right after they got married. But she ended up being infertile."

"Oh my God."

"Yeah." Willow nods and points out Ryker's office. "But they had me, and then the boys, and they always had each other."

She opens a door at the end of the hallway, and we step inside.

The walls are covered in what must be soundproofing. There's a desk with a laptop and lots of notes, and then there's a corner with another computer, an iPad, a mic, and lots of other things that I don't understand.

"This is *incredible*."

Willow grins, looking around. "Ry built it for me."

"Swoon." I take a sip. "Okay, I want to hear you."

"You want me to *demonstrate*?"

"Yes, please."

"I might be a little too drunk for that. We've almost polished off this second bottle. But I can play what I recorded this morning for you."

"Ooh, that's perfect."

She turns on the laptop and hits some keys, and then her voice comes out of the speakers, all sultry and sexy.

"Look at what a good girl you are, all spread out for me."

I purse my lips, my eyes go wide, and Willow laughs. She recorded a spicy scene this morning.

"Logan, I can't do this. It's too much."

"You can do it, baby girl. You're such a good little slut for me. Fuck, look at that wet pussy."

"Oh my God." I snort and then keep listening to this *very* explicit scene, and then she stops the playback. "I need that title, please. It's going to the top of my list."

"It's a good one." She winks and then leads me back downstairs. "Let's sit on the couch and gossip some more. I want to know all about the famous people you've met. I'll trade stories with you."

"Have you met a lot of famous people too?"

"A few, because Ryker is a hockey legend. We sometimes attend functions for charities and stuff. You probably know all about that."

"I've attended plenty of those things. I wish you'd been there. It would have been a lot more fun."

"You know, the annual private concert is happening in Seattle just before Christmas for Ry and Gideon's charity. They had to move it from summer because of a scheduling conflict this year. You and Gid should go."

"I'm absolutely *positive* that the drill instructor will not let me off this ranch. He definitely won't let me go to a fancy dinner with a bunch of people. No way. Not to mention, I might not be here by then."

Her bottom lip pokes out in a pout.

"But now I want you there," she says and pretends to cry, making me snort. "Okay, let's gossip. Who's the most famous person you've met? Besides your mom, because duh."

It's in this moment that I realize something alarming.

I really, really like Willow.

Chapter Eighteen

Gideon

"I'll pop in to see Willow before I go back to the house," I say as I pull up to the farmhouse and cut the engine.

"She'll like that. She's missed you," Ry says as he climbs out of my truck, and we walk to the front door. "We both have. She's mellowed out a lot since Lena got here. Calmed down. We've had some good talks."

Nodding, I follow him inside, and we hear two women scream.

Without hesitation, I push Ryker behind me and run into the living room, ready to kill an intruder, and then stop short when I take in the scene before me.

There isn't a rapist or murderer here, hurting my girls.

No, said girls are sitting on the floor, their backs against the sofa, laughing like lunatics.

Ryker steps up next to me and we both cross our arms over our chests, taking them in. Neither of the women has noticed that we're here, and we share a grin.

Lena's here. And it looks like she's having fun.

"Five!" Lena says, trying to catch her breath. "I've only fucked *five* men . . ."

What in the actual fuck? I'd like to hunt down any asshole who's had his hands on my girl and kill him. Slowly. Painfully.

"SAME!" Willow exclaims, hopping up and down on her ass, and Ry growls next to me. Sounds like he shares my sentiments.

"Those five were a miracle," Lena says, wiping tears from under her eyes. "Well, the first four, anyway. Because my security guys didn't let men near me. It was like constantly having my dad with me."

"She's talking about you," Ry mutters, and I shoulder check him, making him chuckle.

"You poor thing," Willow says.

Poor thing, my ass.

"How did you even lose your virginity?"

"I was seventeen—"

"Nope," I say, loud enough to get their attention. "I don't need or want to hear this fucking story, Rebel."

Both women blink at us, and then slowly smile.

"They've had sex with more than five girls," Lena says to Willow, who nods in agreement. "Like, we could combine our numbers, and they've had sex with more than *ten* girls. Each."

"I mean, look at 'em," Willow says, gesturing up and down. "The muscles. The tattoos. The broody expressions on those faces."

"The freaking chiseled jaws," Lena continues. "How did they both hit the gene pool jackpot with those bodies?"

They're drunk as fuck.

"And I know for a fact that Ryker's fucked way more than ten," Willow says as Ryker mutters *fuck*. "I've seen it firsthand."

"WHAT?" Lena screeches. "You *watched* them fuck other girls?"

"No. Ew. I would cut a bitch. Fuck that." Willow shudders. "Someone sent me pictures of *my husband* fucking other women, and let me just say right now, you can't get that shit out of your head."

"For fuck's sake," Ryker mutters next to me. "We don't need to talk about this."

"It wasn't his fault," Willow adds, slicing her hand through the air. She gets so *aggressive* with her arms when she's drunk. "Someone was trying to blackmail him. Anyhoo, hi, guys!"

"Hi, guys," Lena echoes, giving us a little wave. Her cheeks are rosy from the alcohol, her eyes a little glassy, and that long, dark hair is down around her shoulders. I want to wrap that hair in my hand and kiss the fuck out of her. "Want some wine?"

"How much wine have you had, baby?" I ask. I've changed my mind. I want to toss my girl over my shoulder and carry her home, so I don't have so share her with anyone.

Willow fills both of their glasses, and then they clink them together in a *cheers*.

"Two and a half," she says proudly. Both women climb to their feet and wobble, and we rush forward to steady them.

"Hey, big guy," Lena says softly as she leans in to kiss my chest. "You have *really* great muscles. We've been talking about it."

"You've been talking about my brother's muscles?" Ry asks Willow, who rolls her eyes.

"*Both* of your muscles," Willow clarifies. "We like 'em. It's unanamisses."

"Unanimous?" I ask.

"That's what she said," Lena whisper-shouts, making me snort. "I helped make lasagna. I don't think it'll kill anyone. And I brought Wills a present."

She called her Wills.

Does this mean that they're friends now? I fucking hope so.

"You have to see it," Willow says, directing us into the kitchen. "And we're having the nonpoisonous lasagna for dinner."

"You don't have to love it," Lena says, rubbing her hand up and down my chest and stomach, and I have to take her hand in mine and kiss it—otherwise, I'll have to boost her up on the nearest wall and fuck her until she can't breathe.

"Love what, baby?"

"The present for Willow."

She suddenly looks nervous, and I kiss her temple. Ryker's watching me with a grin.

He figured out that we're sleeping together on our drive today, and he hasn't stopped giving me shit for *robbing the cradle* all fucking day.

Asshole.

"Behold," Willow says, gesturing with her arms and jazz hands at the gorgeous sketch sitting on the kitchen counter.

"Jesus," Ryker whispers as we both step closer.

My girl, my perfect Rebel, has sketched a picture of Ry, Aiden, and me here on the ranch. The barn is in the background, along with the mountains, and the three of us are laughing. Aiden's in the middle.

Christ Jesus, this woman. I have to rub over the sudden ache in my chest.

"It's my men," Wills says as she wipes away a tear. "She captured you all so perfectly. My guys."

"You loaned me all those books, and I just wanted to get on your good side," Lena says, leaning into me shyly.

She hasn't looked up once.

"Rebel." I hook my finger under her chin and tip her head up. "This is fucking incredible."

She bites that delicious lip and then buries her face in my chest. "Thanks."

"I don't have words," Ryker says and then makes a *come here* motion with his hand. "Give her to me."

"Fuck you."

"For real, pass her over."

"I will kill your stupid ass."

Lena's giggling when Ryker takes her hand and pulls her into a hug, making me growl at him.

He grins over her head.

"Thank you. I know it's not for me, but it's going to hang in my house, and it's fucking awesome."

"It's not that big of a deal," Lena says shyly.

"You're wrong," Willow says, getting in on the hug action, wrapping her arms around them both. "It's a big fucking deal. Gid, get in here. Group hug."

"You're all weird."

"Come on." Ryker opens an arm, and I give in, hugging them for a second and then pulling away.

Seeing them all together, actually welcoming Lena, laughing and talking, has something shifting in my chest.

God, she looks right here. Like she belongs here, with us. Like she should never leave.

She's going to leave.

But today isn't that day.

"I'm hungry," Lena announces, wiggling her way out of the group hug.

"Me too," Willow says. "We had a *lot* of wine."

"You don't say." My voice is dry as fuck, but they just laugh at me.

"It's not like I'm driving anywhere," Lena says as she leans on the counter. "Or drunk dialing an ex to piss him off or turn him on. Or both."

I narrow my eyes at her and lean in so only she can hear what I'm about to say.

"I've been reminded twice tonight that other motherfuckers have had you, Rebel. I don't like it. Not even a little. Keep it up and see where it gets you."

"Yeah, okay." She snorts.

"I don't think I've seen Gideon possessive," Willow tells Ry, as if I'm not even in the room. "It's fascinating."

"He's definitely not usually like this. It's new." He steals a slice of garlic bread and bites in. "I'll set the table."

"So you won the Stanley Cup?" Lena asks him.

"Twice," Ry says with a shit-eating grin.

"That's impressive."

"But has he protected a fucking president?" I glare at my brother, who just laughs. "I don't think so."

"You're both impressive," Lena says, patting my chest, and I catch her hand in mine, linking our fingers. I fucking missed her this afternoon. "But I don't know anything about hockey. I know all about your job."

"Hockey isn't all that great," I mutter, and Ryker laughs out loud.

My brother is a dick.

"I was also the MVP. Twice." He winks at my woman, and now I know he's just trying to piss me off.

"I wonder if I ever saw you play," she says, tipping her head to the side. "When I was a kid, before Mom won the presidency, my dad would take me to games. Hockey, football, basketball, pretty much everything. He's a huge sports fan."

I didn't know that.

"Then, Mom went into politics, and we couldn't go anymore. I loved going with him. It was the only time that it was just the two of us out doing something together. My dad was an attorney, so he worked long hours, but we went to a game at least twice a month."

"Did you watch together on TV once you couldn't go in person anymore?" Willow asks, and Lena shakes her head.

"Nah. Things got busy for them after that. Lots of politicking." She sips her wine, and I dish up a big slice of lasagna for her—she needs to soak up some of that wine—and she takes a big bite. "I don't really know my parents all that well, when I think about it. God, this is *so good.*"

Ryker frowns. "What do you mean?"

"The lasagna is delicious."

"Not that, sweet girl—what do you mean about not knowing your parents?"

I glare at him. *Call my woman by anything other than her name again, jackass.*

He just smirks again.

"After the age of about ten, maybe eleven, I hardly saw them. I had nannies. I heard my mom talking to a friend of hers once. She said that they didn't *mean* to have a kid, but it worked out because it looked better for her on the campaign trail. More relatable to voters and such. It really helped her family values platform."

Willow gasps and Ryker scowls, all humor long gone from his face.

I want to punch a fucking wall.

"Please don't misunderstand. I have a ton of privilege, and really no room to complain. They love me the best they can. Dad was the softer one, the one who liked to spend time with me, but then things got really crazy."

"Your parents pretty much neglected you for all intents and purposes," I reply, shaking my head. "If they hadn't been wealthy and provided a nanny, CPS likely would have been called on them at some point."

"Maybe they would have paid attention if Mom hadn't decided to go into politics," she murmurs with a shrug. "We'll never know. They're not bad people. Just bad parents. They love me in their way. They just don't love to be inconvenienced by me, so I'm sure that *this* whole situation is really irritating the hell out of my mom. But when I was small, and Dad took me to those games . . . those might have been some of my favorite memories. So I probably saw you play at some point."

"It's very possible," Ryker says with a wink. "Do you enjoy sports now?"

"Um. Sure?"

The mood lifts with the laughter from her response, and I lean over to kiss her cheek. She's so precious. So fucking sweet. How anyone could ever ignore her is a mystery to me. Even all those years ago, when our relationship was strictly professional, it was impossible to ignore her. But her parents?

You come from far worse. Don't forget that.

"It's official," Willow says. "All four of us came from people who weren't great parents. But I think we all turned out pretty fucking fantastic."

Lena blinks in surprise, and then she turns to Willow, and I can see that she's about to change the subject. "What's the spiciest book you've ever narrated?"

"Oh, there have been some doozies." Willow thinks about it and then glances at Ryker and me. "I'll have to tell you about it when they're not listening."

"Deal."

When I wake up the next morning, the bedroom still cast in darkness, Lena isn't in bed with me.

Part of me panics. Did someone get into my house, through all my security, and take her while I was sleeping?

Unlikely.

But I don't like that she's gone, and I have no idea where she is.

I tug on some sweats and a T-shirt, throw on a flannel over that, and start searching the house. She's nowhere upstairs.

The downstairs is quiet, too, and then I notice that the back door is unlocked.

Before I can freak out, I find her.

My girl is bundled up in blankets, and it's snowing.

She's sitting in the snow.

I shove my feet in boots and step outside, and Lena tips her head back, letting the flakes fall on her gorgeous face.

"It's the first snow," she says softly. "And I didn't want to miss it."

"Baby, it's too cold."

"Come here, I have blankets." She holds her arms out, opening up the blankets, and I pick her up, sit on a snow-covered outdoor chair, and cuddle her in my lap. "Now you're going to get wet."

"I want to take you inside where it's warm, but I have a feeling you'll fight me on that."

"Can we sit out here for just a little while?" Her voice is soft in the stillness of the snow falling around us. "It's so pretty."

"You do know that you can watch this from literally any window in the house."

"It's not the same." She drags her knuckles down my cheek. "Were you mad that Willow and I drank too much last night?"

"Of course not. You weren't hurting anyone. I'm just glad that you had fun and that Willow has finally come around."

She nods and rests her forehead against my cheek, snuggling close. "I like her a lot."

"I'm glad. She's not so bad."

"She told me a lot of things."

I scowl. "Seems she has a big mouth."

"I don't think it was anything you wouldn't have told me yourself." She kisses my cheek, and it soothes my soul. "Just more about Ray and Debbie and how much you all loved them."

"Yeah, we loved them, baby." I kiss her head and lift her in my arms, taking her inside. "It's too cold to sit out here, but we'll watch from the sofa."

"Okay."

She holds on tight as I walk through the house to the living room and take the wet blankets off her, then bundle her in dry ones and go upstairs to change my wet clothes.

When I get back, she's leaning on the arm of the couch closest to the windows, her eyes glued to the huge flakes falling.

"You've seen lots of snow before," I remind her as I sit next to her and wrap my arms around her.

"It's always magical, and there's something extra special about the first snowfall of the year. It gets dirty so fast in the city. I bet it's gorgeous here for a long time."

"Hm." I kiss the crown of her head, enjoying the quiet with her.

"Gideon?"

"Yes, sweetheart."

"I'd like to ask you a question, but I don't want to upset you or hurt you."

I frown down at her and tip her chin up. "You can ask me anything. No guarantee that I'll answer."

Her lips tip up in a smirk. "Your standard response. Okay then."

She takes a deep breath, as if she's gathering her courage, and I press a kiss to her forehead. I haven't been able to keep my hands off her. And for as long as she's here, I *won't* stop touching her.

Because for now, she's *mine.*

"What happened to your biological family, big guy?"

I sigh and push my fingers into her damp hair, brushing it back from her face.

"It's not a good story, Lena."

"I'm trying to get to know you, and I feel like that's kind of a big deal."

Fuck. I hate talking about this. I haven't in *years.* Since I was interviewing for the Secret Service, and it was brought up in that meeting.

"My birth certificate says that my name is Gideon James, and that my parents are Debbie and Ray James." I swallow hard and drag my hand down my face. "And after I talk to you about this tonight, I'll never speak of it again."

She nods, her lavender eyes full of compassion and tenderness, and I know without a doubt that I'd give her anything she asked for right now.

Even this.

Even this horrible, twisted darkness that I come from.

"I'm originally from Bozeman. My parents were normal middle-class people. Dad ran a construction company, Mom was a teacher."

She tilts her head to the side, listening intently. She links our hands together and kisses my knuckles, easing some of the tension in my shoulders.

"Dad was an alcoholic, and had a gambling addiction. He owed money to the wrong fucking people. Got arrested for theft, starting hitting Mom and got arrested for domestic abuse. He was a piece of shit."

She clears her throat but doesn't interrupt.

She also doesn't pull away from me.

"I don't know what happened that last day. Not for sure. I was about twelve, and I'd been at school. When I got home, I found my mom dead from a gunshot wound to the head, and my father nowhere to be found."

Lena gasps, but she still doesn't pull away from me.

"Gideon."

"He'd killed her. He was probably high on something, who knows. They found him and arrested him, and he pleaded no contest because the evidence was *everywhere*. Because Montana has a three-strikes rule, he'll never get out of prison."

"He's still living?" she asks.

"Last I heard, which was when Ray and Debbie petitioned the state to adopt me. He contested."

Her jaw drops. "He fucking *contested*?"

I love that she's pissed on my behalf.

"He didn't have any rights to me anyway. I don't know how he heard about the adoption. Obviously, it went through, and I've never heard from him again. I don't care to. He died along with my mom and my unborn sister. Did I mention she was pregnant?"

Lena climbs into my lap, straddles me, and hugs me tight, her face pressed to my neck.

"Fuck, I'm sorry," she whispers.

"It's not your fault." My hands rub up and down her slender back, down her sides. She feels so right pressed against me.

"Still sorry," she murmurs. "I know your mom would be happy that you landed here, with these good people."

I smile softly and drag my hand down her soft hair. "Yeah, she would."

I'm not the angry kid that I was when I came here. I've healed, and I've been loved. But thinking about that time always leaves me a little off.

"You know," she says quietly, "it's not lost on me that you came from all that, your mom died the way she did, and you ended up protecting a woman. You've done for me what I know you would have done for your mom if you'd been there."

This woman. I don't know what to say. Because she hit the nail on the head, and it has my chest aching with emotion.

"Gideon."

"Yes, little rebel."

I feel her smile against my skin.

"Let's go back to bed."

Chapter Nineteen

Lena

"We'll get there," he murmurs, his voice growly as his big hands glide under the T-shirt of his that I grabbed off the floor before I ran outside this morning. He groans next to my ear. "Do you have any idea how fucking beautiful you are?"

He nibbles his way along my jawline, and then his mouth is on mine, kissing me as if he'll never get enough of me. He grips my hips and pulls my core against his hardness, making me whimper.

"You're incredible," he whispers, his lips still against mine, and I can taste every beautiful word. "The most unexpected, amazing thing in my life."

His hands glide under the shirt again, he pulls it over my head and casts it aside, and then his lips wrap around one metal-clad nipple, making my core clench.

"Need you," I murmur, rocking over him. "Please, Gideon."

"I'll take care of you." His lips pop off one nipple and then move to the next, licking and nibbling, moving that metal around, and I swear to God, I could come just like this. His hips move up, grinding against me. "Are you needy for this cock, baby?"

"Yes." I'm starting to sweat from the need building within me. I have to get naked. I need *him* naked. "Gideon."

"Tell me what you want. Use your words, Rebel."

"You." I lick my lips and press my forehead against his, breathing him in. "I need you inside me. I need you to fill me up."

He sits forward, cups my face, and devours my mouth, and then I'm on my back and he's stripping my leggings off, leaving me naked and wanting. I can't stop staring as he sheds his own clothes and covers me with his body, nestling his cock in my slit, and pushes his hands into my hair.

"You're perfect," he whispers.

"I'm not perfect. Not even a little."

"For me, you are." His nose brushes back and forth over mine. His eyes are soft, full of an emotion I don't dare hope for.

I can't fall in love with him.

Pulling my legs higher against his hips, I glide my foot over the back of his leg, loving how warm his skin is.

"You have a *stellar* body," I inform him as I drag my nails down his shoulders.

"It's all yours."

I wish it was all mine forever. I want all this forever.

But I don't dare ask for it because the rejection might just kill me.

"I'm going to fucking worship you," he growls as he kisses down my neck. His hands are *everywhere*, gliding, stroking, and pinching, then soothing as he nibbles his way back to my nipples.

Getting them pierced was the best fucking thing I ever did in my life.

"Shit." I suck in a breath when his hand covers my pussy and he taps his fingertips over my clit, gently at first, and then harder, all while he sucks on my nipple, driving me absolutely out of my mind. *"Gideon."*

"We're not even close to you coming yet, Rebel." He grins up at me and then presses wet kisses over my navel before moving farther south to my center. "I'm going to drive you wild. And you won't come until I say you can."

"How can I control it?"

"You'd better figure it out." He nibbles the sensitive skin right next to my pussy, and then his mouth covers me, his tongue laps at me, and I cry out, gripping onto the edge of the sofa with one hand and his hair with the other.

"Oh, God. Yes. *Yes*, Gideon."

He hums, and the vibration sends sparks up my spine. The pressure building in my core rocks me, almost makes me panic, it's so all consuming.

"I've got you," he says, pushing two fingers inside me and hitting that spot, the one that only this man has ever been able to find. "Let go, baby. Go over for me. God, you're so fucking beautiful."

His words, the way he's touching me—it sends me over the edge, and I scream as I come, my hips bucking up, meeting his lips.

"Breathe." He works his way up and kisses my cheek, his fingers still inside me. "You have to breathe for me, Rebel."

"Can't." I do gasp in a breath and feel him smile against me. "I think I died."

"Not funny." He slaps my pussy, making me gasp again.

He moves me effortlessly onto my side and spoons up behind me, lifting my leg and notching the head of his cock at my entrance. When he pushes inside, he steals my breath once more.

"So fucking deep," I groan as he kisses over my shoulder. "Holy shit, Gideon. You're so damn big."

"And you take me so fucking well." With my leg resting over his thigh, he reaches around and pets my clit, making me clench around him. "Like a fucking glove. You were made for me, Lena."

Why does that make me want to cry?

I swallow hard and push back against him, wishing he'd pick up the pace and come so I didn't feel so vulnerable, but he doesn't do that. No, this amazing man pulls out and turns me around, so I'm facing him, and pulls my leg up, then slips back inside me and cups my cheek, brushing his thumb over my skin.

This is tender.

This is connection.

Christ, he's making love to me.

"Gideon."

He kisses me so softly, it makes my stomach clench.

"Mine," he whispers against my lips. "Do you hear me?"

I can only nod, because if I speak, I'll cry.

"Tell me."

I shake my head no, and his eyes narrow. He grips onto my ass, pulling me closer, moving a little faster and harder, and *this* I can do.

I can give him this.

"Tell me," he says again, louder and more insistent.

Closing my eyes, I press my lips to his. "Yours."

"Fuck." His fingertips are rough now, surely leaving bruises that will make me smile later. I want his roughness. I want to make him lose control because Gideon *never* loses control.

The head of his cock keeps brushing over that sensitive patch, and before I know it, I'm coming harder than ever, and with a groan, he follows me over, splashing inside me, and I know without a doubt that this has changed everything for me.

I'm in love with him.

"You're not concentrating."

Duh. How am I supposed to do that when he's standing there looking like the epitome of sex?

We're in the ring, and I'm supposed to be hitting him. Or trying to. I've only ever landed one punch, and that was to his stomach after flashing him my tits.

He's been extra vigilant since then.

"We need a day off," I tell him, but he scowls at me and crosses his arms over his chest, showing off his biceps. He's in a black tank top, revealing not only the muscles but his tattoos as well, and it's not fair that he looks that good.

Not fair at all.

"You're not getting a fucking day off."

"Well, not with that attitude." I smile, hoping he'll laugh at my joke, but he just stares at me. "I'm exhausted, big guy. *Someone* has seriously disrupted my sleep schedule lately. You woke me up to fuck me *twice* last night."

His lips twitch up into a smirk. "You weren't complaining when I was nine inches inside you and you were squirting all over my cock, Rebel."

Jesus, the mouth on this guy.

"It's not a complaint—it's just a fact." I bring my foot up behind me and press my heel to my ass, stretching out my quads. "Don't you ever want to sleep in? Be lazy?"

"No."

"Well, not all of us are superhuman like you." No reaction. He doesn't even crack a smile. "You know I just *love* the drill sergeant routine. So broody. So grumpy."

Nothing.

"Okay, hard-ass, what next?"

He circles me, looking me up and down like I'm a horse he wants to buy. It's unsettling and heats me up from the inside out.

"Come on. You're not concentrating in here, so you'll just get hurt."

"Where are we going?"

"Shooting range."

Honestly, shooting is my least favorite thing. I don't hate the obstacle course anymore, but we've been avoiding it because of the snow. The gym is okay. I'd rather run outside, but it's slick, and I don't have the proper shoes for it.

The shooting range makes me nervous. I know I'm safe, but I hate the noise, and I often have to breathe and count in my head to keep myself in the present and not get thrown back to that horrible night.

My nightmares are usually worse after we've worked in the range, especially if it's been a long lesson.

I haven't told him that, though. I refuse to complain, and he's not wrong when he says that it's stuff I need to learn. It could save my life someday.

It's snowing like crazy as we hustle from the gym over to the indoor range.

"Come here," Gideon says, crooking his finger at me. He's standing in front of the door to the armory. I never go in there. I've never been invited, and he keeps it locked down so tight, I assume it's off limits to me. "You can choose your weapon today."

"You're letting me in there?"

"If I'm with you, it's okay. You'll never come in here without me, though. Not until you've been trained on everything in here."

I stop just inside the doorway, my jaw on the floor, as I take it all in.

"Uh, Gideon?"

"Hmm?" He's already holding a weapon, checking it.

The room is so much bigger than it looks from the outside. The walls are lined with all kinds of different guns and rifles, and above each one is an illuminated LED light, so you can see exactly what you're reaching for.

It looks like something out of *Mission: Impossible*. Seriously, Tom Cruise could come walking in here any minute, and it wouldn't surprise me in the least.

"Pick your poison," Gideon says, turning to me. He looks like he *belongs* here, in this room with these weapons. Like he's completely at home here.

Because he is.

I swallow thickly. I can't take my eyes off him.

"Are we in a hurry?" My question comes out as a breathy whisper, making his eyebrow come up in surprise.

"Not particularly."

"Have you ever had sex in this room?"

That has his jaw flexing. He sets the gun down and then walks to me and frames my face in his hands.

"Does this turn you on, Rebel?"

"It's a surprise to me too," I admit, not able to look away from his incredible eyes. "But yeah, seeing *you* in here is a turn-on."

I drop to my knees and grip his belt, making him swear under his breath. He doesn't stop me as I unbuckle the belt, then work on his pants, and finally, his cock is free, and I lick it from the base to the crown, already dripping precum.

"Fucking hell, beautiful girl." His hand fists in the back of my hair, but he doesn't pull me down on him as I sink over him, taking him all the way back.

My gag reflex engages, but I don't stop. I *want* to choke on him. I want to feel helpless and at his mercy in this room.

"You didn't answer my question," I say when I pull off to catch my breath. Sinking over him again, I keep my eyes up and on his, working him with my lips and tongue.

"No, baby. This room is for work. I've never fucked anyone here."

Good. That's the right answer. I don't want to think about him having sex with anyone else, ever. The thought makes me nauseated.

I raise up on my knees, wrap both hands around him, and work him hard. His hand tightens in my hair, and then he *does* urge me down farther.

"You can take all of me. Relax your throat, breathe through your nose. That's my good girl."

Holy shit, my pussy is pulsing with need, but this is for him. I don't need him to fuck me. I need to get him off. I want to taste him, feel him come undone.

I hollow my cheeks, and he groans as his fingertips ghost down my neck. And when I add just the tiniest bit of teeth, he starts to come down my throat, and I swallow every fucking drop.

"Jesus Christ, Lena. Fuck, your mouth is . . . *fuck*."

He pulls me to my feet and kisses me, not seeming to care at all about what I was just doing, and then he brushes my hair back from my face.

"Your mouth is going to be the fucking death of me. What brought that on?"

"You look sexy as hell in here, big guy." I lean in to plant a kiss on his chest. "Okay, what am I shooting?"

He blows out a breath as he tucks himself away, but rather than turn to help me choose a gun, he pulls me into his arms and hugs me close, and I *soak it in.*

God, I love his hugs.

"You're the sweetest fucking thing," he whispers by the shell of my ear, and then he pulls away and gestures to the room. "And your mouth is fucking kryptonite. What do you want to shoot?"

"I don't care." I nibble my bottom lip, shifting from foot to foot.

"What's wrong?"

"Nothing."

He narrows his eyes at me. "Are you nervous, Rebel?"

"The shooting isn't my favorite." I shrug, as if it's no big deal. "But I understand why I'm learning. You go ahead and choose for me."

"First, you decide whether you want to shoot a handgun or rifle."

I haven't shot any of the rifles yet. I've managed to talk him out of them. *He* used a rifle of some kind on that horrible night, and I can't bring myself to do it.

"You've got this, Lena." His voice is tender, so different from how it usually is while we're training.

"Handgun." I turn so he won't see my lower lip quiver.

I don't apologize anymore because he told me not to, but I'm still not okay. I don't know if I'll *ever* be okay.

"Rifle it is."

"You said I could choose."

"We're going to get you past this fear of yours." His chin is firm as he pulls an automatic rifle off the wall and walks toward me with it.

I back away.

His eyes narrow.

I do *not* want to touch that weapon.

"No."

"Lena, you've got this. It's not any different from any of the dozen handguns you've shot since you got here. This one is just bigger."

"I won't do it." I shake my head and turn to leave, and then I'm suddenly in his arms. He's wrapped around me from behind, kissing my head, trying to soothe me, but everything inside me is shaking.

"You are so strong, baby. You're in control here, not the weapon. It won't hurt you."

"Please don't make me do it."

"I won't make you do anything." He turns me around so he can see my face, and his own expression falls. "Please don't cry, Rebel."

"I'm not." I sniff, but I refuse to acknowledge the tears running down my cheeks.

"You'll feel so much better after you shoot it. You'll take that power back."

I swallow hard because I *want* that. I don't want to be afraid.

"You can't be there." I shake my head, and he frowns down at me.

"I'm not leaving your side."

"I'm not leaving your side, Blackbird. You'll be safe."

"What if you're there and I shoot it wrong, and you get hurt?" The last few words are barely audible, but he hears me. He lifts my chin and kisses me tenderly.

"You won't hurt me."

I start to shake my head, but he holds me firm.

"Baby, you literally can't shoot me. I'm fine. Do you want me to shoot it first, so you can see that it's safe?"

I nod slowly, and he kisses my forehead.

"Okay, I'll show you. We'll be shooting down the range, at a target. Just like always. There's no way that the bullet can come back to hurt either of us."

I'm not convinced.

But I follow him out of the armory, and we walk into the range, grabbing eye and ear protection before we walk down to a lane.

"It's the same concept as when you're handling a pistol. Feet planted and spread. Keep your core engaged."

He's going through all the instructions, but I don't hear any of the words. I can't take my eyes off the rifle.

Then, he raises it and points it downrange and pulls the trigger.

Bang! Bang!

"No!" I scream as Gideon is suddenly on top of me, pushing me to the ground. He and Richie have their own weapons drawn, but there's so much chaos, screams, running people.

"I can't see the shooter," Richie yells to Gideon.

"It came from the front entrance."

Bang! Bang! Bang!

More shots are fired, and suddenly, the guys are carrying me through the room toward the back door.

But then another shooter enters that way and starts shooting people too.

We're trapped.

"We're going to let them start working the room," Gideon says, sounding so damn calm. How is he calm? This is all my fault. I just had *to see this new exhibit, and now we're in the middle of a mass shooting.*

I'm sobbing, clinging to Gideon as he and Richie make a plan. There's so much screaming, so much blood.

I can smell the coppery scent in the air, and I can hear the whimpers, the cries for mercy, as the two men continue to shoot the black rifles in their hands.

Oh, God, we're going to die.

"We're not going to die," Richie says. I must have said that out loud. "He's moved from the door."

"Move," Gideon says as he points his gun and shoots. "One down."

"You killed one?" I ask.

He doesn't answer me. He and Richie rush me out the back door and into the darkness. Into the rain.

There's a roar behind us and then hard, fast steps, as if someone is running after us.

"Take her," Gideon shouts, turning to the door we just ran out of. "Get her out of here!"

"No!" I'm clinging to Gideon. "I won't leave you here."

"Go with Richie." He looks my way just for a second. "Get the fuck out of here, Lena."

Bang! Bang!

Gideon's body jerks, and then he falls with me on top of him. Richie fires, taking out the second gunman, and then he pulls me off Gideon, but I can't stop screaming.

He's bleeding. The rain washes the blood into a pool around him, and I wiggle out of Richie's hold and fall back over Gideon.

"No! No no no. You're okay. It's okay. Oh, God, I'm so sorry."

"Hey, it's going to be fine." His voice is raspier, and he's breathing hard, but he doesn't seem like he's close to passing out. "I need you to get out of here, Lena. Let Richie get you somewhere safe."

I can hear sirens in the background.

"I'm not leaving you. We'll get you in an ambulance." I rip off my jacket, and then my sweater, and wrap the sweater around his leg to help stop the bleeding.

Richie isn't trying to get me to leave.

"The threat is gone," Richie says grimly. He's talking into his phone. "Two down. James was hit. Blackbird is secure."

"Shit, I'm going to pass out," Gideon says. "I don't want you to see this, Lena. Go with Richie."

But I'm shaking my head, unwilling and unable to move away.

And then he keeps his promise, the way he always does. He passes out, bleeding in an alley in the rain, and it's all my fault.

Chapter Twenty

Gideon

After emptying the magazine, I replace it with a full one and turn to talk to Lena, but she's no longer standing right next to me.

She's leaning against the wall, her eyes glassy, her face white as fuck, and she's shaking all over. After setting the weapon aside, I rush to her.

"Shit. Baby, look at me." Framing her face, I nudge her up to meet my eyes, but she doesn't look at me. She looks . . . *vacant.* It's like I'm not even here at all, and it's breaking my fucking heart. "Come back, Rebel. I need you to leave that nightmare and come back to me."

She whimpers. Her whole body is shaking so hard, her teeth chatter, and I wish with my whole heart that I could go back in time and kill those motherfuckers all over again.

"Baby, you're safe." I pull her against me and rock her back and forth, cradling her against my chest. "Listen to my heartbeat, Lena. Do you hear it?"

I fucking hate how terrified she is. How her slim body trembles beneath my hands.

"Why won't it stop?" It's a whispered question, so quiet I almost didn't hear it. "I'm not this weak—I just can't make it stop."

Shame on every single fucking person who didn't get her into therapy the morning after it happened.

"Baby, I have to put the weapons away, and then I'm taking you home, okay?"

She nods, but she's clinging to me now, still shaking.

"Can you stand here and wait for me for two minutes?"

Now she shakes her head no. "Don't go."

Christ.

I sink to the floor and pull her into my lap, and she immediately curls into me. Then I grab my phone out of my pocket and call Ryker.

"Hey, man," he says when he picks up.

"I need you in the shooting range ASAP."

"Be there in five," he says and hangs up, and I set my phone aside and press kisses to Lena's soft dark hair.

"I'm right here. I'm not going anywhere. You're perfectly safe."

"I'm not w-w-worried about me." She sniffs, and I brush her hair behind her ear. "You got hurt. Oh, God, you were so hurt, and it was raining, and I couldn't—"

"Shh." Cradling her close, I rock us back and forth. She's not afraid for herself. She's afraid for *me*, and it's so fucking humbling and infuriating all at once.

"I'm sorry," she whispers.

"You don't have anything to be sorry for. *I'm* sorry that I pushed it. That's on me."

She sniffles and presses her face into my neck. "It shouldn't be so hard. It shouldn't feel like you'll die every time I see that gun. But I c-can't."

She starts to sob again, and I just hold her and let her cry it out. It feels like my chest is being torn open.

Ryker comes running into the range and pulls up short, his brow furrowing when he sees us on the floor. His eyes skim over us both, looking for an injury, I'm guessing.

"What's wrong? Is she hurt?"

"We're not injured. I need you to secure that rifle in the armory," I tell him. "And then I need to get her home."

"I'm sorry," she says again, but I simply kiss her temple. "Gideon got shot, and there was so much blood, and it was all my fault—"

"Shh." I shake my head when Ry's face falls. "It *wasn't* your fault, Lena."

"I just *had* to go to that exhibit. I begged you to go until you finally gave in, and it could have killed you."

Ryker isn't supposed to be privy to this information, but fuck it. He's my brother.

Framing her face, I make her look me in the eye.

"Listen to me right now. It was a *random* mass shooting. They didn't know who you were. It had nothing at all to do with you, Lena. We were in the wrong place at the wrong time, and it's as simple as that."

"It's not simple." She shakes her head slowly. "It was the worst night of my life, and I regret it so much."

"Baby, you just wanted to look at pretty art. There's nothing wrong with that. You didn't lure me into an active war zone."

"Fuck," Ryker whispers, dragging his hand down his face.

"I can't get the image of you lying in that wet alley, bleeding, out of my head. I *can't*." She breaks down again, and I finally stand with her in my arms as Ryker grabs the weapon and secures it in the armory for me, then locks it and the range up behind us as we climb into the back seat of his truck.

The tears calm a bit as we get closer to the house, but Ryker keeps checking us in the rearview mirror, his brows pulled together in concern.

"What can we do?" he asks when he parks by the house.

"I have her," I reply as I open my door. "Thanks for the help, brother."

"I'll have Willow make extra for dinner. Come over later."

I nod, and then pat him on the shoulder. "Thanks, man."

After stepping out of the truck, I lean in and take Lena's hand, helping her out of the truck, and then lead her inside. I don't like how pale she still is, or how flat her gorgeous lavender eyes are. She's always full of life, full of fire.

"What do you need, baby?" I ask her.

"Can we just snuggle on the couch?"

With a small grin, I lead her through to the sofa and take a seat, and she curls up next to me, resting her head on my shoulder and linking her fingers with mine.

"I need you to talk to me." I take a deep breath and kiss her head. "*Really* talk to me. I know that we were both there that night, but I think there are some holes for both of us that need to be filled in."

Her deep breath is shaky, but she sits up and faces me, sitting criss-cross, her legs pressed up against my thigh. She won't let go of my hand. It's like if she stops touching me, I'll disappear.

Again.

"I should have listened to you and Richie when you said that it wasn't safe for us to go to the museum at the last minute. I was being selfish, and you know how I hated having a security detail in the first place."

"First of all, you were not being selfish, Lena," I reply, frowning over at her. "I know you didn't like the security, and you tried to rebel against it, but you never said *why*."

She rubs her lips together, thinking about it.

"I was seventeen when Mom was elected. I'd always struggled to fit in because teenagerhood is horrible, and suddenly having big, mean-looking guys following me around in high school made me *so* different. I've never been the person with a ton of friends. And that's okay with me, because I'm pretty introverted, but no teenager likes to feel different."

Been there, done that. "I can understand that. I was a foster kid with a murderer for a father. I know what it's like to be different."

She rubs her hand down my cheek, and I press a kiss to her palm. "I wasn't really the rebellious one, you know. That was Chelsea. *She* was my friend, and she knew that the constant security drove me bananas, so she encouraged me to try to escape. We made it a game."

"She's a shit influence. She's also a shit friend, Lena. I wish you could see that."

She shrugs a shoulder. "She's a selfish person, sure. And she has a lot of faults. But since we were five, she's been a constant in my life when my own parents weren't. Nannies came and went. Security came and went. But Chelsea was always there. So yeah, she has her faults, but she's my friend."

Sighing, I lean over to kiss her cheek and brush my nose over her skin. "Okay, baby. Keep going."

"I always felt guilty when we pulled off sneaking out. *So guilty.*" She shakes her head and bites her lip, looking lost and *sad*. "But that night, I didn't want to sneak away as if I was doing something wrong. I was an adult, and I wanted to go to see the art of an artist that I'd admired for a long time. It didn't feel dangerous to me, Gideon."

"It shouldn't have been dangerous," I agree, rubbing my thumb over her knuckles.

"It felt like such a normal thing to do. Chelsea had no interest in going, but that was fine with me. I don't have an issue doing things alone. Sometimes it's better, actually. I was enjoying myself. And then all hell broke loose."

She swallows hard, frowning.

"At first, all I could think was that some maniac had followed us there, and that I'd fucked up so bad."

I shake my head but let her speak.

"And then it all happened so fast. But all that blood, and the cries and screams. Those shooters had dead eyes."

Yeah. They did.

"They didn't care that they were killing innocent people. They didn't look excited, or angry, or *anything*. They had no expressions at all. And they weren't wearing masks to even cover up their identities."

"It was likely one of two things," I reply. "Either they didn't think they'd get caught, or they didn't expect to leave alive."

"Did anyone ever find out *why* they did it?"

I scowl and squeeze her hand and feel frustration bubble in my gut. "You weren't kidding when you said that no one would speak to you about this."

"No. I was completely shut out. I wasn't allowed to know *anything*, and it drove me crazy. How was there nothing on the news? I know that some things can be covered up, like what happened that night before I came here. But a mass shooting in a museum? Gideon, there was *nothing* on the news, and I searched for it. No mention of you being hurt, of me being there, of any of those people dying."

Taking a deep breath, I push my hand through my hair. "The press releases what your mother and her people want them to release. Whether it's the death of one man near a restroom in an art gallery or the deaths of sixteen people in a museum. She's in control of that."

She blinks, clearly not understanding.

"I don't know why the shooting itself wasn't reported. I can tell you that she didn't want anyone to know you were there, or that I was injured, because that would show weakness. Weakness makes your whole family more vulnerable."

Lena rolls her eyes, making my shoulders finally relax.

"There's my sassy girl."

"I thought I could do it today, out there with you, but as soon as I saw that weapon, it took me right back there. You got shot, I was trying to stop the blood, and then you passed out on me."

"I told you to go so you wouldn't see that." I use my pinkie to brush her hair off her cheek and behind her ear. "You shouldn't have had to see that. I didn't want that for you."

"But it was the last time I saw you until you walked into my bedroom, and damn it, Gideon." She blinks furiously, trying to keep the tears at bay.

"Did you miss me, Rebel?"

She huffs out a breath. "Yeah. I did."

That fills me with immense satisfaction, and I pull her onto my lap, needing her closer.

"If I hadn't been shot, I would have stayed on your detail until your mother was out of office, and things would have been strictly professional between us. I *never* would have allowed myself to look at you differently, Lena. Even now, I know that I'm skirting some serious lines when it comes to what's appropriate."

"Gid—"

"No, let me say this. I would absolutely, without a fucking doubt, do it again. There isn't anything I would do differently, because if I hadn't been shot that night, we wouldn't be here like this, and there is *nothing* I want more than having you here with me. You're mine, and it took that incident to take me out of the job so I could have this with you all these years later. And this?" I kiss her lips softly as they tremble. "There's nothing better than this, Lena."

"Gid, what if I don't want to go when all this is over?"

"Then you don't have to go."

She blinks in surprise. "I don't?"

"You're welcome to stay here for as long as you want. Always."

Don't ever leave.

I'm so gone over her, I'd marry her today. But my life is here on this ranch, and I know it's not for everyone. She hasn't experienced a winter, dealing with forty-below-zero temperatures. Being isolated out here. That'll get old for her.

But for as long as she wants to stay, she has a home here, because if I had my way, she'd be with me for the rest of my life.

"I'll try again tomorrow," she says with a sigh, wrapping her sweet little body around me.

"Try what?"

"Shooting that fucking gun."

Scowling, I drag my hand up and down her back. "You don't ever have to shoot it. I'll take it off the table right now."

"No, I *do* need to. I need it for my own self-confidence. It's just metal. It can't think or react. It can't hurt you, and I need to remind myself of that. So I'll suck it up and shoot the fucking thing, and then we'll get on with our lives."

Taking her chin in my fingers, I kiss her lips softly. "You're the strongest woman I know. You don't have to shoot that rifle to prove anything to me or anyone else."

"I'm proving it to *me*." She straddles me and wraps her arms around my shoulders, and when she presses her center against me, it makes me hard as fuck. "Thanks for talking it out with me. I think it helped a lot. But I have some questions."

"Shoot."

"First of all, *do* we know why they targeted that museum?"

"One of them was a security guard who had been fired because he took his job a little *too* seriously and pulled his gun on a customer who touched a painting. The other guy was his brother."

She blinks at me, then looks out the window. "That is *so* . . . It wasn't a political statement? Or, I don't know, *something*? All those people died because he was *mad*?"

"It was literally an act of revenge because he lost his job." My hand slides around to her ass, and I give it a little pat. "What else do you want to know?"

"When you went to the hospital, what happened then? I went back to my apartment and my life, but I don't know what happened to *you*."

I feel my lips twitch, and she scowls.

"It's not funny."

"No, but I like knowing that you were worried about me." I lean up and kiss her chin. "I was in the hospital for close to a week. I had to have emergency surgery because one of the bullets grazed an artery—that's why there was so much blood, but I obviously didn't bleed out. They got me stitched up, but I *did* almost lose the leg."

Lena gasps, her face going pale again, and I frame her face in my hands and pull her forehead against mine.

"I *didn't*, though. I stayed in DC for a year, working with the best PT team in the country because I was determined to go back to work, but the leg will never be at a hundred percent. Once that was decided, I came back home to the ranch, built this house, and started my business."

She closes her eyes for a minute and then pushes her hands into my hair.

"And you never got married?"

"No." I nuzzle her nose. "I didn't."

I stand and carry her to the stairs, and she wraps her legs around my waist, nuzzling my neck.

"Gideon?"

"Yes, baby."

"I'm so fucking glad you didn't choose anyone else."

I smile against her shoulder and hug her to me when I stop by the bed.

"There is no other choice for me, Rebel. Just you. Always you."

Chapter Twenty-One

Lena

The bed is empty.

Well, aside from me.

Waking up alone isn't unusual. Ever since I adjusted to the time change, I rarely wake up before six. And since I've been sleeping in Gideon's bed, I sleep like a baby. Nightmares are rare now, and sleeping in his arms is an addiction I don't want to recover from.

I think it would drive me crazy if I had to go back to sleeping without him. And the best part is, I don't have to.

He said I can stay.

Gideon almost always wakes up before me, leaves me to sleep in this big, cozy bed while he gets some work, or a workout, in before I get up and start my day.

It's become a routine, and I kind of love it. It feels so . . . *easy.* So perfect for us. And this morning is no different.

It's been a week since the incident at the shooting range, and I'm determined to get back out there today to shoot that damn rifle. Gideon's kept me away from there, focusing on hand-to-hand and other exercises, but I'm ready to try again.

I will succeed today.

I *know* I can do it. I feel so much stronger since I've lived here with Gideon. The bad moments are fewer and farther between, and since our conversation last week, I've felt a shift in me and how I feel about the entire incident.

It's still the worst night of my life.

But I realize that it wasn't my fault. Those shooters would have been there with or without me in attendance. I'm not the reason that Gideon was shot.

I still hate it, but I've let a lot of the guilt go.

And today, I'm going to shoot the rifle that scares me and let that go too.

I climb from the bed and wander into the bathroom to do my business, pull my hair up into a ponytail, and after I brush my teeth, I wash my face and then move to the closet to pull on some leggings and a baggy sweatshirt over a sports bra. No matter what we decide to do today, this outfit will work for it.

After I leave the bedroom in search of coffee, I hear Gideon's voice in his office, and I stop in the doorway, watching him.

He's in his usual uniform of black tee and black tactical pants, and his tattoos are delicious in the early-morning light. Just looking at him makes me wet.

But I don't like the way he's rubbing his forehead in agitation or the hard set of his shoulders.

"Yes, Madam President."

I lift an eyebrow. *He's talking to my mom.*

His eyes lift to mine, and he offers me a half smile, making my thighs clench.

Christ, he's handsome.

His eyes fall to where I'm clenching my legs together, and he smirks.

"She's doing well. Would you like to speak to her?"

No, she likely won't.

Gideon scowls, confirming my suspicions.

"It's no trouble, she's right—yes, ma'am. Understood."

He hangs up and sighs, and I cross the room to him. Gideon shoves his chair back from the desk as I move to stand in front of him, and he buries his face in my stomach as his arms come around my hips and he hugs me.

My hands dive into his hair, enjoying him.

"This isn't the longest I've gone without speaking to my parents," I inform him softly. "Once, when I was in high school and they were on a tour of Europe, I didn't see or speak to them for about four months."

He tips his head back so he can look up at me with those hard steel eyes. "I fucking hate that."

"It just is what it is." Dragging my hands down to his cheeks, I bend down to kiss him. "I'm fine, Gideon. Better than fine. Are things resolved in DC?"

"No." He kisses my stomach, and then he pulls me into his lap and nuzzles my neck, making me laugh. He probably won't tell me any more than that.

I'm on a need-to-know basis when it comes to my own life as far as my mother's concerned.

"I'm going to make us breakfast today," I inform him. "I've been watching YouTube videos to learn, and the other day, Willow walked me through making French toast."

"You need protein with that," he informs me, still kissing and nuzzling my neck.

"I'll make bacon and eggs too."

His hand drifts up and down my thigh and around to my ass.

"What are you doing?" I ask him.

"Trying to seduce my girl," he growls, making me grin.

"Aside from that."

He lifts his head and kisses my nose. "I was at war with a spreadsheet."

"Why?"

"Because I fucking suck at spreadsheets."

"Well, lucky for you, I'm good at them. I can help."

The idea thrills me, and my chest clenches in excitement. I can help him. I can be helpful and put some of the classes I took to use.

I turn around and, still sitting in his lap, wait while Gideon types his password into the computer, and the spreadsheet that comes up has my eyes crossing.

"Jesus, big guy."

"Told you." He points to numbers on a page, information in two different emails, and I can figure out quickly what he needs in the spreadsheet. "It's taken me three days to get that far."

"I can do this in less than two hours."

He stills behind me, and then his lips land on my shoulder. "You're hired."

Excitement stirs in my belly, and I turn to smile at him over my shoulder. "Really?"

"Hell yes. If you can do this for me, I'll give you anything you want."

With a snort, I turn back to get to work, opening a fresh spreadsheet to start from scratch, and Gideon moves my ponytail over the front of my shoulder and kisses the back of my neck, making my nipples pucker.

"I'm supposed to be working," I murmur as I try to concentrate.

"Good girl. So dedicated. Such a work ethic." His hands roam under the baggy sweatshirt, slide up my sides and over to my breasts. "Have I told you lately how much I love the metal right here?"

"Once or twice." Jesus, my panties are already soaked, and my fingers tremble as I try to focus on the task at hand. Gideon flicks one nipple, and I gasp. "Shit, I can't work like this."

"You'd better." He lifts the sweatshirt all the way off and lets it fall aside, then works my sports bra off, and goose bumps pebble up from the cool air. "Be a good girl and keep working for me, Rebel. If you stop, you don't get to come."

His teeth graze the ball of my shoulder as his hands drift down my stomach and into the waistband of my leggings, working down until he's cupping my pussy, and when he finds how wet I am, we both groan.

"Look at how wet you are, baby. Goddamn, you make me insane. What do you need?"

"You."

"More specific."

I swallow thickly, my hips circling with every movement of his fingers. "I need you inside me so bad I ache with it."

"Mm, I like that." He bites the side of my neck, making me whimper. "I fucking like that a lot. I want you aching for me all the damn time. Did you wake up like this?"

"No."

"What turned you on? What made this pretty pussy so fucking wet for me?"

"Just . . . *you*."

His fingers move between my lips, then back up to swirl around my clit, and I lean back into his touch, abandoning the keyboard altogether.

"You stopped working," he growls against my ear as he pulls his hand out of my leggings, making me gasp in outrage as he licks his fingers clean. "I told you what would happen."

"Gideon."

"Don't forget who's in charge here, Rebel." He bites my earlobe and then pushes me forward until I'm standing and bent over his desk. "I think I'll edge you for a little while, just to remind you who the boss is."

"Fuck."

"Oh, we will. Don't worry about that." He grips onto the sides of my leggings and yanks them down and off, and I'm bent over his desk completely naked. "God, you're gorgeous."

His hand glides up over my spine from my ass to my neck, and I curl into his touch like a cat. I never get enough of his hands on me. After I've gone without touch and affection for so long, being with Gideon every day is absolute *bliss*.

"You're so good at that." My voice is breathy and quiet, and I feel him grin against the small of my back before he bites my ass cheek, making me squirm.

"You have the softest skin," he says. "Like velvet."

"It's all in the lotion you use."

He smacks my ass, and I gasp before chuckling.

"Keep running your perfect little mouth, Rebel, and see what it gets you."

"Hopefully more of that."

He swats me again and then rubs his hand over it, soothing the sting. "I love your sass." His fingers trace the crack of my ass and down over that puckered muscle on their way through my sopping pussy.

He comes back up again without touching my clit, which has my legs scissoring back and forth.

"Are you all worked up, baby?"

"You know I am."

"Good." He bites my butt cheek before kissing it and then leaves wet kisses up my spine to my neck, and he wraps a hand around my throat, pulls me upright, and kisses my lips. His tongue licks into my mouth, and he grinds his hardness against my backside, but he's still fully dressed.

"You need to get naked."

He quirks an eyebrow. "You're. Not. In charge."

"Please get naked?"

His lips quirk, but they don't smile.

"I need you to fuck me, big guy." His fingers dive into my pussy, *hard*, and he starts to finger fuck me, and holy shit. "Oh, yes. Yes yes yes."

"God, you're tight." He nips at my shoulder, and then he pulls his fingers out and spins me around, kissing me as he unfastens his pants.

When his cock springs free, he lifts me in his arms and walks me to the wall, pinning me there.

"You make me lose control," he growls against my lips as he slides inside me, making me whimper. "And I *never* lose fucking control, Lena."

"You're safe with me."

At my whispered words, he starts to pound mercilessly. He pins one of my hands above my head and fucks me harder, more intensely than ever before.

"Rub that clit and come for me." He licks my bottom lip, and I know I can't tell him no.

I lick my middle finger, making his eyes blow wide with so much lust, my pussy clenches around him tighter, and then I move my hand between us and circle that little bundle of nerves, making us shudder.

"Just like that. You're going to come all over my cock." He bites my lower lip, and I gasp, right on the edge. "Make a mess of us."

"Gideon."

"That's right. Say my name while I fuck you, baby."

"Gideon."

"Go over. You're so fucking gorgeous like this. Come *now*."

His voice is like gravel, his cock hard and hitting *just* the right spot, and I couldn't stop this orgasm if I tried.

I clamp down on him, and he ruts into me, growling as he follows me over the edge and splashes his cum inside me.

His lips find mine, but they're softer now. Tender. And when he lets go of my wrist, I wrap them both around his neck, and he buries his face against me.

"Mine," he whispers.

"Yours," I agree.

"That was really good," Gideon says with just a hint of surprise in his voice as we clean up the breakfast dishes.

"I told you, I'm learning. I have to earn my keep." I snort at that, and then suddenly, I'm in Gideon's arms, and he's kissing the top of my head.

"You don't have to *earn* anything."

"I know my mom's paying you—"

"No, she's not."

I spin and stare up at him in shock. *"What?"*

"I turned it down." He kisses my nose. "She thinks I'm doing her a personal favor. I can't accept money for having you here when I have no intentions of ever letting you leave, and I'm happy to protect and care for you, Lena. No one needs to pay me to do that. This is no longer a job for me. It's a relationship."

Holy mother of God.

I don't know what to say.

I'm at once overjoyed and annoyed.

"But—"

He steps away, not touching me at all now, and I need his hands on me, so I step with him and wrap my arms around his waist.

"Don't pull away from me."

"Then tell me what the hell you're thinking."

I lick my lips and frown up at him. "You spent a *lot* of money on me when I first got here, and we weren't in a relationship then."

Holy shit, we're in a relationship.

"I already *have* plenty of money, Lena. If you'd ever like to see my portfolio, I'm happy to show you. Ryker's a finance guy, and he's made us both very rich men. I can afford to buy you anything in the world you might need or want. Your clothes and art supplies were no big deal."

I blink at him for a full ten seconds. "Whether you're wealthy or not isn't the point."

He brushes a piece of my hair off my face and behind my ear in that way that I love so much.

"Then what is the point, baby?"

"I think you should be reimbursed for those things, at least. I understand not wanting a paycheck, but it's *her* fault that I couldn't bring anything at all with me. She should have to pay for that, and she'd expect to."

He sighs, narrows his eyes, and cups the side of my neck in his big hand. "I'll let her know she owes me for that initial night of online shopping, but that's it, Lena. That's as far as I'll compromise."

"I can live with that. And now I *really* have to pull my weight around here."

"What are you even talking about?"

"I *want* to cook and clean up and help you with your spreadsheets and anything else you need. I can't just work out, learn how to kick someone's ass, and sketch all day every day. That'll get old fast."

He swallows hard. "I'm going to warn you right now, baby, living out here isn't easy. You'll start to feel isolated, and eventually, you might want to move back to the city."

Frowning, I stare at him again, and then I roll my eyes.

"Did you just *roll your eyes* at me, Rebel?"

"Yes. For fuck's sake, Gideon, I've been here for *weeks*. I'm not bored. I don't miss crowds of people, or being harassed by the paps, or anything like that. Sure, I could use a restaurant meal once a week, but when things die down, we can do that. I'm not telling you I want to leave—I'm telling you I want to be a *partner*. I want to do my part for this household. Because if you don't intend to let me leave, and I don't intend to do the leaving, this is my house too."

A slow grin moves over his impossibly handsome face, and he pulls me in tighter and ghosts his lips over mine.

"It's all yours, baby. Learn to cook, do whatever you want. But you need to tell me if you ever start to miss the city. Because we can take trips. I want to make sure you never start to hate it out here."

"Did Debbie start to hate it?"

"Fuck no, getting her off the ranch took bribery and tears."

"What about Willow?"

"She loves it here, with the occasional trip to town, or Seattle."

"So what makes you think that I won't be content too?" I tilt my head and thread my fingers through the hair at the back of his head. "I love the quiet. I love your mountains. I don't want to go anywhere."

“Good.” He slaps my ass and steps away from me. “Now, let’s go to the gym.”

“Can we go to the range?”

His brow furrows. “Baby, we don’t have to—”

“I want to. I need to shoot that damn rifle.”

He’s already shaking his head, but I take his hand and give it a squeeze.

“I’m good. I’ve got this. Let me kick some ass today.”

He sighs, examines my face, and then nods. “Let’s kick some ass, Rebel.”

Chapter Twenty-Two

Lena

"Wait." Willow spins around from where she's washing potatoes in the sink and pins me in her wide-eyed stare. "You *shot it*? You really did it. And no freak-out this time?"

My smile is smug. "I did it, girl. I made that rifle my bitch."

"Yes!" She rushes to me, her hands dripping wet, and hugs me to her, and I don't even care that she's soaking the back of my shirt. "I knew you could do it. I bet you're so relieved."

"I definitely am because now I don't ever have to do it again." I snort and chop some peppers for the salad. Willow and I are getting dinner ready while the guys are off doing something or other. They weren't specific. I enjoy hanging out with Willow. She's become an unexpected friend, almost like the big sister I never had, and I never feel like I'm walking on eggshells around her, even after our rough start. She wouldn't ask me to do something I'm uncomfortable with. She wouldn't encourage me to be someone I'm not. She's shown me what real friendship looks like, and it's kind of sad to think that I've never had this before. "Oh! Before the guys come back, I have to show you this. I want your take on it before I give it to Gideon."

I wipe my hands dry and then rush over to my bag so I can pull out my sketchbook and open it to the page I've been working on for Gideon.

When I turn it so Willow can see it, she immediately crumbles into tears.

"Oh, God, I hope those are good tears and I didn't butcher this."

She nods and stares down at the page, taking it in.

"I love it so much, Lena. I love that you captured them when they were younger, from around the time when Ry and Gid came to live here. God, they look so happy." Ray and Debbie are smiling at each other, his arm is around her, and they're sitting on the big wraparound porch on this house.

"I thought it would bring happy memories." I loop my arm around her shoulders, and she leans against me. "Do I need to tweak anything? Change anything? You knew them, and I want to make sure it's as accurate as possible."

"No." She wipes her cheeks and continues to stare at the paper. "No, there's nothing here to change. You'll make the guys cry too."

"I don't necessarily want to make anyone cry. I just want Gid to like it."

"He's going to go crazy for it." She takes one more look before I close the book and return it to my bag. "You know, his birthday is at the end of the month. That would be an incredible gift. If you want, I can order a frame for it so you don't have to use his accounts."

"That would be *perfect*. Thank you."

We resume making dinner, and we hear the front door open and the guys' voices carry through the house.

"We're in the kitchen," Willow calls out.

"Oh, good, you're making my favorite."

Willow gasps and spins, and then she's crying again and running to Aiden, who's standing just inside the doorway. She wraps her arms around him and squeezes him, and he wrinkles his nose, as if he's only tolerating the hug because it's from her.

"Surprise," he says when she pulls back to look up at him. "I came home for a couple of days."

"You don't have a game this week?"

"Not until Monday," he says and smiles at me. "Hey, Lena."

"Hey, Aiden, welcome home."

"So that's where you two ran off to," Willow says to Ryker and Gideon, who are both grinning at her proudly.

My man is seriously a smoke show when he smiles.

"Someone had to get the kid from the airport," Gideon says as he ruffles Aiden's hair and then walks over to kiss my forehead. "You okay?"

"I'm great. So how's hockey?" I ask Aiden. "Do you love it? Is everyone being nice to you? Do we have to kick someone's ass?"

Everyone stares at me for a minute, and I shrug.

"What? They better be nice to him. Because if they're not, I have a *lot* of new skills that are going to waste right now."

"Good girl," Gideon whispers in my ear.

Ryker smirks at me. "He's a rookie. They're giving him all kinds of shit, Lena. That's how it works."

"But I'm also *really* good at my job, so they're not giving me too much shit. It's all pretty much what I expected. Met a girl." He shrugs as if it's no big deal, and Gideon and I grin at each other.

"Name. Age. Job. Tell me everything," Willow says.

"Do you want her Social Security number and blood type too?" Aiden asks. "Maybe some tax returns and her family tree?"

"I can find those things out for you," Gideon adds, and Aiden smirks. "It'll just take one phone call. I don't even need her full name."

"That's kind of scary," I decide, watching my man, and he turns to me with a raised eyebrow. "Do you know everything about *me*?"

"You're fucking adorable," he says and kisses the tip of my nose.

"Is that a yes?"

Everyone laughs, and I decide to take the focus off me and shift back to Aiden.

"What's your girl's name?" I ask Aiden sweetly and wink at Willow.

"Miranda," Aiden replies and finds a cookie in the pantry. "She's forty."

Now, we all stare at him because I know for a fact that Aiden is only twenty.

Willow sputters, and both of the guys start shaking their heads.

"Wow," I say, the first to find words. "Okay. What does she do?"

"She's some kind of entrepreneur. Met her after a game." He bites into his cookie. "Super rich. So I decided that I'd quit hockey and let her be my sugar mama. The sex is fucking out of this world. Older women know what the fuck they're doing."

I start to laugh, but everyone else is stunned speechless.

Aiden's smirking behind his cookie. "You guys are too gullible. She's twenty-one, and she's a barista. She works in the iceplex."

"What's the iceplex?" I ask as the tension in the room evaporates and Willow pulls out a bottle of wine, making me smirk. Poor mama bear just had a stroke.

"It's where the team has practices and stuff," Gideon tells me, rubbing circles on my back. "It's big, with restaurants, shops, several rinks for practice. But it's rented out for leagues and such as well. We'll visit sometime when we go to watch his games."

We're going to watch his games!

"Count me in for that. Okay, so she's a barista, and she's . . . *pretty*?"

"Hot as f—hell," he says, eyeing Willow. "I like her."

"You never talk about girls," Willow says, staring at her kid as if he's grown a third leg.

"I guess there wasn't anyone to talk about before."

"That's the *sweetest.*"

Aiden winks at me and plucks a slice of cucumber out of the salad, tosses it in his mouth.

"Are we having meat loaf?" he asks.

"Yes," Willow replies.

"Awesome." He kisses her head and then turns to leave the room. "Gonna go wash up."

He strides up the stairs, taking two at a time, and Willow blinks back tears.

"I miss that little jerk."

"I know you do," Ryker says as he pulls her in for a hug. "He's doing great. Mac told me that no one's giving him a hard time, he likes his roommates, and he's kicking ass on the ice. Mac must not know about the girl."

"Who's Mac?" I ask Gideon, trying to get caught up on all the who's who.

"Teammate," Gideon says. "Played with Ry from day one."

"It's Mac's last year," Ryker adds. "He was holding out so he could play a season with Aiden. The two of them have been close for the past five years or so."

"I love everything about this." I sigh happily and lean against Gideon's side. "Thanks for including me."

"Of course. You're one of us," Willow says, tilting her head to the side. "We got drunk and talked about how much sex we've had. You're my bestie now."

I snort and feel Gideon stiffen next to me.

"Oh, lighten up." I smack his chest with the back of my hand, and he's so fast, he catches my hand and lifts it to his mouth.

"No more talking about sex with anyone but me," Ryker says to Willow, but I decide to be a smart-ass.

"I have no experience with that, so—"

"And you fucking won't," Gideon adds, his voice hard as granite as he pins me in his angry stare. "Don't push me, Rebel."

"Wow," Willow whispers as Ryker hides his smile behind his hand.

"Or what?" I tilt my head, enjoying myself *immensely*.

Gideon simply picks me up and carries me out of the kitchen.

"Hey! I don't want to go home. I'm hungry."

"Not going home," he mutters and carries me into an office and closes the door behind us. "Talk about sex with another man again, and I'll spank your ass until it glows. I'm a jealous man, Lena. You may think it's funny, but I don't."

"You don't have anything to be jealous *over*, big guy. I had no idea what all the fuss was about until you. I don't even think about anyone else. Willow and I joke around and talk because we're women, and when you get some alcohol in us, that's what we do. But now that I know that it bothers you so much, I won't do it when you're around."

He's glaring at me, his hands in fists, and I drag my palm up his chest and cup his rough cheek.

"You weren't a virgin when I met you, either, you know," I remind him softly.

"No one in this world matters but you," he says, wrapping his arms around my shoulders. "*No one*, Lena. It doesn't matter if I fucked five women or five hundred—"

"I'm not one for sex shaming, but *please* tell me it wasn't five hundred."

"—it doesn't matter because they weren't you. No one has ever made me crave simply being in her presence like you do. Hell, I'm jealous that anyone else gets to *talk* to you."

"Okay, that's a little unhinged."

"So don't push me. I don't care that you weren't a virgin when you came here, but I don't want to ever hear about it again. Unless any of them hurt you. In which case, I'll make them pay."

I blink up at him.

Is this a good time to tell him that Howey was an asshole in bed? I mean, it wasn't *bad* sex, but now that I know how good it can be, I realize Howey was selfish as fuck.

Nah, I shouldn't say anything.

"No need to go all murdery on me."

He kisses my forehead. "Are you sure I can't take you home so I can fuck that sass out of you?"

"I'm *hungry*," I repeat. "And it would be rude to leave now. I like those people."

"I love them, but I'd ditch them right now."

I snort and boost up on my toes so I can kiss him, but he still has to bend down to meet me.

"Let's go enjoy dinner, and then you can take me home and fuck me seven ways to Sunday."

"Christ," he mutters as he opens the door, and when we get to the kitchen, Aiden's back downstairs, and Willow has pulled the meat loaf out of the oven.

"Dinner's ready."

"I need a favor."

We're riding back to the house from working out in the gym. Aiden left for Seattle this morning, and we all met at the farmhouse to have breakfast together before Ryker and Willow took him to the airport. Then Gideon and I went right out to work in the ring.

I'm extra sweaty today. He worked me hard, but I managed to get a punch in that he wasn't expecting, so I'm taking that as a win.

"Ask away," he says, reaching over to hold my hand.

The weather has gotten cold enough that we rarely run outside or walk to the workout facilities anymore, so we're in his truck.

"I need to call Chelsea."

His gaze whips around to mine, and he scowls. "Fuck no."

"Just listen to me. Her birthday is in two days, and I want to call to wish her a happy birthday and chat with her for a few minutes. It would be completely out of character for me *not* to do that, even if I was on a world tour for my mother. I'm shocked she hasn't been asking about me."

"She did finally reach out to Richie to ask how much longer you'll be gone and when you'll be answering your phone," he admits, and I stare at the side of his head.

"Why didn't you tell me?"

Now he looks over at me with his Secret Service face firmly in place. "Because you didn't need to know."

"*Gideon.* I had the right to know that. I want to call her for her birthday. I have done everything you've said, and you know it. I haven't even asked to call my *family*. You can do this for me."

He sighs and drags his hand down his face, but finally says, "I'll figure it out. You'll use the landline because I can scramble the trace. But you can't talk for more than ten minutes."

"I haven't spoken to her in too long. We never go this long without talking. No limit on the call."

"This isn't a negotiation, Rebel. It's ten minutes or nothing."

"I don't like you like this."

He parks at the house, and I push out of the truck and march to the door.

"Like what? Keeping you safe?"

"All grumpy and broody and a hard-ass."

"News flash—*this* is who I am, baby. Like it or don't."

"Fine, I'll take the ten minutes, but I need this to be over. I need to be able to make phone calls and use my own cell and live like a normal human being. Willow can't even text me recipes, or tell me when she's popping by here. This is getting ridiculous."

"I know." He seems to deflate. "I agree. They're not telling me much, so I can't tell you how much longer this might go on. I'll get you a burner phone so you can at least talk to me and Willow. I didn't expect it to go on this long, honestly."

"Okay. I need a shower."

I go to walk to the stairs, feeling frustrated and dejected, but he takes my hand and pulls me against him, into one of those perfect hugs that always melt me.

"I'm sweaty and gross."

"You're never gross. Before you get in the shower, I have something to show you."

I frown up at him, and then he's guiding me through the house. But he doesn't lead me upstairs. Instead, we walk down a hallway, and he stops in front of a closed door.

"Go ahead." He gestures to the door, and I frown up at him. "Open the door, Lena."

I turn the knob and push the door open, and then feel my jaw drop, and I haven't even walked across the threshold.

This used to be another guest room, but now it's . . . *not.*

The windows in here face the lake and the mountains, and all the coverings have been removed. There's a big desk with all my art supplies in front of it. Against one wall is a small couch with fluffy pillows and a throw blanket. It's colorful and beautiful, and I turn to Gideon.

"What is this?"

"The beginning of an art studio," he says, looking inside. "It's too cold for you to sit outside to sketch. I know you still do in the morning, but it has to stop until spring, baby. I don't want you to get sick. This way, you can still work and look at the mountains, but I know you're safe and warm."

He gave me an art studio.

"I know you'll want to hang stuff on the walls and finish furnishing it the way you want, so I kept it simple for now. You'll have exactly what you want in here."

I turn into him, bury my face in his chest, and hug him close.

"Thank you," I mutter, the sound muffled by his impressive muscles.

"You're welcome." He presses his lips to the top of my head. "I want you to be happy here."

"I *am* happy. Now, I'm even happier."

His chest rumbles with his laugh, and I turn away to run my hand over the desk.

"This is beautiful."

"It was my mother's."

I spin around and find him smiling softly at me.

"It was in their office. She always had a desk in front of the window so she could work on things while Dad was at his desk. There was so much space in that house, she could have had her pick of a room for an office, but she wanted to be with Dad."

I swallow hard and blink back tears.

"You don't have to let me use—"

"It's yours. You're not using it, Lena. It's yours to keep."

I shake my head slowly, but he walks to me and tips my chin up.

"I had a talk with Ry and Wills, and they're good with this. You'll use this desk often, and I want you to have something of hers."

I blink up at him for a minute and then find myself frowning.

"Question."

"Shoot, baby."

"Come with me," I reply, leading him out of the room and up the stairs to his office, where I see that he has the same view as the one downstairs. He's facing the mountains. But then I glance around, and I remember the confidentiality involved with his work, and I realize that he'll tell me no, and that I should be grateful for what I have. "You know what? Never mind."

"What's going on in that gorgeous head of yours?"

"Well, I was going to ask you if there was room in here for the desk, so I could work with you, but you have to deal with a lot of super-secret stuff, and probably don't want me listening in—"

"I'll move it today."

Surprised, I take a step back and feel my cheeks heat. "I know I can't be privy to—"

"Nothing I do is off limits to you. Not anymore. I don't need a high security clearance to train new men. If I need to take a call that might be sensitive, I can leave the room for it. If you want to work in here with me, I'll make it happen. I just didn't want to distract you from your art."

I lick my lips and look around again, taking in the big space in front of the windows.

"I love what you gave me downstairs," I tell him, "and I'm so grateful. But given a choice, I'd rather be with you."

His face softens. "Then you'll be with me, baby. Ryker and I will move the desk up today."

I jump into his arms, wrap my legs around his waist, and kiss him. "Let's go take a shower."

Chapter Twenty-Three

Lena

"I swear, I won't talk to her for longer than the ten minutes. If it makes you feel better, it'll be *nine* minutes."

Gideon's tense, his face tight, his hands in fists. I can see that he doesn't want me to make this phone call, but damn it, it's her *birthday*, and I'm her best friend. I want to talk to her.

"I'll be nearby," he says grimly. "I have to keep an eye on the time, and—"

"I don't mind if you listen," I assure him. "I don't have any secrets."

"Fuck," he whispers and paces away, and then comes back to me and frames my face so gently, it almost brings tears to my eyes. "I don't want to risk you. You're too damn precious, Rebel."

"Hey, you're not risking me. It's going to be okay. You can scramble the call, and I'll follow the rules to a T." I kiss his lips softly and rub my nose over his, desperately trying to reassure him. "She might not answer, you know. Especially if it shows up as an unknown number or something, she could send it to voicemail, and then I'll just wish her a happy birthday, and that's that."

"I'm not going to get that lucky." He shakes his head mournfully. "But it seems I can't tell you no, so against my better judgment, here we go. You'll use this phone on my desk, and you'll wait for me to give you the signal before you dial. You know her number, right?"

"She's had the same number since we were fourteen. I know it."

He nods, and we sit at the desk. He hits some keys on his laptop, and then he picks up the receiver and passes it to me.

"Go ahead and dial," he says.

I quickly tap out the number and put it on speaker, so he can hear everything. I really don't have anything at all to hide from him. If she says something stupid, that's on her.

And it's entirely possible.

On the third ring, Chelsea picks up.

"Hello?"

"Hey," I say with a smile. "Happy birthday, friend."

"Oh my God! It's about time you freaking called me. It's been *forever*, Lena Elizabeth. You can't just fall off the face of the earth without giving me a heads-up, especially after you ran out of that gallery that night."

"It's been crazy," I reply, and watch Gideon's jaw clench. "Are you having a good birthday?"

"So far it's been fine. Mom is sending me to that little spa we love so much for the day, so I'll get buffed and polished, and then I'm going to dinner with a group of people. Hey, where are you, anyway?"

Not *How are you, friend?* Not *Are you okay?* Not *I miss you so much, tell me everything that's happened.*

"It changes daily," I reply, keeping my voice chipper. "All over the place. I always did want to travel, I guess."

"No, you didn't," she says with a scoff. "You're *such* a homebody. Getting you to leave your apartment is like pulling teeth. Living in the city is wasted on you. Anyway, I'm glad you called, because I need a loan."

"Chelsea—"

"I know, I know, but I swear this will be the last one."

"You say that every time."

Gideon's shaking his head, his eyes full of rage, but I keep my gaze on the desk in front of me.

"But you always come through, don't you, bestie? You *know* my parents are stingy as fuck with their money, and the ten grand they give me every month isn't enough to tide me over. I just need a few thousand."

She sniffs, and I *know* that sound.

I know her.

To anyone else it might sound like allergies, or a head cold, but *I know this woman*. And that's not what that was.

"Chelsea." My voice is hard, full of accusation.

"Don't start."

"You're fucking using again, aren't you?"

"Listen, you don't get to judge me. You've been *gone* without a word to me. What was I supposed to do?"

"Don't blame your drug habit on me." *Oh, hell no.* No. Never again.

I've done this with her before. The endless worry, the late nights, the overdoses. It took me forever to convince her to go to rehab, and she was clean for two years.

Two years, down the goddamn drain.

I can't do this with her again. I won't put myself through it.

"Just send me the money." Her voice turns whiny. "Please, Leens. You have all the money in the world, and you can share some more of it with me. I love you."

I blow out a breath, feeling close to tears.

"No, you don't. You haven't even asked me if I'm okay. We've been on the phone for"—I check the time—"seven minutes, and it's been all about you, Chelsea."

"I mean, it's *my* birthday, so—"

My laugh is humorless as I press my fingertips into my eyes.

"Two minutes," Gideon says, keeping his voice low.

"Wait." Chelsea's voice is clipped. "Is that *Gideon*?"

"No. All the guys on the detail sound the same."

"No, they don't. But whatever. Are you going to send me the money or not?"

"Not."

"Then why did you even call me?"

"Because it's your fucking *birthday*, and I haven't seen you in weeks. But don't worry, Chels, I won't be calling you again. Ever. I'm done. I'm not your ATM, and I'm not your enabler anymore."

"What the fuck? This is *not* Lena. It's an AI modulator or something, because there's no way in hell that the Lena I know has the balls to talk to *anyone* this way."

Maybe not before. But I've grown stronger since I got here.

"It's me. Just a better me. Good luck, Chelsea. I hope you get clean someday."

I hang up and then rest my head in my hands, elbows on the desk, and take a long, deep breath.

"What the fuck," I whisper. I know that Chelsea is selfish, but *seriously*?

"I'm so fucking proud of you."

I shake my head, in disbelief over how that call just went.

"I should be sad." I look up and lean back in the chair, staring at the mountains out the window. "I just broke up with my best friend of twenty years, but I'm just . . . *relieved*."

"It was a long time coming, from what you've said."

"She's right. I *never* would have spoken to her like that before. I wouldn't have had the guts. But damn it, she's never been a good friend to me. She got me in trouble *all the time*. She set me up to fail, and she used me more times than I can count. I was the one who picked up the pieces when she overdosed, and I'm the one who worried about her, begged her to get clean. I even paid for the damn rehab."

I shake my head, and Gideon stays quiet, just listening to me.

He's a good listener.

"I think it took coming here and becoming friends with Willow and seeing you with your chosen family for me to understand what true friendship looks like. I don't want to put up with Chelsea's shit anymore."

"Good for you," he murmurs, and I look his way, and see pride and love on his face.

Love.

We haven't said that word. We've made love. We've laughed and hugged and even confided in each other.

But we haven't said the word out loud.

And I'm feeling too bruised to say it now. Because if he didn't return it, well, I would be a mess, and I don't want to risk it.

"What do you want to do now, baby?"

I sigh and rub my hand over my face. "Let's go to the gym. I need to punch something."

"I've created a monster."

With a laugh, I let him pull me out of the chair. "Just don't piss me off, or I'll be punching *you*."

Chapter Twenty-Four

Gideon

"You can't be serious."

Leaning on Willow's kitchen counter, I drag my hand down my face. These women are going to be the fucking death of me.

"Why?" Willow stares at me as if I'm being unreasonable. But *I'm* not the unreasonable one here. "Come on, Gid, she's been stuck on this ranch for *such a long time*. It's just one night out. One dinner. And I'm not even suggesting we go without you and Ry. I want you both there, armed to the gills if need be."

"We'll be with them," Ryker says, and I stare at him like he's lost his fucking mind.

"No one knows I'm here," Lena reminds me and folds her hand into mine, twining our fingers together. "I won't be dressed up the way I am for the press. No one will even recognize me."

"It's just dinner and drinks at the pub in Paradise Valley," Willow says. "Just a couple of hours, and then we come right back here. It's your *birthday*. We want to celebrate you, handsome."

"Great, make me some spaghetti and call it a birthday."

Lena and Willow both roll their eyes, making Ryker laugh.

I don't think it's fucking funny.

"Please," Lena says and kisses my biceps. "I have a present for you and everything."

This is a bad fucking idea. Every instinct I have tells me to say no. To stand my ground and refuse them.

But damn it, her gorgeous lavender eyes do things to me, and against my better judgment, I sigh. They're not wrong. It *has* been a while, and there's been no sign of danger. Paradise Valley is tiny. It should be fine.

"That's his 'yes but I'm pissed' sigh," Willow says.

"We've got them," Ryker tells me and squeezes my shoulder. "Nothing will happen to either of them."

"Fuck."

"Let's go before he changes his mind." Willow grabs her purse and wraps her arm around my girl. "We're having cocktails."

"I could *so* go for a dirty martini," Lena says with a nod. *"Filthy."*

Why does that word sound so fucking sexy coming out of her little mouth?

"I won't drink," Ry assures me. "I know, I'm not an expert, but I'll keep my eyes and ears open. We've got this."

I'm uneasy during the entire fifteen-minute drive into Paradise Valley, but the girls are excited, chatting it up in the back seat of my SUV.

When I pull into the parking lot of the pub, I park near the entrance and turn to look at my girl. "Stay here until I tell you it's safe to get out. You know the drill."

Her face sobers, and I feel like a fucking prick for tossing a wet blanket on her fun, but *fuck me*, nothing bad can happen to her.

I love her too much.

"Say you understand, Lena."

"I understand." Her voice doesn't shake, and then she smiles at me, and the knot in my chest loosens just a bit. "It's okay, big guy. Do what you need to do."

I pull my GLOCK out of the center console and tuck it into the waistband of my pants, under my shirt, and then I nod at Ryker and we push out of the SUV.

My eyes automatically skim the area. The parking lot is only about a third full, with no one currently pulling in or out, and there are no vehicles currently occupied.

"Seems quiet," Ryker murmurs beside me, and I nod but take one more moment to look around. "Also, you're intense as fuck when you're in work mode. I've never seen it before."

"If anything happens to her, I'll burn this world to the motherfucking ground."

I feel his eyes on me, but I don't turn to him.

"When we go inside, I want you in the front and the two women between us. I'll bring up the rear. At the table, I want a booth, with us on the outsides. They're surrounded by us at all times."

"You're in love with her."

I don't even hesitate. "Irrevocably."

My brother blows out a breath. "I love her to pieces. She's great."

"Good. Let's keep her alive tonight."

"Let's keep them both alive until we're old as fuck." He nudges me with his shoulder, and then we move to opposite sides of the vehicle to open the doors for our girls.

"It's safe," I say to Lena, offering her my hand. She has a wrapped package in her lap. "When did you grab that?"

"It was in the back." She grins at me, and then boosts up to kiss my jawline. "Thank you."

"Don't thank me yet."

Ryker moves to the front, leading us inside, and I hear him give instructions for where to seat us to the hostess.

Finally, we're in the back of the room, in a booth, with the girls tucked safely against the wall, and I take a breath.

I won't breathe completely easy until we're back on the ranch, but for now, this works for me.

"What can I getcha to drink?" the waitress asks as she approaches. She does a double take at Ryker and me, and then a slow smile spreads over her lips. "Hey, fellas."

"Hey, Sarah," Willow says with a fake smile, making Ryker and me share a grin.

Willow is territorial as fuck. It's adorable.

But then Lena's hand lands on my arm and she tips her head onto my shoulder, also fake smiling.

"Oh, uh, hi, Willow," Sarah says.

"You know my *husband*, Ryker," Willow says. "This is my friend, Lisa."

"And this is my boyfriend, Gideon," Lena says, not batting an eye at the fake name that Willow gave her.

I love these girls.

"Of course, we all grew up together," Sarah says. "What can I get you to drink?"

"Two filthy martinis for us," Willow says, pointing to herself and my girl.

"Water for me."

"Same," Ry says, and then Sarah's gone. "That wasn't obvious at all, Trouble."

"Sarah *always* had a crush on you guys," Willow says, rolling her eyes. "And I'm not convinced that she really cares that you have a ring on your finger, but she won't fucking flirt with you while I'm sitting right here."

I lean over and kiss Lena on the head, breathing in her oranges. "What do you want to eat, baby?"

"I want a burger and onion rings. But I need you to get french fries so I can steal a few."

"Deal."

"Oh, can we do the same?" Willow asks Ryker, who just nods and sets his menu aside. "Good idea. Okay, before the food gets here, Gid needs to open his present."

"I need a drink first," Lena says, and just then, Sarah returns with all our drinks. We place our food order, and Lena takes a few sips of her martini. "Oh, that's good."

"They used the good gin," Willow agrees with a nod. "Okay, presents."

"You guys didn't have to get me anything at all. It's just another day."

"Wrong," Lena says. "It's the best day of the year because you were born on it."

Christ, my heart.

I ignore Willow's *aww* and Ryker's grin, and lean over to kiss her lips.

"You're all the present I need, Rebel."

"You guys are way too gooey," Willow says as she takes another sip of her drink. "Come on, the wait is killing me."

Lena bites her lip, then grabs the long, thin wrapped box that she stowed between her and the wall and hands it to me.

I don't bother to try to save the paper as I tear into the gift, then open the lid of the box and feel the breath catch in my lungs.

"Holy shit," I whisper, and drag my finger over the glass covering my mom's face. It's a sketch of my parents, sitting on the porch of the farmhouse, laughing and looking so in love, my heart aches. It's exactly how I remember them from the time when Ry and I came to live at the ranch.

I pass the frame over to my brother, and then I cup my girl's face in my hands and kiss her.

"Thank you. That's the most beautiful gift I've ever received."

"You're welcome."

"This is *incredible*," Ryker says, shaking his head as he stares at my girl's art.

"Right?" Willow wipes a tear from her cheek. "You're so talented, Le-Lisa." She winks at Lena, making her laugh.

"I'm glad you like it."

Very few people come in and out of the pub, and soon, I start to let my guard down just a little and let myself enjoy this time out with my favorite people.

"What kind of book are you recording now, Willow?" I ask after our food is delivered and we start eating. Lena puts two of her onion rings in my basket and grabs a small handful of fries.

"It's a hockey romance, actually. I'm enjoying it. Next up, I have a dark stalker romance."

"I bet it's fun to work on such diverse projects." Lena licks some ketchup off her finger, and it has my cock standing up and paying attention.

"I love that it's always different," Willow agrees. "I have a fun job."

"Gideon mentioned that you have a degree in finance?" Ryker lifts an eyebrow at Lena. "That's my jam, girl. What kind of portfolio do you have?"

"Mostly IRAs, but the bulk of my money is in trust, from my parents. I come into the rest of it when I'm twenty-five."

"When is that?" Willow asks. "Not because I need any of your money—I'm just curious when your birthday is so I can prepare."

Lena laughs at that. "I turn twenty-five in January."

January 14.

Maybe I'll propose to her on her birthday.

Because if she thinks I'm not marrying her, she doesn't know me at all.

Ryker and Lena keep talking about dividends and stock trades, and Willow and I stare at each other with glossed-over eyes.

"This is *not* a fascinating conversation," Willow finally says.

"Yes, it is," Lena objects, shaking her head and passing her empty glass over to Sarah in exchange for a fresh one. "I just learned like three new things from your husband. Whoever said that jocks can't be smart are wrong."

"Who says that?" Ryker asks with a scowl, making the girls laugh. "I'm fucking smart."

"I mean, you married me, so you're brilliant." Willow kisses his arm, making him smirk.

I hear the back door of the pub open and assume it's someone taking out the trash. We're not far from the hallway that leads to the restrooms and the back door.

"I have to pee," Lena whisper-shouts. "Can you please let me out?"

"I'm going with you."

She blinks up at me. "I'm not into that. It's not my kink. Sorry, big guy."

Ryker laughs, and Willow spits out her martini.

"I'm going to make sure the bathroom is safe, Rebel."

"It's safe. You don't have to hold my hand. There's hardly anyone in here, Gideon."

I shake my head.

"The hallway is ten feet away." Lena points and then kisses my hand, which is linked with hers. "No one has even gone back there in a while."

"I'll go with her," Willow says. "I have to pee too. It's all these martinis, which are delicious, by the way. But yeah, they go right through you."

"We'll be fine."

"Trust me, if anyone tries any funny business, I'll scream," Willow says.

"Plus, I'm totally badass now. I know how to punch, kick, and bite my way out of just about anything." Lena flexes her arm, showing off an impressive biceps, if I do say so myself.

"Damn, look at the guns on your girl, man," Ryker says with a low whistle.

"Told you." Lena looks smug as she smiles up at me with glassy eyes. "Willow and I can pee alone."

I slip out of the booth and peek down the dark hallway, then nod at the girls, who slide out of the booth and walk past me. As I sit across from Ry, I hear the bathroom door swing open and then closed and let out a breath.

"I hope you plan to marry that girl."

"That's my plan," I agree. "I'm so fucking glad that Willow came around."

"Me too. She was not easy to live with there for a while." He sips his water, but before he can say anything else, we hear Willow's scream.

And my blood runs cold.

Chapter Twenty-Five

Lena

"I've never seen Gideon *that* intense," Willow says as we walk away from the table toward the restrooms. "I mean, he's always been broody, and I know he's badass, but wow, that's a lot. Is that how he always was when he worked for you?"

"Yeah," I reply with a nod and push the door open, and Willow follows me in. There are only two stalls in here, and we each take one. "I could probably count on two hands the number of times I ever saw him smile. He's *very* serious about his job, and frankly, it always made me feel so safe. I never felt safer than when Gideon was the head of my detail."

After finishing up, I step out and wash my hands, waiting for Willow. I brush my fingers through my hair and smooth some ChapStick on my lips.

"I've never seen Gideon look at someone the way he looks at you," she says, and the words echo in the small bathroom, making me smile.

"And how is that?"

"Like you hung the damn moon." She snorts, and then I hear the toilet flush, and she steps out to wash her hands. "Gideon was no saint, and I won't give you the gory details because no one wants to know what happened before they came into their man's life."

"No thanks." I shake my head.

"But *no one* has ever impacted him the way you have. I can see it written all over his face that he's in love with you."

I bite my lip and lean on the counter.

"We haven't said the words," I say quietly as we look at each other in the mirror. "But I love him so much, I ache with it, Wills."

"The age gap doesn't bother you?"

I shake my head. "I don't care about that. I'm in my mid-twenties. We don't see each other the same way that we did when I was a teenager."

"Time apart would have helped with that," she agrees with a nod. "I get it. I sincerely hope it works out between the two of you because I *love* having you out at the ranch with us. I've always wanted a sister."

My lower lip trembles, and Willow wraps me in a tight hug.

"Thank you so much," I whisper. "I've always felt like such an outcast in my life. And you've made me feel so welcome. Like I belonged here the whole time."

"Maybe you did," she says. "I'm sorry I was such a bitch in the beginning. We lost so much time."

"I understand," I remind her. "And I appreciate that Gideon has people in his life who love him so much."

"You both do," she says with a wink. "Now, we'd better get back out there before they come looking for us. Gideon's already on edge."

"I feel bad that we talked him into it. I hate that he's so uncomfortable on his birthday."

"He's fine," she says, waving me off. "And we'll be home soon enough."

I open the door, and she walks out ahead of me. I step out behind her, and strong arms band around me, picking me up off my feet, and I start to flail as I'm being dragged backward.

"You're coming with us, you little bitch."

My heart is in my throat as I hear Willow's scream, and I frantically look around to see if they're taking her, too, but I don't see her. Just three other big men as I'm pulled out the back door and behind the pub.

I can't stomp on the asshole's instep, but I can use my elbows, so I drive one into his side, making him lose his breath, and I slam my head back into his nose.

"Fuck!"

I'm dropped to my feet, and I spin and kick the asshole in the stomach, and he falls backward.

A different set of arms reaches for me, but I hurry out of the way. I can hear shouts now, and I know that Gideon is coming to help me. The last few seconds have felt like an eternity.

He's right there. He's armed. It's okay.

I kick another guy in the knee, and he crumples to the ground, but then I'm pulled against someone else, and I feel metal press against my neck.

"Again?" I demand, more angry than scared right now because I know Gideon's about to kill this fucker.

"Drop it," this asshole screams in my ear as Gideon comes barreling out the door, his gun drawn, face set in rage-filled hard lines. His eyes hold mine for just a millisecond before they move to the man holding me, and the three others around us. Two of which are all kinds of fucked up, thanks to me.

"Training worked," I say with a sassy grin, but Gideon doesn't smile.

"You're going to drop that gun, Lieutenant," the asshole sneers, and I frown.

"You *know him*?"

"You and I both know that I'm not putting my weapon down, Rogers," Gideon says, not acknowledging my question. "If you don't want to die tonight, let her go."

Rogers snorts. "Right. Not happening. I have orders to take her with me."

"You won't be doing that."

"You're good, James, but you're not *that* good. There are four of us."

"And two of you are on the ground," I remind him, but no one acknowledges me.

I could get out of this guy's hold, but he's got a gun on me. I don't know what to do.

But before I can even think about it, Gideon shifts his aim to the guy writhing on the ground with a broken nose and pulls the trigger, shooting him right between the eyes.

Holy fucking shit.

"Mistake" is all I hear before Rogers pulls the gun away from my head, but instead of hearing a shot, I feel something slam against my head, and everything goes black.

Chapter Twenty-Six

Gideon

That motherfucker pistol-whipped my girl.

As soon as she's crumpled in his arms, I lift my weapon and shoot Rogers between the eyes and then kill the other two who were with them, and rush forward to grab Lena before she falls to the ground.

Sirens blare in the distance, and the next thing I know, Ryker and Willow are next to me.

"What the hell?" Ryker asks. "How?"

"I had a bad feeling." Rage has a pulse as it flows through my body. "*No one* knew she was here."

"But she made that call," Willow says, her voice shaking like crazy, and Ryker pulls her into his arms to comfort her. "Gid, she called Chelsea."

That little bitch was the mole.

"Chelsea had to be in on it," I say grimly as I dial the number for Eagle and first responders pull in.

I don't leave Lena's side as I climb into the back of the ambulance, still on the phone with the president and Bishop, and also talking with the local police.

"Her pulse and blood pressure are fine," the EMT says.

"We'll be on the ground in four hours," Bishop says in my ear. "You stay with Blackbird."

"I want answers, Bishop. This came to my fucking doorstep."

"Four hours," he repeats and hangs up, and I turn to my girl, looking so pale on this goddamn gurney. The drive to the hospital takes minutes, and then we're running through the ER to a room, and I'm pushed aside as Lena is surrounded by doctors and nurses.

"I need this whole hospital locked down," I bark at the security guard by the ambulance bay, who looks startled. "That's the First Daughter of the United States, and I need this place locked down *now*. Do you understand?"

"On it," he says, speaking into his radio.

I don't let Lena leave my sight as the doctors work on her, and finally, the one who seems to be in charge steps over to me and shakes his head.

My heart fucking *stops*.

"If you tell me she's dead—"

"No, she's not dead. If you're not her immediate family, I shouldn't be telling you—"

"If you don't tell me, I'll fucking break your legs."

His face hardens, but he must see the truth in my face, because he continues. "She's unconscious, which tells me that hit to the head was harder than any of us would want it to be. I need to get images of her brain so I can see what's going on."

"Do whatever you have to do."

He nods and drags his hand down his face. "The skull *is* fractured."

No.

Baby, no.

My whole world is in that hospital bed. My life doesn't work without her. She has to be fine.

This is all my fucking fault.

Why did I listen to them? Why did I cave when Lena ganged up on me with a friend *again*, only to have her end up in this hospital bed?

Fuck, I don't deserve her. She should not *be with me.*

"Get the tests done. Her mother will be here in less than four hours, and we need to have answers for her."

"I'm on it," he says, and I run beside the gurney as Lena's wheeled down to an imaging lab. I have to stand on the other side of a window while the test is run, and then she's with me again as we return to the room, where Ryker and Willow wait.

"Oh, sweetie," Willow says as she takes Lena's hand and sits next to the bed. "Gideon, it happened so fast."

"Yeah, well, that's usually how it works, baby girl." The guilt is eating away at me more and more with every passing second. "It's my fault."

"Whoa." Ryker shakes his head. "No, it's not."

"It one thousand percent *is*. Goddamn it, I *knew* better. Until that threat was gone, we were to stay put, and I fucked up. I can't work with a clear head because I'm too in love with her to think straight. She shouldn't be in my care. I'm not safe for her."

"We talked you into it," Willow says softly. "What now? Does this mean that it's over?"

"No, it means that four men are dead, but they were just foot soldiers." I can't stop pacing. "But now we know who, and I know who the fucking mole is."

Bishop should be taking care of this as I speak, even from the air. They'll have to land Air Force One in Missoula, and then they'll come to Paradise Valley by helicopter.

As I stand at the foot of her bed, nurses bustle around, cleaning the wound on Lena's head and bandaging it up. They change the fluid bag when it's empty, and they take several vials of blood.

What for, I have no idea.

Finally, the doctor comes back, his face still in grim lines.

"The bad news is, there is definitely a small fracture in the skull, and a contusion on the brain. It's caused some swelling. However, I don't see a bleed anywhere, which is good news."

"Is it normal for her to still be unconscious?" Willow asks, her eyes brimming with tears.

"Absolutely. Her body is protecting itself. Until that swelling goes down, it's best if she's asleep. In fact, if she were to naturally wake up now, I'd put her in a medically induced coma."

Jesus fucking Christ.

I can't stand any of the words coming out of his mouth.

My Rebel, my baby, is lying there, hurt and in a fucking *coma* because of my incompetence.

"Rest is the best thing for her," he continues. "We'll keep monitoring her closely. I'll come talk to her parents when they arrive."

"I'm shocked he told you so much," Ryker says.

"I fucking threatened him," I reply with a sneer.

"Gid, come hold your girl's hand."

I shouldn't. I shouldn't be allowed near her. I had *one goddamn job*, and I couldn't do it. But even now, I can't stay away from her.

I circle the bed, take her free hand in mine, and kiss her knuckles, and then, as if my body is moving on its own, I crawl onto the bed with her and hold her gently against me, wrapping my body around her as if to keep her safe from anyone who might come storming in here to try to hurt her.

"I'm so sorry," I whisper against her ear. "I'm so fucking sorry."

I press my lips to her forehead and feel tears fill my eyes when I realize that I can't smell her oranges. All I smell is the antiseptic of the hospital, and it makes me want to rage.

"You're going to be okay, baby. I promise, it's going to be okay."

"We're going to step out," I hear Willow say as she pats my back, and then I'm left here, with my girl. Someone turns off the overhead light, covering us in darkness, and I let the tears come.

I never want to relive those moments behind the pub. It's too fucking close to what happened five years ago.

Lena in danger, all because I didn't listen to my gut and tell her no. Because I wanted to give her the world, and I caved when she batted those gorgeous lavender eyes and asked me so sweetly for just one night out.

I can't trust my own judgment with her.

"I need you to be okay, baby. I need you to get better and open those pretty eyes for me. We have too much to do, Rebel. And you're too hardheaded to let something like this keep you down for long. Christ, you were amazing out there. When I came out the door and saw you shove your foot into that asshole's knee, I was so proud of you."

I keep talking to her, holding her, kissing her. I need this amazing woman to be okay. Because she's the best part of my life.

Finally, noticing the time, I ease out of the bed, careful not to jostle Lena, and sit in the chair next to her. The president and her husband should be here soon.

Not fifteen minutes later, the door opens, the light flips on, and Lena's parents, along with Bishop, step inside.

I stand as Lena's dad rushes to her side, not even sparing me a glance, and takes her hand.

"Report," Madam President says as she stands at the end of the bed and stares at her daughter with fear in her eyes.

"Since arriving at the hospital," I begin, and fill them in on all the tests and the diagnosis. "She needs rest but is expected to make a full recovery."

"Give us a minute, please," she says, and I nod, give Lena one final look, and then join Bishop in the hallway.

"Tell me you got this under control," I say as soon as we're alone.

"You were right," he says, dragging his hand through his thinning hair. "Chelsea was the snitch. She'd been seeing Rogers for months, and she's been questioned. It seems Rogers was feeding her addiction in exchange for information."

"I'm glad I killed the fucker."

Bishop exhales. "Yeah, well, he wasn't the mastermind. He was just young and Chelsea's type, and she fell for his shit."

"Who the fuck—" I break off when he meets my gaze evenly, and cold settles into my bones again. "Richie."

"He was working with a small faction of people who don't like the president's war policy, and they thought they could manipulate her if they had her daughter."

"And they were able to infiltrate the motherfucking *Secret Service*?" I demand.

"They paid a lot of money." He leans back against the wall. "Of course, this is treason. Everyone has been arrested, including Chelsea. We have proof. The idiot woman didn't delete anything from her phone, and Richie's singing like a fucking canary."

"The night of the gallery—"

"Chelsea was in on it. All of it." He shakes his head. "She thought Lena was dead, and we were covering it up. Until Lena called her the other day."

He lifts an eyebrow at me, and I wince.

"It was a secure line, but that's no excuse. I fucked up."

"Yeah, well, if you hadn't, we would still be chasing our goddamn tails." He watches me as I look longingly at the door. "Did you fall in love with her?"

I don't answer for a long minute, and then Bishop swears under his breath.

"Christ, James."

"She's staying with me."

"No, she's not." I turn to see the president standing at the threshold, looking exhausted. "Leave us, Bishop."

In interviews, this woman projects such a warm persona. Like she's the best, most loving and devoted mother in the world.

Privately, she's so *cold.*

"I'm taking my daughter home tonight."

I frown, but it's been ingrained in me not to argue with the commander in chief.

"You won't follow her," she continues. "You'll let her get on with her life, and you'll stay here, living your own."

I narrow my eyes, still not speaking.

"You are not who I want for my daughter, Mr. James. You have no place in her life. I entrusted you with her safe keeping, and you couldn't even provide that without failing. I need to know that my daughter is safe, no matter what."

"Lena is a grown adult," I reply, speaking for the first time. "She can choose what she wants."

She lets out a small, shaky laugh.

"The life of a president's child is not their own. She has responsibilities. And if you try to step in, if you so much as think about trying to be with her because you're *in love* . . . I can make things very difficult for you, Gideon. For your family. It would be a shame if Aiden lost his new job."

I blink at her, nausea filling me.

"I could ruin that entire ranch of yours. It would be a pity, since it's so beautiful."

I'm shaking my head, but she keeps talking.

"None of that fills me with joy. It's disgusting. But I want what's best for my daughter, and that's just not you, Gideon. It's nothing personal, it's just the facts. Now, we're leaving immediately."

"Surely she shouldn't be moved—"

"Goodbye, Mr. James." Her eyebrow lifts. "You are dismissed."

"Let me—"

"Don't make this harder than it needs to be," Bishop says as he joins us. "You have to go, Gid."

"Can't I just say goodbye?" My voice is so rough, so strained, and for the first time since I've known her, I see the president soften, just a little.

"You can have five minutes," she says.

I swallow hard and step back into the room just as Lena's dad approaches me to leave. His eyes are wet as he pats me on the shoulder, and then, without a word, he walks away, shutting the door behind him.

She looks so fucking small.

I approach the bed, take her hand in mine again, and lean down to kiss every knuckle before I push up and kiss her cheek, soaking in her softness. Her *goodness.*

"You're the sweetest fucking thing," I whisper shakily, and decide *fuck it* and climb onto the bed with her once again and pull her against me.

This is the last time I'll hold her in my arms.

Because her mother's right. I'm not good enough for her. I can't keep her out of harm's way. I've failed her twice.

"I love you, baby." I pepper kisses on the top of her head, careful to avoid her injury. "You're the best thing that ever happened to me. I'm so sorry that I failed you tonight. Fuck, I'm sorry."

I draw in a shaky breath. Christ, my heart feels like it's been torn from my body and set on fire. How am I supposed to do this? How am I supposed to say goodbye to the person I love most in the world?

"If you ever need anything, you reach out to me. Fuck, I wish you could hear me." My hand drags up and down her bare arm, and even though she's unconscious, it makes goose bumps pebble on her skin. "You're everything good in this life, Lena. You deserve nothing but the best, and I—" I swallow hard. "I hope you find it, baby."

I lie with her for another minute, and then I kiss her lips softly before pulling away and standing from the bed.

Christ.

I have to go. If I don't go now, I won't ever do it, so I stride out of the room, ignoring Bishop and the others, and down the hallway, my chest aching more and more with every step that I take away from the love of my life.

Every cell in my body is screaming for me to go back in that room and hold her to me. To *never* let her go.

I promised that she could stay with me forever, if that's what she wants.

She was supposed to be my wife.

But the president wasn't wrong. I couldn't do my job or keep her safe. I failed. How can I possibly think that I'm good enough for her to spend the rest of her life with?

I walk out to the waiting room, where Willow and Ryker both stand and rush over to me.

"What's going on?" Ryker demands, his jaw firming when he sees my face.

"Where's Lena?" Willow asks.

"She's leaving." My voice is hoarse. My world is falling the fuck apart. "It's all over. She's going home."

"The ranch is her home," Willow says, shaking her head.

"No." I head for the doors, needing to get out of this hospital. Needing to get back to my house. "It's not. Her parents are with her, and they're taking her back to DC where she belongs."

They're flanking me, keeping up with me as I march to the SUV parked close by.

"But you'll go with them, right?" Willow asks. "And then when she's better, you'll both be coming back?"

I shake my head and climb into the vehicle.

"No. It's over. It's all fucking over. Let's go home."

Chapter Twenty-Seven

Lena

I have a headache the size of the Grand Canyon, and every inch of my body hurts. I'm afraid to open my eyes, so I start by stretching out my fingers and toes, and even that aches.

What the fuck happened?

I feel like I fell off a cliff and was unlucky enough to survive.

I bend my knees and elbows and whimper with the ache of it. My shoulder is singing in pain.

"Someone's waking up." I don't know that voice. "Take your time, Lena. Take it slow. You've been unconscious for three days."

Three days?

That can't be right.

"Gideon." I try to say it out loud, but all that comes out is a croak.

"Here's some water for that dry throat." The top of my bed starts to rise, and when I'm somewhat sitting up, I blink my eyes open and scowl at the brightness of the fluorescent lights, but there's a straw in front of my lips, so I lean in and take a pull of the cool water.

That feels good.

"I want Gideon." I glance around the room. "Where am I?"

"The White House, of course," the nurse says. "I'll be right back."

Why am I in Washington?

And where is my man? Where's Willow?

Don't panic. They're probably around here somewhere. Grabbing food, or getting some fresh air.

I'm taking a deep breath, trying to calm down, when my father walks into the room and offers me an encouraging smile.

"Hi there, pumpkin," he says. "I'm so damn glad you're awake."

"What's going on?" I ask him as he sits on the bed, by my hip, and takes my hand in his. "Why am I here?"

"Do you remember the attack?"

The attack?

And then it comes back to me. We were at dinner, at the pub, and those men grabbed me.

"Oh, God, is Gideon okay? Did they hurt him?"

I sit up straight, panic shooting through me.

"Whoa, Lena, calm down."

"Is. He. Okay?"

Dad nods and kisses me on the forehead. "He's okay. No one was seriously hurt but you. Well, and the ones who tried to take you. I can't tell you more than that right now. I don't want you to stress yourself. You have a head injury, sweetheart, and you need to rest."

I feel tears track down my cheeks.

"Dad, is it all over?"

"Yes, baby. That I can tell you. You're home now, and you can get back to your life."

I swallow hard.

Back to my life.

"My life is at that ranch, Dad."

He shakes his head once, and then I hear my mom's voice.

"Your life is here," she says and crosses over to kiss my head. "I'm so glad you're awake. You worried me."

"Where is Gideon?" I ask her.

"I assume he's in Montana," she replies simply, as if my world isn't falling apart. "And you're where you belong."

"Mom—"

"No." Her voice is sharp now, and I shut my mouth because I know there's no talking to her when she's like this. "Get some rest. We'll move you upstairs out of the infirmary later today."

"I'd like to go home."

I need to go to the ranch.

"You can move into your apartment in a few days, once you're well on your way to recovery."

"Has Chelsea been in to see me?"

Mom and Dad share a glance, but they don't answer me, and that pisses me off.

"We'll be back," Mom says. "I have a press conference."

They both walk out, and I'm left with no answers.

"I need my phone," I say to the nurse, who's walked back in to check my vitals.

"It's right here," she replies, setting the device on the bed next to me. "You really should nap."

"I've been asleep for *days*," I remind her. "I think I'm fine."

Picking up the phone, I go right to my contacts, but they're gone.

I have literally *no* contacts.

"I was told that it's a new phone," she says with a wink.

Why do I need a new phone? And where's my old one?

I'm feeling sleepy again, and that frustrates me, but I let the nurse lay me back, and I close my eyes.

It's been two weeks since I woke up.

I'm back in my apartment, and I *hate* it.

Not that I'm not in a great part of town, in a beautiful building. I have a new security detail, and no one will tell me where Richie is. No one will give me Gideon's number, and when I tried to google it, I got an immediate call from my mother telling me to stop.

What the fuck? They're monitoring my internet use?

Mom has been much more attentive since I've been back. Every minute of her day is always scheduled to the second, but she finds time to call or text me, just to check in. I know that what happened in Montana scared her, and I understand that, but why are they keeping me from Gideon?

And why isn't he burning the world to the ground to get to me?

None of this makes sense.

Not to mention, I haven't heard even one peep out of anyone. And it reminds me how fucking isolated I am in my life. I don't want Chelsea back in my orbit. She's toxic as fuck, and I'm so much better off without her.

But I miss Willow and Ryker. And oh my God, every bit of me aches for Gideon.

He's my person.

Is it because I fucked up again? It was my fault that we went to that dinner. Willow and I talked him into it. I just wanted to celebrate my man's birthday, and it all fell apart in the *worst* way. I just had to have it, he caved and gave it to me; and it blew up in our faces.

Hell, I wouldn't want to be with me either.

But God, how I miss him.

To keep myself busy, I've been sketching like a madwoman, and I even decided to reach out to my favorite gallery to see if they'd exhibit some of my work under a pseudonym, and I'm meeting with them later this afternoon.

It'll be a soft launch, since I'm not well known, but the fact that they agreed to give me gallery space meant a lot to me.

It sucks that no one I care about will be there.

Fuck, I'm lonely.

There's a knock on my door, and I open it to find Bishop standing there.

"Hello, Lena. I just have some questions for you, if you have time."

"I have nothing but time. Come on in." I step back, giving him room to pass. "This is convenient because I have some questions for you too."

We walk into the living room and have a seat across from each other.

"How are you feeling?" he asks me.

"Fine. I have headaches once in a while, but I'm told that's normal."

He nods. "Good. I'm glad you're healing. Lena, I have to ask questions about Chelsea."

I frown over at him. "Is she in trouble?"

His eyes narrow. "You don't know."

My stomach rolls. *I never know anything.*

"Well, why don't you tell me?"

Bishop blows out a breath and pulls his hand down his face. "Chelsea was the one responsible for feeding information to the people who tried to take you."

No.

"She was having an affair with Rogers, and he was feeding her drug addiction in exchange for inside information on your whereabouts."

This is impossible.

"She's currently in jail, awaiting trial, and she'll end up in prison for the rest of her life for treason."

I'm simply staring at him, not even blinking. I don't want Chelsea in my life anymore, but I wouldn't wish this on her. She was on . . . *their side*? She was my best friend!

"This is impossible."

"I'm sorry, but it's not. It's the truth. I need to ask questions about specific times and dates that the two of you were together and what she was privy to."

"She was privy to fucking *everything*. She was my best friend. My only friend, thanks to this fucked-up life I live. Jesus." I stand and pace the room, my heart hammering. "She could have had me killed. She could have had *Gideon* killed."

I hate that her weakness was used against her, but she knew that I would get hurt, and *she didn't care.*

She didn't care.

I spin and stare at Bishop, who's now also standing.

"Please tell me he's okay. Dad said he is, but—"

"He's in Montana," Bishop says with a nod. "The three of them are safe, Lena."

My shoulders drop in relief. "Why isn't he *here*? Or better yet, why am I not there? No one will fucking talk to me, and I can't get his number."

Bishop's face is hard, and he doesn't look like he's going to answer me.

"*Please* talk to me. I'm not a child, Bishop. I deserve to know what in the hell is going on."

He's quiet for so long, I'm convinced he's not going to answer me, and my heart sinks.

Finally, he whispers, "Shit," and sits down again.

"You're here because your mother wanted you to be here. The threat was eliminated, and it was time for you to come home. Gideon is in Montana because that's where he lives, Lena."

I shake my head. "You know what I'm asking you. He would *not* just abandon me. If my mom insisted I come back here, he would have come with me. Why isn't he here, Bishop?"

"Because he was given very specific orders to *not* be here," he replies. "Not because he didn't want you, Lena. He was a fucking mess in that hospital. I've never seen him like that."

Oh, thank God.

He didn't abandon me.

"We don't question the commander in chief's orders. We follow those orders to a T. It's what we do. He left that night because he'd been given the order to do so, but that isn't what he wanted."

Tears fill my eyes, and I cover my mouth with my hands, holding the sobs in.

"What do I do?" The question comes out as a hoarse whisper. "I want to be in Montana. I need to be with him."

"I think you need to take a little time," he replies slowly. "You're still healing, and if you're going to fight your mother for what you want, you need to be at the top of your game for that."

He's not wrong.

"Keep getting well. Work on your art. If you want, I'll set you up with a therapist to help you navigate all this, and when the time is right, Gideon will be there. Trust me, he's not going anywhere."

"I want to call him. I need to tell him what the plan is and hear his voice. I was with him every single day for weeks, and now *nothing*? This isn't right, Bishop."

He nods slowly. "Gid's not taking calls right now."

I narrow my eyes at him. "What do you mean?"

"He's shut off his phone. He's back to work, and he's isolating. He's healing too, Lena."

My heart aches. Fuck, poor Gideon.

"If this were any other situation, I'd call him and get him on a plane. Or I'd send you out there. I'm on your side in this, but if you tell your mother that, I'll deny it."

My lips twitch.

"But it's not normal circumstances," I murmur, glancing out my windows.

"No. It isn't."

"I'll follow your advice. I'll work on myself. I think I have an art exhibit happening, but no one will know it's mine. I'm working under a pseudonym. That's the deadline, Bishop. Because after that day, I'm moving to Montana, whether my mother likes it or not."

His lips twitch. I don't know if I've ever seen Bishop smile before.

"That's a good plan. I'd like to know more about that exhibit."

"All the contacts were removed from my phone. Otherwise, I'd call you."

That news has him pausing, a crease forming between his eyebrows.

"May I see?"

I pass it to him, and he taps the screen. He sets my phone aside and taps his own phone, then puts it up to his ear.

"Reinstate Blackbird's contacts immediately."

Holy shit, Bishop's on my side!

For the first time in two weeks, I don't feel so alone. I don't feel like everything I love is lost to me.

I have a plan.

I like having a plan.

He shuts my phone off, then turns it back on and passes it to me.

Magically, all my contacts are back.

"Thank you. It's not like I call many people—"

"It doesn't matter. That's yours, and no one has the right to take that away. My number is in there. If you need anything, call me."

"Please give me Gideon's number," I say, my voice strong. "I need it."

After another pause, he takes my phone back and programs it in.

"I'm not lying to you, or trying to hurt your feelings," Bishop says. "I haven't been able to reach him since I left Montana."

"I understand."

He nods and stands, and once he's gone, I let myself have a good cry.

I wish he was here.

But now I have his number. He probably doesn't want to hear from me. If what Bishop said is true, he won't read anything I send him, or answer my calls.

Gideon is my person. After all that time together, he's the one I confide in the most. He knows everything about me, inside and out. That man is the only one I want to talk to.

So after wiping the tears from my cheeks, I open a new text thread and start talking to him.

Me: God, I miss you so much.

I hit send. It doesn't deliver.

Bishop wasn't lying.

After taking a long breath, I type some more.

Me: It's been two weeks since I saw you, and it's freaking killing me, Gideon. I hate it so much. I get it, though. Now that I've talked to Bishop, I understand why you're not here, but I miss you and the ranch so much. This isn't the end for us.

I hit send, and with a renewed sense of determination, I pick myself up off the floor and get to work.

Chapter Twenty-Eight

Lena

Texting Gideon over the past couple of weeks has helped me keep my thoughts straight. It's almost like a diary, a way for me to mark the time while I'm separated from him. I send him messages every morning and night, and throughout the day as well. It's become my closest friend.

And it makes me feel closer to him.

None of the messages are ever delivered, but I know that someday they will be, so I keep sending them.

Me: Good morning, big guy. I hope you're doing okay. What did you have for breakfast? Don't forget to add protein. Ha! Are you still going for runs? I need a session in the ring with you. I have some aggression to get out.

Me: I've hired another trainer because I'll be damned if I went through all that work at the ranch to lose all of it. He's not nearly as hot as you. And he's a taskmaster, so you'd probably like him.

Me: There are days that I'm sure that my time at the ranch was a dream because I've been without you for so long now that it feels like I was never there. And that makes me so sad. I wish I'd had my phone with me when I was with you, so I'd have some photos. We never took even one selfie, not one picture together. It's like the olden days, before cell phones. You know, like when you were a kid. LOL JK I wish you were seeing these messages so you could send me pictures. I bet everything is covered in snow and so pretty! We could have a snowball fight and I'd kick your butt. And then we could make snow angels. And have cocoa. And make love in the shower so we warm up.

Me: I've been talking to the owner of my favorite gallery here in DC and she's going to show my work! She loves all the charcoal drawings of the mountains, so we're going to focus on that because she's even offered to host a show. I'm doing what you said and using a pseudonym, so even though I'll be in attendance, people won't know it's me. I don't care, I want to see what people think of my work. Hopefully it doesn't crush my ego to dust. I wish you would be here for it. I can't imagine doing this without you.

Me: Have you completely destroyed the spreadsheets I made? Ugh, I don't even want to think about what kind of shape they're in. Don't worry, I'll fix everything when I get there.

Me: The exhibit sold out! All fifty tickets sold, which boggles my mind. Now I'm so nervous!

Me: The headaches are bad today. I wish I could curl up in your lap and lay my head on your chest and listen to your heart. There's nothing better than that. Well, maybe when you'd make me come. I wonder if that would help the headaches? I'll report back on that . . .

Me: Well, the orgasms didn't help the headache. And they didn't help me missing you. And it's not nearly as good as when you do it, so maybe I'm not ready for that. Fuck, I miss you. I MISS YOU!!

Me: I think we should take a trip somewhere. Maybe somewhere tropical, like the Maldives, and we can be lazy in a hammock that sits over the water. I know, you're not good at being lazy, but maybe you'll do it for me. We'll have lots of tropical sex. God, I think about sex way too often for a woman who isn't getting any. This is all your fault, by the way. Why do you have to be so sexy?

Me: I had Mexican for dinner. It wasn't nearly as good as that place we get takeout from.

Me: I had to kill a spider today. By myself. BY MYSELF, GIDEON! I'm not okay.

Me: I had lunch with my parents today. How Mom found time for a lunch, I'll never know. It was fine. I make it no secret that I don't want to be here, and I want to go back to Montana. Mom ignores that part. I hate being ignored.

Me: So, here's the thing. After this exhibit, I'm coming back to Montana. Whether you read any of this or not, I'm coming back. I need you. I need the ranch, the mountains, even that fucking obstacle course. If you turn me away once I get there, so be it, but I have to try, Gideon. I have to. Please let me come home.

Me: Merry Christmas, big guy.

Me: The gym kicked my ass today. *pout*

Me: Happy New Year!

Me: Do you remember that day when we went to the hardware store and you made me walk in front of you, pushing the cart? That was hot as fuck, Gideon. I was thinking about that today. I don't even need to go to the hardware store, but I kind of want to. Not that it'll be any fun without your sexy body pressed up against me.

Me: It's my birthday. Willow sent me a cake! I mean, she didn't bake it because it would get torn apart in the mail, but she had it delivered, and it was so sweet of her. It's even my favorite. I plan to eat this whole thing myself. Don't tell my trainer.

Me: I wish you'd answer your phone. Or just read my messages. Although, if you read them and don't reply, my heart will be so broken, I don't know what I'll do with myself. You wouldn't do that to me. You'd say something, even if it was just GO AWAY, REBEL.

Me: I want to sit outside and look at your mountains tonight.

Chapter Twenty-Nine

Gideon

"I don't fucking care how cold it is—get your asses moving!"

No one dares glare at me as my recruits trudge through the snow on a run. It's cold as fuck out here. And it should be. It's January in Montana, for fuck's sake.

January 14.

We pass by the obstacle course, and all I can see is Lena, climbing those ropes, running through the tires, walking the balance beam.

Fuck.

Not ten minutes goes by without my thinking about her, and it's been almost two fucking months. Two long, agonizing, terrorizing months.

Because the ranch, the one place on this earth that has always been my safe place, is a fucking torture chamber.

She's everywhere.

In my gym, in my bed, in the kitchen. I can't escape the memory of her, no matter where I go. I packed up all her things in a fit of rage and mailed them to the White House weeks ago. I've cleaned and scrubbed the house, and yet I swear I can still smell her oranges in my pillows.

It's a madness that I wouldn't wish on anyone.

Today is the last day with this round of recruits, and I decided to bring them out for one last run before they head to the airport. I can admit, I've been a complete asshole. I'm never here to be their friend, but I've been worse than usual.

And if they can't handle it, they shouldn't fucking be here.

One of the guys trips in the snow and almost takes a tumble, but he corrects himself fast enough and keeps going.

Finally, we make it back to the house, where the bus is waiting to take them to the hotel.

They all shake my hand before they leave, but I feel no connection to any of them. It's as if they weren't even here.

I'm walking through every day like a motherfucking zombie.

Once they're gone, I go inside and take a shower, and wander into the closet to put on clean clothes.

A little piece of red fabric catches my eye from under the dresser, and when I tug it free, I see that it's the little red satin panties that Lena had when she first arrived, before her new clothes got here.

Fuck me.

Without overthinking it, I press the material to my nose, and I can smell her.

I can fucking smell her.

Christ. It feels like the torment will never end, and this is the little piece of fabric that brings me to my knees.

I can't do this. I can't be here, on this ranch, without her.

I have to move.

Shaking my head, I pull on some boots and find my jacket, then get in my truck and drive to the farmhouse.

I've hardly seen Wills or Ryker. I stay on my side of the ranch, do my job, and keep to myself.

But today, I need to talk to them. Because I'm losing my goddamn mind.

"Hey," Willow says in surprise when I walk through the front door without knocking. She walks to me and wraps her arms around me, hugging me tight. "I've missed you."

"I'm just down the road."

For now.

"Sort of," she says and pulls back, scowling as she looks up at me. "Gid, are you eating?"

"I'm fine, Wills."

She barks out a laugh, and I notice Ryker coming down the stairs.

"You look like shit," he says and then walks into the kitchen. "Come on, let's eat something. I'm fucking hungry."

"I don't need food."

"Sure you do." Willow pats my shoulder. "I have homemade pizza. How did this round with the trainees go?"

I can't honestly remember. They just left, and I couldn't pick any one of them out of a lineup.

"They're fine." I sit on the stool and shove my fingers through my hair. "I think I have to move off the ranch."

The room goes still. They both just stare at me. Willow's eyes fill with tears, and if my heart wasn't numb, it would break me.

"I can't do this," I admit in a low voice, shaking my head. "I'm in hell."

"Fuck," Ryker whispers.

"Okay, so hear me out," Willow says, holding her hands up. "Don't yell at me."

"I never yell at you."

"There's a first time for everything. What if you went to see her?"

"I was given an order. It was made very clear to me that I'm *not* to go near her. If I do, my family could be harmed."

"That's bullshit," Ry says, shaking his head. "There's no way."

"She's the *president*. She can do whatever she wants, and when you add mama bear to that, it's scary. I'm not willing to risk either of you.

Not ever. I've been in touch with Bishop, and I know she's healing. She's doing fine without me."

"Or, you know, she's *surviving* without you."

I narrow my eyes at her as she bites her lip and looks like she regrets saying anything. "What do you know?"

Willow blows out a breath and leans on the counter. "Look, I'm not stupid enough to *not* talk with her. She and I became good friends, and I love her. So I found her email address and I reached out about a month ago, and I've spoken to her once or twice."

I swallow hard, my heart suddenly in my throat.

"Is she okay?"

Willow smiles softly. "She's okay. She's getting her stuff figured out."

"What does that mean?"

"Exactly what I said." She shrugs. "Don't give up, Gid."

"It's not giving up," I insist. "I'm following orders."

"You're no longer an employee of the motherfucking government," Ryker cuts in, his voice hard and full of anger. "You're a man. You're entitled to a goddamn life. Maybe more than the rest of us, given all you've done for this country. You're the best man I know, and if the president can't see that, and doesn't think you're good enough for her daughter, she's a fucking idiot."

"I really hope this house isn't bugged," I mutter. "She didn't say anything that wasn't true. I *didn't* protect her. She was hurt on my watch."

"I'm gonna call bullshit on this," Willow says with a sigh. "First of all, why did it take the powers that be all that time to figure out what was going on? Come on, they should have figured it out before she was ever sent here. They weren't *looking*, Gideon. Because they had other fish to fry, and it was easier to tuck her away, safe and sound, in the boonies than it was to launch a full-scale attack, or whatever. You didn't do anything wrong."

"I. Didn't. Follow. Protocol."

"You're a human being."

Fuck. I'm so damn frustrated. I have to stand and pace the room.

"It doesn't matter if I'm human. It doesn't even matter if none of it was my fault. It's over. She's not coming back."

My voice falters on that last word, and I have to clear my throat.

"And I'm reminded of her everywhere I turn. I can't do it. I can't stand to be haunted by the one thing in this world that I want more than anything, knowing that I can't have her."

Willow brushes a tear from her cheek.

"Maybe we do some remodeling."

I shake my head.

"You're not going anywhere." This is from Ryker, who looks so fucking pissed off—I haven't seen him like this in years. "We're a family. You're not leaving this ranch. We'll tear that house down and build a new one if we have to, but you're staying here."

Before I can reply, there's a knock on the door, and we all stare at each other before we make our way to the entrance.

Ryker pulls it open, and there's a man standing on the other side.

"Gideon James?"

"That's me." I step forward. Fuck. Has something happened to Lena?

They wouldn't come here to tell if me if it had.

"You're not an easy man to reach," he says with a half smile. "I'm Dustin Harding, the warden at the Montana State Prison. I've been trying to call you but couldn't reach you."

I haven't turned my phone on since she left.

Willow steps up next to me and slides her hand into mine. It's sweet. Meant to comfort me.

She's not who I want.

"I'm sorry to inform you that your father passed away last month."

"My father died five years ago," I reply with a hard voice.

Dustin nods and then shrugs. "Well then, Nicholas Peterson died last month, and I wanted to let you know."

"I'm sorry you came all this way, because Nicholas Peterson doesn't mean shit to me. He killed my mother and my unborn sister. You know that, right?"

He nods again. "Understood. It's policy to notify next of kin. I'll let you get back to your day."

He walks out the door, shutting it behind him, and I'm suddenly in a group hug with my two best friends.

"Ryker's right. You're not going anywhere," Willow says against my chest. "You're right where you're supposed to be, and you're going to stop hiding. Because we're your family. *We are your family*, Gideon. This is your home, and that hasn't changed."

"She's right," Ryker says.

"What are you feeling?" Willow runs her hand up and down my arm.

I blink down at her and then exhale. "Actually, I feel lighter. That asshole is gone for good, and he can't hurt anyone I care about ever again. Even me. He should have died a long time ago."

"He wasn't your family," Willow says. "And you were right, we lost our dad a long time ago. Gid, Ray and Debbie would be so fucking sad for you right now. Not because that murderous piece of shit died, but because of everything that happened with Lena. And they would be livid that you're thinking about leaving."

I pull away from them. "Don't give me parent guilt."

"I'm not. I'm telling you the truth. They worked so hard to leave this ranch to us. To all of us. But if it's not whole for you without your girl, then *go fight for her*. Bring her home with you. Ryker's right, you don't work for the president anymore, and everyone has had time to calm down, to take a breath. The fear is over. Those responsible are either dead or in jail. Maybe now is the time to have a conversation with people, to see Lena."

My heart stutters.

I'd give just about anything to see my girl right now. To hold her, kiss her.

To sink inside her.

I dream about her every night and then wake up in this nightmare.

I nibble on my lip, thinking it over.

"The worst she can say is no," Ryker says.

"No, the worst she can say is *get the fuck away from me, I never loved you, you need to go to hell.*" I shrug. "Same thing, I guess."

"His sense of humor is back," Willow says. "That's a good sign."

"I know that I can't go on like this," I admit. "I've never disobeyed an order, but fuck. I *can't* keep living without her. If she says no, I'll respect that."

Please, don't fucking say no.

"But maybe I have to try."

"That night," Ryker says, "you told me that if anything happened to her, you'd burn the whole fucking world to the ground. Well, something happened, and I don't see any flames, James."

I stare at my brother for a moment. "Are you saying I should have tried harder?"

"That night? No. There was nothing you could do that night. But now? I don't see why you wouldn't fight for what you want. For what you love and need in your life. Lena loves you, Gideon."

Willow nods, and then takes a deep breath. "Okay, I think I have a plan. The only downside is that you can't rush to the airport right now."

"When can I rush to the airport?" I ask her.

"In ten days."

"Fuck that." I pace back and forth, ready to pull my hair out.

"It's a *really* good plan," she insists. "And if you need convincing, let me show you something."

She disappears down a hallway and then returns to the room, carrying another framed piece of art.

It's the mountains at sunrise.

Fuck, my Rebel is so fucking talented.

"She sent this to me as a gift," Willow says. "The rest of her work is going on exhibit in ten days."

My eyes snap up to hers. "Where?"

"In DC. She's getting a whole exhibit, Gid. But I want you to look at this a little closer."

I take it from her and stare at the colors. The oranges and pinks, how perfectly she captured the mountains with snowy peaks.

There's no denying that this is the view from my back deck.

As my eyes skim down, I see that she signed it *L. James.*

James.

You could always use a pseudonym, you know . . .

My gaze whips back up to Willow, and she smiles smugly.

"Tell me about this plan."

Later that night, I crawl into bed, still missing the warmth of my woman, but feeling hope for the first time in so long, I'm scared to trust it.

Scared to believe that this could work.

That she will want me back.

She's using my name as her pseudonym.

Out of all the names in this world, she chose mine. And if she wants my name, I'll give it to her for good.

For real.

I pull my cell out of the drawer of my bedside table and power it on, and then watch in shock as hundreds of texts start coming in.

Hundreds.

From a DC number, and when I page up to the beginning, my heart stumbles.

Unknown number: God, I miss you.

Fuck.

Fuck.

Settling into the bed, I change the contact information to "Rebel," and then start to read every single message from my girl.

Chapter Thirty

Gideon

Every single day, my Rebel sends me texts. They haven't stopped. I also haven't replied.

I want to tell her everything that I have to say in person. I want to hold her and bury myself in her, my nose in her neck, and never let her go as I explain in precise detail how fucking badly I've missed her.

I'm a shell of a man without her.

But I'm on my way to her. With every mile this plane takes toward DC, my anxiety lessens. I'll see her tonight.

I only have to endure a few more hours without her.

And then, I'm never letting her go again. I've also been in contact with the president, and I've made it clear that I'll do whatever I need to do to make sure that Lena is mine. Even if that means I have to leave the ranch and move back to DC to be with her.

Because this life doesn't work without her in it.

Settling into my seat in first class, I open the phone and page back to the beginning to read all her messages to me. I've read them a hundred times at least, and could likely recite them from memory, but it calms me to read her words.

Just as I get to the end, a new one comes in.

Rebel: I wish you were here.

I'm coming, baby.
I'm coming.

Chapter Thirty-One

Lena

My texts started being delivered sometime after the night of my birthday. My heart flew into my throat when I opened the text thread and saw that little word *delivered* at the bottom of the page. And every day since, I've been on pins and needles, waiting for him to reply. Or to call me.

Anything.

But he's been silent.

So I've continued as normal, sending messages and talking to him, sharing my thoughts and feelings, and every day, they're delivered.

Why isn't he responding?

"You must be excited," Mom says as she sips her coffee. "You're hardly speaking. I'm so proud of you, sweetheart. I know this showing is going to be a huge success. I wish you'd let us scream about it. I wish you'd use *your name.*"

I shake my head and set my phone down, then turn my attention to my mother.

It's the morning of the show, and we're having breakfast together. Mom and Dad won't come tonight because it would be a security nightmare, and I'm honestly okay with that.

I want it to be as low key as possible.

"You know why I don't want to," I reply. "We've been over this."

She sighs, watching me.

"Mom, I need you to know that once this show is over, I'm going back to Montana."

I already have my travel plans in order, I've alerted Bishop so he can arrange the detail accordingly, and I've packed up everything I want to take from my apartment.

I'm going home.

Her eyebrow climbs and her eyes narrow, but she doesn't interrupt me, which honestly shocks the hell out of me.

"I'm proud of you, Mom. I know that I've never told you that before, but I am. You chose this life for all of us. You've been a good president. But I don't want this life for myself, and I don't have to choose it."

"Lena," she says with a sigh. "You would make an excellent First Lady. Howey plans to go into politics. You know what it takes—"

"Absolutely *not.*" I shake my head adamantly. "I would never choose to marry a politician. *Never.* That's not the life for me. I can't wait for your term to end so I don't have to have Secret Service anymore. I want Gideon, Mom. I love him with my whole heart, and being away from him for two months has only reiterated that for me. I choose him, and the life on the ranch."

She slowly shakes her head and takes a deep breath.

"Of course, I only want what's best for you. I'm a shit parent, Lena. We all know it. I've never denied it. But that doesn't mean that I don't love you and want wonderful things for you."

"*Wonderful things* doesn't have to mean the life *you* would choose," I remind her. I've never been this frank with my mother, and it's only because of Gideon, and how he's empowered me, made me feel loved, that I'm able to stand up to her now. I know what I want, and I'm going to make sure my mother knows it too. "I'm taking happiness in both hands and holding on tight. Because let's be honest, Mom, there hasn't been a whole lot of that in my life. My own best friend betrayed me so horribly, she was willing to get me killed."

Mom swallows hard, but I keep talking.

"Gideon is my happiness. I love him. And it honestly pisses me off that you gave him orders to stay away from me."

"I was terrified," she admits, sitting back in her chair. "You'd been in harm's way, and I needed to blame someone."

"It wasn't his fault."

"He was hired to protect you, Lena, not fuck you and fall in love with you."

I recoil at the harsh words, scowling at her. "Don't demean what I have with that man."

God, I hope I still have it.

"It's the truth." She shrugs a shoulder. "However, with some time to calm down, I can see that you love him. He loves you too. So if the two of you can make it work, I won't do anything to stop you."

I blink at her in surprise. I expected much more of a fight over this.

"You're giving us your blessing?"

"I'm shocked too." She finishes her coffee. "Now, good luck tonight. Call me tomorrow and tell me all about it."

"Okay. Thanks, Mom."

I've never been so nervous in my life.

No one knows it's my work.

No one will be looking at me, judging me. As far as anyone else is concerned, this artist can't attend tonight.

I'm just here as an art lover.

"I hope you enjoy the showing." Kylie, the owner of the gallery, winks at me. "I think it's extra special. You look stunning, by the way."

I glance down at the red dress I chose for tonight. It fits me like a second skin, and makes me feel beautiful. Maybe no one knows that I'm the artist, but I still wanted to feel special for tonight.

"I'm sure I'll enjoy it." My smile is shaky at best, and Kylie slips a glass of champagne in my hand. "Thank you. For everything."

"It's just some bubbly." She winks and then slips away to work the room.

I don't have any friends here. Not that I have many friends anyway. I guess Javier, my trainer, could be considered a friend. And Kylie. But I'm here alone, and I wander around, pretending to check out the pieces hanging on the walls.

I wish Willow and Ryker were here. Aiden would get a kick out of this.

And God, how I wish Gideon were by my side. I ache with how much I miss him.

I notice that Kylie has put several *sold* stickers by my pieces, and that makes me happy.

"Fancy meeting you here."

I glance up in surprise, and then feel my lip curl at the sight of Howey.

It shouldn't surprise me that he's here. One of the reasons I was attracted to him in the beginning was his love of art.

But I really don't love that he's *here* at my show. I hope he doesn't buy anything.

"What do you think of this?" I ask him and sip my drink.

"Boring." He shrugs, and I want to slam the heel of my hand into his nose. "I mean, the artist has talent, but it's not my taste."

Good. He won't buy any of it. The thought of my work hanging in his home makes me nauseated.

"I like it," I say with a shrug. "I love the mountains."

"Figures. You always had simple taste in art."

I fucking hate this guy. If Gideon were here, he'd tell Howey to fuck off.

"Well, I hope you enjoy your evening." I turn to walk away, but he catches my elbow and spins me back to him, making me bump up against him, and my skin crawls.

I sense my detail step toward us, but I put my hand up.

I can handle this asshole.

"You're going to want to take your hand off me."

Howey smirks, and his eyes flick over my shoulder. "You gonna sic your guard dogs on me, little one?"

I smile back at him. "No. I don't need to. Last chance, hotshot. Let me go."

"Lena, I miss you—"

I stomp on his foot and shove my knee up into his groin, making him double over as I back away.

"When a woman tells you to let go, it means *let the fuck go*. You're such an asshole."

"That's my girl."

Oh, God.

That voice. I hear that voice in my dreams.

I spin, and there he is. He's in a black suit that molds over that sexy-as-hell body perfectly. Holy shit, nothing has ever looked so damn good.

His steel eyes soften as he takes me in from head to toe, and without another thought, I pass my glass to Howey and launch myself into Gideon's arms, wrapping my arms around his neck and kissing him for all I'm worth.

He catches me easily, those arms banding around me, and then his lips are at my ear.

"I'm so fucking proud of you, Rebel."

"You're here." I can't believe it. "Oh my God, you're *here*."

We're causing a scene, so I take his hand and pull him through the room and out the front door so we can talk outside, where there are no prying eyes.

"Wait, do I have to go back in there and kick that motherfucker's ass?"

"Nah, I already did that."

He smirks and frames my face, then presses his lips to mine again. This time, the kiss is slow and lazy, and when he licks into my mouth, I melt against him. My hands slide under his suit coat so I can feel the muscles over his dress shirt, and I moan.

"You never replied to me," I say when we come up for air.

"I needed to say everything in person," he replies, his voice gruff. "I had to get some shit in order. I needed to make sure that once I had you in my arms again, it was forever. Because the past two months have been *hell*, Lena, and I can't do it again. Not for one more day."

"Thank God." I lean my forehead against his chest as relief washes through me. "I thought, once you saw the messages, that you just weren't interested and didn't know how to tell me to go the fuck away."

"No." His hand goes to the back of my neck, and he tips my face up. "No, baby. Those messages were a lifeline. I found them just when I needed them the most, and I'm so grateful that you sent them."

I lick my lips and take a deep breath.

"Okay, I want to keep freaking out that you're here, and I want to take you to my place immediately and get naked, but first I have to go inside and talk to Kylie real quick."

"We have time," he assures me. "We should go in and enjoy this show, baby. Fuck, it's amazing."

"I won't stay much longer." I drag my hand down his tie, reveling in how solid, how *real*, he feels under my touch. "Because I *need* to get you alone. Gideon—"

"I'm not leaving you," he assures me. "I'm stuck to your side. Let's go in and enjoy this night for you, and then we can talk."

I nibble my bottom lip and then give him a nod, and he leads me back in. My detail is hanging back farther than they normally do, and I know it's out of respect for Gideon and me.

I'm surprised to see that almost all the pieces have *sold* tags on them.

"Holy shit," I whisper, and Gideon presses his lips to my temple.

"You're so fucking badass," he says into my ear, making me grin and my heart fill with so much love, it's brimming over. "I had no doubt that this would be the case."

He's here.

He's with me.

And he's mine.

Chapter Thirty-Two

Gideon

"Every single piece sold," Lena says as we walk into her apartment. "I can't believe it."

Before she can say anything else, I spin her around and boost her up in my arms, pinning her against the door.

"You're so fucking beautiful, Rebel." I nibble her neck, breathing in the oranges that I missed so fucking much.

Christ, she feels like heaven in my hands.

"You killed me all night in this dress."

Her thighs clench around my waist.

"You are so damn hot in a suit," she says, and I set her down so she can work my jacket off, and then I pick her up again and carry her through to her bedroom. "But I need you out of it, big guy."

"You can have anything you fucking want."

We shed our clothes, and then I nudge her into bed, pull the covers over us, and tug her into my arms, where she hugs me so tight and buries her face in my neck, and I can feel the tears running over my shoulder.

"I missed you *so much*," she says.

"I missed you too, baby." I brush her hair back from her face and tuck it behind her ear. "Now, I'm going to eat that delicious pussy, and make love to you, and I'm going to pound you into this mattress, and then I'm going to make love to you again, but first, I have a couple of things to say."

"Can we do the pounding-into-the-mattress thing first?" she asks, batting her eyelashes, and it makes me truly smile for the first time in months.

"God, I fucking love your mouth." I bite that lower lip. "And no. We need to talk. I need you to know why I didn't come with you."

"I know why," she assures me. "I know you well enough to understand that you're a soldier. You follow orders, Gideon, and my mother is your commander in chief."

"Walking away was the single most horrific moment of my life, and I'm not exaggerating, Lena. I found my mother shot to death when I was a kid, and this was worse than that."

Her eyes fill with so much sadness as she cups my face in her sweet hand and leans up to kiss my lips.

"It was pretty horrible waking up without you."

Fuck.

I gently run my hand over her head.

"How are you feeling, baby?"

"A lot better. But I was disoriented, and I hurt everywhere, and all I wanted was you. I threw fits, I begged, and no one would tell me anything. It was five years ago all over again."

"Fuck, I'm sorry." I have to pull her closer, so I tighten my hold, and she weaves her legs through mine.

"Finally, Bishop explained everything to me, and it actually made a lot of sense. I'm not mad, Gideon. Not at all. But you need to know that I have a flight plan for tomorrow. I'm going back to Montana, and you can't get rid of me. My mom is aware. I'll fight tooth and nail for you, because you're *everything*. And you said that I could live with you for as long as I wanted. You can't take that back."

I kiss her forehead, and then her nose, love filling every pore of my body. "You're coming home with me, Rebel. By this time tomorrow, everything will be back the way it should be."

She relaxes in my arms, and then she curls into me again and takes a long breath.

"I love you, baby."

Her head comes up, those gorgeous lavender eyes wide, and that bottom lip quivers, splitting my heart in two.

"I love you so much. Nothing works without you. I've been haunted by you, and I can't stand the thought of being without you for another minute. My spreadsheets are shit, by the way."

"You're really bad at them. It might be the only thing you're bad at."

I nibble on the side of her mouth, and she purrs.

Fucking purrs.

And she's naked, in my arms, and my hand roams down her back to her ass, pulling her against my hard-as-fuck cock.

"Oh, I really missed this," she says with a moan. "Like, *really* missed it."

Grinning, I kiss down her shoulder, then turn her onto her back and nibble her perfect nipples, tugging the metal into my mouth.

"Fuck, I missed these."

She smirks, and then groans when my hand moves down between her legs and I glide my finger over that bundle of nerves that's already hard and begging for my attention.

"You're already fucking wet, baby."

"One look at you was all it took," she says. "I've been a quivering mess all night."

With a growl, I spread her thighs wide and lower my face to her, lapping from her entrance to her clit and back down again. Fucking her with my tongue has never tasted so goddamn amazing.

"Gideon." Her hands dive into my hair and fist there, pulling me closer as I lick and nibble. Two fingers join the party, and her back arches up beautifully.

"I want you to soak my face, Rebel." I pull her clit into my mouth and suck, and she comes apart, her pussy squeezing my fingers.

Before she can come down from the high, I cover her and push inside that wet heat, groaning as I tip my forehead to hers.

"Fuck, baby."

Her arms circle my neck, her legs hitch up on my thighs, and I'm buried balls deep, afraid to move.

"I love you too, big guy," she whispers against my lips, and that's all it takes for me to start thrusting hard and fast, unable to get enough of her.

"You're so damn perfect." I'm hammering into her, unable to be gentle. "Christ, I missed you."

She moans, and I know she's almost there.

"You're going to give me another one, Rebel." I bite her neck, and she clenches down on me. "Come on, gorgeous, come on my cock."

"Oh shit!"

She takes me with her. I'm unable to hold back, and I come inside her, filling her until I'm leaking out of her, and then I pull out and walk into the bathroom to fetch a warm cloth to clean her up.

When I pull her into my arms again, she lays her head on my chest and ghosts her fingers through my chest hair.

"Can we go home tonight?" she asks, tilting her head back to look up at me. "Can't we just *go*?"

Dragging my fingers down her cheek, I smile at her. "I can make some calls, but it's past midnight. Let me make love to you for the rest of the night, and we'll leave first thing in the morning."

Lena smiles softly. "That sounds like a good compromise to me."

Chapter Thirty-Three

Lena

"You're home!" Willow comes running from the kitchen, her arms outstretched, but Ryker got to me first and has me in a hard hug that makes it hard to breathe. "Oh, thank God you're home."

She doesn't pull me away from her husband—she just wraps her arms around both of us and squeezes.

"Gid, get in here," Willow says, and then I'm in the middle of a James family group hug.

It's so fucking nice.

"I'm so glad you're finally home," Willow says. "We have so much to talk about and so many things to do. Now that you're not in jail here at the ranch—"

"She was never in jail," Gideon says with a scowl.

"—we can go shopping in Missoula, and we can go to Seattle to watch Aiden play. We're going next week."

I grin up at Gideon, whose eyes are soft and pinned to me. I spent the whole flight in his lap. We had to take the private jet for security purposes, and he held me all day.

He hasn't stopped touching me since he found me at the show last night.

"I'm *so* excited to see Aiden play," I tell them, and then go to follow Willow into the kitchen, but Gideon takes my hand, tugging me in the other direction. "Where are we going? We just got here."

"We'll come back," he assures me, sharing a smile with Ryker. "But I need a little bit of your time before I share you with them for the rest of the day."

I roll my eyes but follow Gideon out of the house and down to his SUV, and he drives me to the house. We haven't been here yet. We stopped by to see Wills and Ryker as soon as we pulled onto the property.

"You want to unpack first?" I ask him. "I mean, that's pretty strict, but okay."

"Keep running your mouth, Rebel." He kisses the top of my head and opens the door for me, and my heart stutters.

Because there in the living room is the biggest bouquet of red roses I've ever seen. It smells *amazing*.

"One for every day you were gone," he says, hugging me from behind.

We walk through the house to the back deck, and he leads me outside. It's cold as hell out here, but I love the crisp air as it fills my nose, and I take in all the snow blanketing the trees, the mountains. The frozen lake is so beautiful, it brings tears to my eyes.

I missed this so much.

"I knew it would be gorgeous. God, how do you not just stand here and stare all day?"

I turn, and then gasp when I find him down on one knee, holding a diamond ring that has the tears falling down my cheeks.

"You are the reason my heart beats, Lena. You're literally my favorite person on this earth and the greatest treasure in my life."

I sniff and brush a tear aside, listening to every beautiful word coming out of his mouth.

"You borrowed my name for your art, but I'd like to give it to you, permanently. I'll give you anything you want, baby. Marry me."

Cupping his face, I lean in and rest my lips on his, brushing them back and forth.

"Of course I'll marry you, Gideon."

He gently pushes the ring onto my finger, and then I'm in his arms and he's carrying me inside, his mouth on my neck, nibbling that spot just under my ear that makes me lose control.

"I thought we were going to back to the farmhouse."

"Later. I have to fuck my fiancée first."

With a snort, I weave my fingers into his hair.

"It feels so good to be home," I tell him as he lays me on our bed. "And not just for safe keeping this time."

"No, baby, you're here forever."

Epilogue

Gideon

She wanted to wait until her mother was out of office to get married. And then she wanted it to be in the summertime, so we could do it in the field by the lake, with the mountains in the background, and flowers chosen from the property.

Which means I waited eighteen long fucking months to make her my wife.

But if it meant seeing this smile on her face, I'd do it again in every lifetime.

"You may kiss your bride."

I wrap my arms around her and dip her back, kissing the fuck out of my new wife, and she smiles against me as everyone around us breaks out in applause.

"I love you, Mrs. James."

"I love you too."

With a smile on my face that feels like it'll never go away, I link our fingers and walk her down the makeshift aisle that leads to the tent where the reception will be held, but I take a detour and sneak her off to the house.

"Gideon, we have people waiting for us."

"They can wait five minutes." I kiss her again and feel her melt against me. "Maybe ten."

"No way. You're not fucking me right before our reception."

"Come on, it's not official until it's been consummated."

She scoffs at that and then kisses my chin. "We consummated this morning."

"Doesn't count."

There was no way that I was going to sleep at Ry's place last night. I don't give a shit about tradition.

I won't ever sleep without my Rebel in my arms ever again.

"I can't believe we found Debbie's wedding dress in the attic," she says, brushing her hands down the lace that hugs her body perfectly.

Debbie was the tiniest person I'd ever met in my life, so we had to have this altered for my girl.

And I know, without a shadow of a doubt, that my mom would be thrilled that Lena wanted to wear it.

"I feel like she's here with me," Lena says softly. "And I didn't even know her."

"She'd love you. My parents would have spoiled the shit out of you, Rebel."

She chuckles and kisses my hand. "We need to go celebrate with everyone, Gideon. My parents look like being in the boonies is getting to them. I'll let them escape in an hour."

I laugh and decide to hold off on sinking inside my girl until later. "I guess that works."

"Also, I'm ready for the Secret Service to go," she adds.

"They're good guys, baby."

"I know. But I love that we don't need them anymore."

We turn to walk back outside, but before we can get through the door, she stops.

"Gideon."

"Yes, baby."

"Are those *kittens*?"

My girl has wanted cats since she first got here, and I decided it was time to deliver.

"Oh my God," she says before I can answer her. "I'm a mom!"

With a laugh, I watch as she picks the two sleeping babies up and kisses them both.

"Hello, babies. I'm your mommy now. Yes, I am."

"Uh, Rebel? We have a party to get to."

She gives them each a kiss and then follows me outside.

"I didn't get you anything yet."

I frown down at her. "You're the present, Lena. Haven't you figured that out by now? You're all I need."

"You're swoony, Mr. James."

Sweeping her up in my arms, I kiss her silly, and then I hear someone clearing their throat.

"Could you just *not*?"

I grin over at Aiden. "What do you want, kid?"

"They want to do family photos, and I was the lucky one who got to come tell you." He shakes his head. "Come on. I think Lena's parents are trying to leave."

"Told you," she says with a laugh.

I pat Aiden on the back, and we walk to where the photographer is already posing my family for photos by the lake.

"I feel them with us today," Aiden says quietly. "I've felt them all day."

"I know." I pat him on the back. "We were just saying the same thing."

"I felt them there when I won the Cup this year too. It's like they're just hanging out with us, here for all the big stuff."

"They wouldn't miss it, kid. They wouldn't miss any of it."

"I hope it never goes away." He stops and looks around at the mountains, at our family. "Because someday, it'll be me out here, and I'm going to need them too."

"They'll be here. We'll all be here. Because this is home."

ABOUT THE AUTHOR

Photo © 2025 Kristen Proby

Kristen Proby is the *New York Times*, *USA Today*, and *Wall Street Journal* bestselling author of more than seventy titles. Making her publishing debut in 2012, she continues to captivate fans with spicy contemporary romances about families and friends, packed with plenty of swoony love. She also writes paranormal romances and recommends leaving the lights on while reading them. When not under deadline, Kristen enjoys spending time with her husband and their fur babies, riding her bike, relaxing with embroidery, trying her hand at painting, and of course, enjoying her beautiful home in the mountains of Montana.